Portrait of a Murderer

Portrait of a Murderer

A Christmas Crime Story

Anne Meredith

With an Introduction
by Martin Edwards

Poisoned Pen Press

Originally published in 1933 by Victor Gollancz
Copyright © 1934 Lucy Malleson
Introduction copyright © 2018 Martin Edwards
Published by Poisoned Pen Press in association with the British
Library

First Edition 2018
First US Trade Paperback Edition

10 9 8 7 6 5 4 3 2 1

Library of Congress Control Number: 2017938966

ISBN: 9781464209048   Trade Paperback
       9781464209055   Ebook

Poisoned Pen Press
4014 N. Goldwater Boulevard, #201
Scottsdale, Arizona 85251
www.poisonedpenpress.com
info@poisonedpenpress.com

Printed in the United States of America

Contents

Introduction

Portrait of a Murderer is a Christmas murder story whose tone, suited to the bleak midwinter, is captured in the opening words:

> Adrian Gray was born in May 1862 and met his death through violence, at the hands of one of his own children, at Christmas, 1931. The crime was instantaneous and unpremeditated, and the murderer was left staring from the weapon on the table to the dead man in the shadow of the tapestry curtains, not apprehensive, not yet afraid, but incredulous and dumb.

The novel earned praise from that most demanding of judges, Dorothy L. Sayers, who reviewed detective fiction for the *Sunday Times*: "The book is powerful and impressive, and there is a fine inevitability in the plot-structure which gives it true tragic quality." *Portrait of a Murderer* also earned Anne Meredith a contract with an American publisher, but despite its quality, it earned her neither fame nor fortune. Soon the book was forgotten, even though its author continued to write (under another name) with considerable success for another forty years.

Meredith was, even at the time *Portrait of a Murderer* first appeared in 1933, a seasoned writer of detective novels, but this book is not a whodunit, and is conspicuously more ambitious than her earlier work. As Sayers put it: "In the 'straight' spot-the-villain kind of detective story, the murderer is apt to be the most unreal character in the book. This defect is inevitable, since we must never be let into the inner secrets of his murderous mind—if we did, we should know him for what he is and there would be no story. His motives, his hesitations, the dreadful spiritual convulsion that precipitates him from dreaming into doing—all must be taken on trust, and frequently we remain, after all, unconvinced."

She contrasted that kind of story with those "told from the murderer's viewpoint. We see the crime committed and watch, through his eyes, with painful anxiety, while the evidence is piled up against him." One of the examples she cited was Francis Iles' masterly *Malice Aforethought* (1931). "A third method," she added, "shows us first the crime from the murderer's point of view and then the detection from the point of view of the detective." Richard Austin Freeman, as Sayers said, used this approach in *The Singing Bone* (1912), "and now comes Miss Anne Meredith, with less emphasis on clues and more on character". Meredith's sympathies were with the killer, and "because he is what he is, we can understand that callous determination… He combines meanness and magnanimity, both in a heroic degree… the detection is throughout subordinated to the psychology."

The book's American publishers added an exclamation mark at the end of the title to add a touch of melodrama to the vivid red and black dust jacket, and solicited a blurb from Carolyn Wells, one of the most popular crime writers of the era: "It seems to me a Human Document, crammed with interest and personality. And a fascination from which there is no escape until the last page is reached." A biographical note about the author informed readers that Anne Meredith came "from a legal family on both sides. Had she been allowed her way, she would have become a lawyer herself, but her aunt was sure that 'no man would marry a lawyer'. So she went to London and spent her time reading up on the law, studying books on detection, and organising a Crime Circle which once a week attempted to solve some unsolved crimes."

The biography is interesting as much for what it conceals as the information that it discloses. It was an attempt—from the commercial perspective, eminently sensible—to reinvent the author who had adopted the pseudonym of Anne Meredith. Her real name was Lucy Beatrice Malleson (1899–1973), and her list of novels produced under two different names, J. Kilmeny Keith and Anthony Gilbert, already ran into double figures. She had also achieved enough success to merit election to membership of the Detection Club, which she later served as Secretary; there is an entertaining account in her memoir *Three-a-Penny* (1940; also published as by Anne Meredith) of her induction into the Club.

She became a good friend of fellow Club member Cecil John Street (two of whose novels written under the name Miles Burton have been published in the British Library Crime Classics series), and dedicated her memoir to him, or at least to his best-known pseudonym, John Rhode. Detection Club members amused themselves by giving each other's names to characters in their mysteries, and Agatha Christie duly gave the name Anne Meredith to a woman in *Cards on the Table* (1936) who has apparently committed murder and got away with it, only to be suspected of another crime.

Anne Meredith novels continued to appear until the early 1960s, but their connection with crime fiction diminished and ultimately disappeared altogether, and none of the books made quite such an impression as *Portrait of a Murderer*.

The Anthony Gilbert novels, however, became increasingly popular. The reason for this was because, in *Murder by Experts* (1936), Gilbert introduced the Cockney solicitor with a gift for solving mysteries, Arthur Crook, who became a popular series character. The Keith pseudonym was abandoned, and with it Keith's amateur sleuth, Scott Egerton, perhaps detective fiction's only crime-solving Liberal Member of Parliament. An Arthur Crook novel called *The Woman in Red* (1941) was enjoyably filmed in 1945 as *My Name is Julia Ross* with a cast including Dame May Whitty, but with Crook removed from the script. The movie was remade in 1987 by Arthur Penn, whose entertaining version, *Dead of Winter*, starred Mary Steenburgen and Roddy McDowall, and bore even less resemblance to the original.

Although Anthony Gilbert novels have been republished from time to time over the years, Anne Meredith's work has long been forgotten. Yet *Portrait of a Murderer* is notable for its portrayal of character and social comment, and illustrates the truth that, contrary to widespread belief, a good many crime novels written during the Golden Age of Murder between the two world wars were anything but cosy.

Martin Edwards
www.martinedwardsbooks.com

Part I

Christmas Eve

1. Adrian

Adrian Gray was born in May 1862 and met his death through violence, at the hands of one of his own children, at Christmas, 1931. The crime was instantaneous and unpremeditated, and the murderer was left staring from the weapon on the table to the dead man in the shadow of the tapestry curtains, not apprehensive, not yet afraid, but incredulous and dumb.

2. The Grays

At the time of his death Gray was in his seventieth year, and had six children living. There had been a seventh, who died as a child, and so long ago that the younger ones scarcely remembered his existence. Only when the bitterness and futility of his parenthood pressed upon the ageing man with a greater sense of weariness than usual did Gray wonder whether the young Philip might not have grown up to be a solace and companion to him. But these moods occurred seldom, and for the most part he, like his children, forgot the little son who had died thirty years ago.

It was his habit at Christmas-time to invite all his relatives to spend the season at his lonely house at King's Poplars. The wife of one and the husbands of two of them made their numbers up to nine, while Mrs. Alastair Gray, the dead man's mother, an old lady of ninety, brought the party up to eleven. There was, in addition, a number of servants, both male and female.

As was shown at the inquest, Gray was on good terms with none of his children, while more than one had good reason to wish him out of their path. His eldest son, Richard, was at this time a man of two-and-forty, ambitious, dogged, and fierce to achieve his objective, which was place and reputation. He was childless, a fact that greatly distressed and humiliated him, was well known in political life, and had a few years earlier obtained a knighthood. He had been for many years married to Laura Arkwright, a notable woman in society.

Gray's eldest daughter, Amy, his only unmarried child, kept his house for him, and was a shrewd and shrewish woman of forty, small, sharp-featured, with reddish hair and thin lips and hands.

His second daughter, Olivia, was married to Eustace Moore, the unscrupulous but intelligent financier into whose hands Gray had allowed the larger portion of his capital to pass.

The dead Philip had come next, and after him Isobel, who had made a brilliant but, as it turned out, disastrous marriage several years earlier. Gray had been delighted when Harry Devereux asked for his daughter. The suitor was rich, handsome, and much sought after. He had a reputation for wit and charm that was not wholly misplaced, but he should have married a woman of his own world, not the young, independent, fiercely idealistic Isobel. Within two years his wife acknowledged her folly, but when she endeavoured to escape from its consequences she found herself powerless. Her husband assured her that she would win nothing but obloquy if she attempted to divorce him; and here she realised that he was right. A man of his popularity had women on every hand prepared to defend him. She thought it improbable that he had not guarded himself at every turn and thus she endured for another year. Then she was delivered of a girl-child, who survived her birth seven months. Isobel attributed the baby's death to a certain brutal action on the part of the father, and spent anguished weeks wondering how she could have averted the tragedy. Finally she asked her father to receive her home, detailing, as best she could, the manner of her life, her intolerable life, in London. Both Gray and Amy wrote, imploring her frantically to consider the position she would occupy if she returned, the manner in which tongues would wag, her own humiliation. They commiserated her on the death of the child, letting it be seen that they thought her request due to mental upset, following her loss, and spoke hopefully of "next time." Isobel left both letters unanswered, and the household at King's Poplars heard nothing more of her, until Devereux himself came down to suggest that Isobel should return home, as she was ill, stubborn, persistently refused him his rights, and he feared some desperate act on her part, such as suicide.

"And you think it would be pleasanter for us to have the scandal of a suicide in the house, rather than yourself?" was Gray's acid comment.

Amy said, "It's a struggle to live as it is, without another mouth to feed."

Devereux made it plain that he would allow his wife a handsome allowance so long as she remained at the Manor House. The attitude of father and sister altered at once. A week later Isobel reappeared. The older servants—there was at that time a housekeeper who had known the family for a great many years, who died twelve months later, besides the long-established Moulton—were openly shocked at her appearance. Isobel had always been the independent, the

courageous one. She had found herself work in the neighbouring market town, had loved solitude, had read, had
gloried in trips to London, had haunted book-shops and
art galleries. Isobel Devereux came back white and listless,
meekly submissive to her father, and handing over to Amy,
without demur, practically all the money with which her
husband supplied her. She scarcely counted as a personality,
but could be relied upon to perform those casual and thank-
less household duties that are invariably shirked by others.

Hildebrand, named for the famous Cardinal, came next,
a difficult, striking, handsome figure, sullen and secretive,
capable of sudden expansion when he blossomed as unexpectedly and beautifully as a miracle or a flower, but among his
own people dark, silent, and morose. From childhood he had
caused his father anxiety; he was original, headstrong, and
hot-tempered, and had early cut himself off from all sympathetic communication with his family, who were antipathetic
to his ideals and intentions, and responded with the utmost
ungraciousness (reasonable enough in the circumstances) to
his perennial demands for financial assistance. He was seldom
mentioned to their acquaintances by any of them, and eked
out a wretched, cramped existence with the woman he had
chosen to marry and their trail of drab, unattractive children,
in a little house near the Fulham cemetery.

The last child, Ruth, had been married for eight years
to Miles Amery, a promising young lawyer whose career
had, unfortunately, stopped short at the promise. Richard
and Eustace were both enraged and disgusted by this wilful
relative, who seemed devoid of ambition, and did not even
want to bring kudos to the family into which he had married. He pursued his obscure way with apparent satisfaction,
never even aiming at anything higher. He seemed to think
that a moderate income and a middle-class house in an
unexceptionable district were the culmination of any man's

desire. If you asked him how he was, he said very fit and having lots of fun.

"Fun!" said Eustace in a sepulchral tone, as Chadband might have said, "Drink!" and believing it every whit as sinful.

"Fun!" intoned Richard, vexed and outraged at what seemed to him a wanton flinging away of opportunity. "What's fun?"

They might well ask. Ruth could have told them. It was the house in St. John's Wood, and the two little girls, Moira and Pat, and all the satisfactions of their happy, full, rich life with one another.

3. Richard

I

On the morning of Christmas Eve, 1931, that was to close so tragically, Richard Gray and his wife, Laura, travelled to King's Poplars in a first-class carriage. After a long silence, Richard lifted his haughty, melancholy face from the pages of *The Times,* and remarked in tones as cold and polished as a brass door-handle, "I beg of you, Laura, to remember my father's views on the question of tariffs. It is most important that he should not be upset before I have an opportunity of discussing the position with him. You know how heated these political dissensions leave him."

Richard invariably spoke as though he carried a reporter in his waistcoat pocket.

Laura, a tall, handsome woman, very beautifully gowned, said lightly, "You can rely on my discretion. I, too, know how important it is that he shouldn't be upset. After all, I want to have a title quite as much as you want to buy it for me."

Richard frowned and returned to his paper. He considered his wife's remark in bad taste. Laura had, in fact, been one of his least profitable investments. As a young man, even before he had completed his term at the University, Richard had decided to make a success of his life. He had worked hard, cultivated a wide acquaintance, travelled, read extensively, taught himself to appreciate golf, spent wet afternoons watching a ball being kicked round and round a slimy field, and even, in certain company, lost money on horses. The result was that, within ten years, he had achieved a reputation. He had started on his political career, and its early honours were falling thick upon him. Flushed with pride and ambition, he extended his circle of acquaintances, and at thirty he met Laura Arkwright. She was three years his junior, handsome, an heiress, possessed an influential circle of relations, was cultured, urbane, and a well-known amateur pianist. She was, in short, in every way suited to be the wife of a rising M.P.

Richard, well pleased with his perspicacity, awaited the enriching of his life through this new tentacle he had put out. In almost every direction he met with bitter disappointment. Owing to ill-advised speculation, his wife's fortune was largely dissipated; she gave up her piano-playing comparatively soon after her marriage, on the extraordinary ground that she objected to commercial art. Richard brooded over that for some time—he was already very like his father—and at last was driven by injured curiosity to ask her what she meant. Laura said lightly it meant that she didn't want to play to his friends any more, and that she'd always been sorry for nice dogs exhibited at shows, another cryptic and absurd remark that Richard failed to understand. But he had had enough of asking for explanations, and took other means of showing his displeasure.

His greatest disappointment, however, was their child-lessness. He had meant to have sons—a daughter or two later, perhaps, since, though daughters were negligible in themselves, they might make advantageous connections for a father by marriage. But they had never even experienced the customary scares and hopes of a young couple. Richard, of course, blamed his wife; sometimes, in very intimate male society, if he felt sufficiently sore, he would acknowledge that she was a cold woman. He was perpetually surprised at the number of quite important people who appeared to think it worth their while keeping up with her, even after she lost her fortune, but supposed they had the sense to realise that she was married to a man who might be precious useful to them one of these days.

Laura said scornfully that of course they hadn't got children; a man like Richard couldn't expect them. He'd be so miserly he'd grudge them their very life.

At the end of three years she detested him. Since his realisation that they would, in all probability, never have children, he had been at first ostentatiously offended. Later, however, his grievance took a subtler form. He persisted in loading his wife up with jewels, handsome clothes, and furs—"Putting his trade mark on me, so that I can't be mislaid wherever I go," said Laura bitterly. This action on his part caused other wives to say in envious tones, "It must be wonderful to have a husband like Richard Gray. That wife of his hasn't done a thing for him, and he's the most generous soul alive. Some women have luck." Which, as Laura knew, was Richard's crafty intention, and a new way of humiliating her. Added to this was the fact that her relations had failed to fulfil her husband's expectations of them, having indeed become an embarrassment rather than an aid. They had seceded some years earlier to an advanced Radicalism that horrified and disgusted Richard, whose mode of argument was that a certain class had held power and lands for centuries, and therefore had proved their ability to govern.

Laura, while maintaining a gay and spirited attitude, was actually extremely unhappy. This was partly due to the humiliation of realising her inability to compare with her own kitchenmaid, who, with admirable composure and no legal sanction, had recently been delivered of twins. But still more was it the result of the dreary ineffectual life she supported with her husband. By nature apt to be reckless and impulsive, she had schooled herself to a cool and polished manner that flaunted its cynicism in the face of an indifferent world. At heart she detested the innumerable political intrigues in which her husband engaged, whose rewards seemed contemptible. In addition, she was deeply in love with a man who, like Richard, was chiefly concerned with the fruits of office, and who heaped humiliations upon her by beseeching her in the most craven manner to be perpetually on guard against revealing a hint of the true relationship between them. Laura had sometimes dallied with the notion of asking Richard for a divorce, but in her heart she knew both men too well to hope that either would lay aside a spark of his ambition to accommodate her.

She was aware of, and utterly sickened by, Richard's present strait. He had for some time been devoured by a passion to obtain a peerage; the amount of feeling he could squander on the attainment of this paltry ambition seemed to her more contemptible than the money entailed. He had not contemplated this step in his original scheme, but since overhearing a club member, a little less snobbish than himself, observe to a neighbour, "What earthly good is a title to a fellow like Gray? He's got no one to follow him," his intention became fixed. He would at all events command respect and notice, if not from posterity, at least from contemporaries. This determination had now become an obsession with him. Already it had lured him to unjustifiable lengths. It was not only the peerage that he coveted, but a certain appointment to which, he believed, a peerage was a necessary step. There was a second competitor in the field, a man in many ways more favoured than himself, and to this silent, heart-breaking, neck-to-neck race he applied himself recklessly. The course involved an expenditure far too heavy for his purse, and he had already entered into obligations he could not meet. The man he must satisfy was a rigid Nonconformist, who would certainly disapprove of his candidate's action in running headlong into debt. Once let the tale of his financial embarrassments come to F——'s ears and he might abandon all hope both of title and political advancement.

The money, he considered, had been wisely spent; a certain proportion had been speculated in good works, the endowing of a bed in a somewhat obscure hospital in F——'s constituency, a handsome subscription to a fund being inaugurated for the unemployed, and various donations to societies for dealing with the destitute and unfortunate. So far, so good, even from F——'s point of view. But, far outbulking these moneys, were enormous sums spent on entertainment, costly wines, fruits out of season, astounding frocks for Laura, flashing jewels, a car whose photograph appeared in various Society journals, prominent positions at fashionable gatherings, all designed to create the impression that where Richard Gray was absent something was lacking. And as if it were not troublesome enough to be bombarded by short-sighted creditors, who didn't appear to realise the position, or the good fortune that would reward their patience, there was the affair of Greta Hazell.

Miss Hazell was a striking young woman of a southern type of beauty, warm-blooded, entrancing, and—oh, very expensive. Quite how expensive Richard was only just beginning to understand. He had supposed himself lavish, if not recklessly extravagant, in his treatment of his wife, but

Greta showed him how, without any of that ostentation, a mistress could prove quite as costly. There, though he would not for worlds have admitted it, even to himself, lay the root of this financial embarrassment that irked him day and night. The rest he might have supported, but this made the burden intolerable. The lady in question, being a woman of business flair and experience, was blackmailing him for an absurd sum. When he protested, she said, "It wouldn't suit your book at all, my dear Richard, to have our connection made public. Whereas it wouldn't injure me at all. Indeed, considering the amount of limelight you've enjoyed of late, it might even be good for me. The woman who seduced Richard Gray." And she laughed.

He looked at her dumbly. Even in the moment of his disillusion and rage he was compelled to realise her charm. Of course, he had met her at an unlucky moment. He had attended a stag dinner, at which an eminent and very out-spoken novelist, whose books even Richard had read, had been the guest of the evening. As the hours drew on, under the influence of this gentleman and the wine, that was excellent, various guests became loquacious, and Richard was left with the shocked recognition that there was a delight to be had for money that he had not yet experienced. His tempered raptures with his bride were effectually quenched by the murmurs and admissions of some of those present; here, it seemed, was a secret well of joy from which other men drank, but not he.

His fidelity since marriage had been a matter of policy and of choice; he had no ethics to bind him, but he had not experienced any temptation to deceive Laura, and had, in fact, been too busy collecting scalps in other fields. The conversation, however, had fired his persistent love of self. Here were actually men less well off, less intelligent, less well connected, less brilliant in every way than himself, and he now perceived them to be richer than he. His view, he saw, had been a one-sided one; he had thought only of his work, and never of personal compensations. He went home in an unusually passionate and warm-blooded frame of mind, prepared to find his wife deficient in response. And circumstances favoured him. She had that afternoon had a most unsatisfactory interview with her lover, and was thoroughly disgusted with men, their evasions and securities. She turned away, therefore, when Richard came up to her and, taking her bare arm, began to stroke it possessively. Richard was rather pleased than otherwise at this exhibition of marital coldness. Three days later he met Greta Hazell, and within a fortnight he had taken a handsome little flat for her in Shaftesbury Avenue—not till later did he realise that its rent was three hundred and twenty pounds a year—and was buying her whatever her fancy of the moment prompted. After some months he realised that he was by no means her only visitor to the flat. Taxed with infidelity, she laughed impudently. Did he suppose she kept all her life for his pleasure? she asked. Richard was dumbfounded. Here was something he had bought defying him. It was intolerable. He determined at once to break off the liaison and never see the wretched creature again. Then she stated her terms. They were staggering; at first Richard could not believe her. She was—in execrable taste—amusing herself at his expense. But she speedily disillusioned him. He could do nothing. She had him on the hip, and it would be dangerous at this stage in his affairs to make an enemy of her. He was puzzled to know how she had learned so much of his precise position. It did not occur to him that a political rival might be among her visitors.

That, then, was the position this Christmas Eve. He had not yet met her demands, was not in a position to do so, but he was aware that he could not much longer defer payment.

Somehow, setting his personal feelings aside, willy-nilly he must compel his father to help him. First he must pay off Greta—who had the name of never returning to plague a discarded or discarding lover—and then he must raise enough to keep the more pressing of his creditors at bay until he had achieved his goal. It would be a difficult task. Adrian Gray accorded his son only a grudging congratulation when he achieved his knighthood; he had not, in Richard's opinion, altogether met the situation by saying, with an assumption of heartiness, "Just as you like, Richard, of course. A gentleman was good enough in our day. We didn't go in for these fancy titles and letters after our names," adding that, of course, gentleman had a more exclusive meaning a generation ago. Nevertheless, he would glean a certain pleasure out of saying, "My son, Lord So-and-So," though it was questionable whether he would consider that prestige worth its price. His own affairs, as his son realised, were in a worse way than the man himself was aware. He, Richard, thought it improbable that Eustace had disclosed the true position, and he was particularly anxious to outwit his brother-in-law and obtain the first interview with his father. Once Eustace had made a clean breast of the position, it would be hopeless for any of them to ask for help. As for Brand—but Brand could be easily dismissed. Brand was a person of little importance and no influence, the kind of relative that even peers may own, though it is rash for mere knights to do so. Eustace's speculations were a subject for consistent gossip in Richard's own circle; people gave it as their opinion that that chap must come to grief pretty soon, and he'd be lucky if he kept out of gaol. Still, any racing man would have bet at high odds, say 50 to 1, on Eustace when it came to a match between him and Richard. The latter felt that his only chance was to be first in the field, and even that was a slender one.

Official business, however, delayed his plans, compelling him to remain in town until the evening of the 23rd, when it was too late to make the tortuous and inconvenient journey to King's Poplars. He had made up his mind to travel by train, which would cost him nothing. To arrive, a suppliant, in the brilliant and much-advertised car that he possessed, would be to alienate Gray at once, and give Eustace an opportunity to point a derisive finger at him.

"Why doesn't he put his car down if things are so stiff?" Eustace would ask. And, even without that prompting, the same no doubt might easily occur to Gray himself.

Moreover, the car was among those luxuries for which he had not yet paid, and it seemed to him safer to leave it in the garage in town. At London Bridge he looked out nervously for Eustace, though in all probability he would motor down; there was no sign of him in the train or on the platform, and he had to school himself to such patience as he could command until they reached King's Poplars. Shortly before the train drew up at the station he spoke again, with chill abruptness.

"My father tells me he has had a very disquieting letter from Brand," he observed. "Asking for money, as usual."

Laura lifted her charming brows: "We seem singularly united for once."

Richard was very angry. It was abominable. This odious comparison of himself with a shabby clerk, tied to a woman with an atrocious history, living in some degraded quarter of London, dabbling with a paint-box in his spare time—that was the kind of thing one's footman might do. He'd make a fine relative for the future Lord X——.

Arrived at last, he was informed that no conveyance was immediately available; he displayed his annoyance in a manner that seemed to Laura contemptible. His undignified rage with the station-master made her feel a little sick, and, standing in the background, she thought, "Why on earth did I do it? What did I think he would become? No one put any pressure on me. I had money and independence and a family whom I loved. What did I see in him? And which of us has changed so completely?"

The station-master thought Lady Gray was a credit to them; such a lady she always looked, quiet and proud, with that lovely sort of red hair she'd never cut, just showing under her fashionable hat. A taxi was presently secured, and they drove up to the Manor in feverish unrest on Richard's part and a bored disgust on hers. The first person they encountered was Eustace himself, prowling round the gardens, looking cold and glum.

Richard asked politely, "Have you seen my father?" and Eustace said that he had, and that he didn't think the old man looked any too well. He talked of a dicky heart; did Richard know if there was anything in it? Richard said firmly that he didn't, and disregarding obvious hints from both Eustace and Amy, whom he scarcely paused to greet, broke into the library and poured out a history of his position.

Adrian was less than sympathetic. He said fiercely, "You can take your title to the devil. I'm ruined, Eustace tells me. Ruined. It's all that fellow's fault—a crooked, slimy sort of chap, not even a gentleman. What in God's name Olivia saw in him beats me. She's a fine figure of a woman to let a little rat like that go messing her about."

Richard, making the best of a deplorable business, responded promptly, "I've never considered Eustace a safe man. He'd play ducks and drakes with anyone's money."

Gray turned on him in a fine rage. "If you were so sure as that, why did you never warn me? You knew I had the greater part of my capital in his concerns."

Richard resembled a man struggling desperately to hold in a panic-stricken horse. He was white with rage, and the effort to control it; his voice was high and strained. He replied, speaking very fast, as though he could not swiftly enough pour forth his rage and disappointment, "You were impossible to warn. You would listen to no one. You were convinced you were a financier, with more courage than any of the rest of us. You filled us up with tales of large dividends and bold investments. At least it might have occurred to you that, with all safe companies paying something under five per cent, you must be running some risk or perpetrating some dishonesty in order to get a regular fourteen per cent. We did remonstrate with you, Miles as well as myself. And how much did you listen? Not a word. I was a beggarly politician out for grab, Miles a lawyer hoping to make something out of both sides."

"Miles—" began Gray uncertainly, but his son would not allow him to proceed.

"Miles is a lawyer, just as Eustace is a financier, and neither of them will lift a finger until he's paid for it. Why should he? An enquiry or two would have told you what you needed to know; ask anyone in the City what Eustace's reputation is. You'll get the answer in one word. You knew he always had money in his pocket; he hasn't got a job like the rest of us. Did you ever stop to wonder how it got there? It came out of other people's pockets, and they were no more willing to lose it than you'd be. Now I suppose he wants more..."

"He won't get it, not a penny. I haven't got it. And I haven't got anything for you either. You're not buying a peerage to please me. It's an expensive luxury, especially as you haven't a son to take it up."

Richard said thickly, "Not yet."

"Not yet?" His father stared. "You mean that Laura, after all these years...?" In the face of his son's possible humiliation he was instantly urbane. "My dear boy, don't you feel a little suspicious?"

"I don't mean anything of the kind," cried Richard in a rage. "Laura will never have children, any more than she'll ever be unfaithful. A woman like that may not be an ideal mate for a normal man, but she realises her obligations, and one of them is not to make a cuckold of me." His anger made him coarse and bitter.

"Then what did you mean? Laura's perfectly healthy, isn't she?"

"Perfectly, I believe, apart from her regrettable inability to bear me children."

"You're taking a very long chance when you anticipate the possibility of an heir, if all that's true. And you surely don't wish to ruin both yourself and me for the sake of Brand's son?"

Richard's comment on that was unprintable. When he had gone, his father, greatly shaken, did a strange thing. He sent for his second son-in-law, Miles Amery, and said, "Do you see much of Richard when you're both in town? He strikes me as being in a very peculiar condition."

"He's aiming very high, sir," returned Amery, a tall, thin, stooping man, with pleasant grey eyes behind rimless pince-nez, dressed in a pepper-and-salt suit. "It's trying to the nerves."

"From his manner in my room just now I should have said he was on the verge of a breakdown. Have you any influence over him at all?"

Miles shook his head. "We're practically strangers. We have nothing in common, you see, and I doubt if we should agree on a single point."

"He's usually inclined to be taciturn, but to-day he's so voluble and so wild in what he says that I feel sure he can't be well. I haven't seen Laura yet. How does she seem?"

"No one would ever guess from Laura that anything disquieted or distressed her. You would have to be very intimate, far more intimate than either Ruth or I am fortunate enough to be, to know what she feels or thinks. As to looks, she was always the most striking woman I've ever set eyes on!"

Gray said nervously, "I hope it's all right. He struck me as being in the kind of mood when nothing would be impossible to him. And—well, between ourselves (you must hear a great many confidences, Miles, and this is strictly without prejudice)—I believe he's developed a regular dislike of Laura. He's actually hinting at the possibility of another marriage later on. And I'm convinced the idea of divorce hasn't gone through his head."

Miles looked troubled. "You seriously think it may be dangerous for Laura to remain with him? That's a very grave charge."

"I'm not charging him with anything. You lawyers always want to see things go wrong. That's your livelihood."

"We shouldn't be human if we didn't watch after our bread as strenuously as anyone else," Miles pointed out tranquilly.

"I only say he seems to me unbalanced. Look at the enormous expense and trouble to which he's going to get this title. And would he do such a thing just for Brand's boy to inherit it later on? Richard's usually so self-contained. I've never seen him like this, and in his present mood he may be capable of any enormity."

Miles said, "Could you persuade him to see a doctor?"

"He wouldn't listen to anything I said. You perhaps…"

Miles looked dubious and said he would try, but he had little hopes of success.

II

Richard meanwhile was furiously repeating the result of the interview to an indifferent Laura. When he had finished, she said, thoughtfully, turning the magnificent marquise ring round and round on her finger, "Do you suppose that was final?"

"I should think, whether he realised it or not, he spoke the truth when he said he hadn't got a penny. It's the end for him all right, if the City gossips are to be trusted. The end for Eustace too, and for us. The end of years of work and ambition. I've subordinated everything to my career, and this is what I reap. I lose everything—my health, position, money, security, natural tastes, liberty—all gone in a single hour."

"It seems quite ridiculous that we failed to realise it earlier," was Laura's unexpected reply.

"Failed to realise…?"

"I mean, that the whole of our effort and ability to possess something can be lost so easily. If it had been something else more stable, more worth while—well, we might have failed, but we shouldn't have to admit that we'd lost everything. There'd have been the pleasure we should have got out of the labour, and the delight of meeting sympathetic minds. As it is we've nothing. Except time. We've still, fortunately, quite a lot of that."

"Time?" repeated Richard foolishly, staring at her.

"Yes. To begin something else. I suppose, if what you say is true, it means exposure—you'll fall out of favour—we shall have to begin something else. Let's choose something better next time."

Richard seemed at length to grasp her meaning. "Exposure?" he exclaimed. "Kindly refrain from speaking as if I were a common thief. I'm not Eustace. Exposure may very well mean ruin of a criminal kind for him. I have done nothing illegal."

"I apologise. I misunderstood you. But at all events you do admit that it means farewell to the peerage. If, as you say, *l'affaire* Eustace will shortly become publicity for the Sunday Press, your name is sure to be mentioned. And your father's. You may have had nothing to do with him, but the descriptions on the hoardings won't be satisfied with 'Financier.' They'll come out in all the glory of 'Famous M.P.'s brother-in-law,' etc."

"A lot you care that my hopes should be defeated," he accused her.

"Not much," she acknowledged calmly. "But, Richard, if only you could take a detached view, see the—the insignificance of it all. A thing that can tumble to pieces so easily is never a safe structure, or one worth wasting all one's life on. It rests simply on money, which is an asset more liable to chance than anything I know. It takes into no account work or idealism or aspiration—it's a mere wastage of life. I can even be glad for this opportunity to realise the truth. And there are so many things we've never even considered that bring satisfaction of themselves, quite apart from rewards."

She seemed, as she turned to him with an ardour he found foreign to her and of which he could not in this connection approve, to have sprung into a new life and colour, a vivacity and gaiety with which he had not for twelve years associated her. As easily might he have expected to see a dead branch put out green buds before his eyes.

He exclaimed feebly, deprived of spirit by her warmth, "What things do you mean?"

They were so clear to her own mind; the hopes she had cherished as a girl, the lofty ambitions of youth, their bare memory irradiated and refreshed her, though she was approaching the middle years and long ago had left youth behind her. Nevertheless, she flushed with pure joy to contemplate them; experiencing a stimulus she had never known during the careful colourless years of her wifehood.

Richard astounded her, breaking into her thoughts, by a sudden return to his most dignified and unapproachable displeasure.

"It is a disadvantage to any man in public life to have a wife who is entirely uninterested in his aims."

"It's not precisely that, Richard, but they don't seem worth all your work and energy. It seems to me rather humiliating for you to spend so much attention on them."

Richard watched her steadily, one hand fidgeting with a book he had picked up from the table. His eyes had a peculiar trick of appearing much lighter when he was angry. Now they were almost colourless.

"I understand. Nevertheless, contemptible as it must appear to you, I do not propose to relinquish my position so lightly. I had hoped at one time that your brothers might see fit to use their influence, but unfortunately they have forfeited their opportunities. They have to be regarded as something less than a forlorn hope."

"Quite forlorn," Laura agreed. "Alastair wouldn't consider promotion ought to go by favour, even before he changed his political views. And Philip would be just as unhelpful."

She moved to the dressing-table, took up a silver-backed brush, and smoothed a strand of red hair that had become disarranged. A sense of amazement filled her. Was this all that portentous dignity concealed, this childish battle for place? Was his armour truly nothing but silver paper and cardboard? She saw life as a landscape stretching into the distance, with no enclosing walls or comfortable house with doors that locked to keep the pilgrim within; and Richard strove to make it secure, narrow, and exclusive. The absurd passion of his last words hung upon the air, deafening her ears and deadening her heart. He was, after all, in earnest. One should feel compassion, not this sense of chill disgust. To him it did matter so much.

4. Olivia

I

Eustace Moore, who married Olivia Gray, was frequently described as a bounder, but he bounded with so admirable a discretion that this peculiarity on his part was nearly always overlooked. He was a man with a vast acquaintance. When he entered any public building—a restaurant, lecture-hall, or bar—he was instantly hailed by several voices. He was an energetic and, in some ways, a mischievous man; his conceit of himself was so great it overleaped all obstacles in his mind before he had approached a problem, so that these obstacles seldom existed by the time he set to work. His imagination was his weakest point. A man given to wild gambles himself, he had neither understanding nor patience to spare for those who feared such risks. He had his finger in a great many pies and possessed an enviable treasury of commercial tips. He sometimes boasted that he could gauge any man's financial standing at the end of half an hour's conversation. In appearance he was short, neat-waisted, clean-shaved, dark, and well dressed. He had very small, beautiful hands and feet and brown eyes, and a smile of great charm and subtlety. He paid a great deal of attention to his finger-nails and hands. He had married Olivia because she represented the world in which he was not at that time altogether at ease. He was under no illusions as to her family, that he considered unintelligent, short-sighted, and snobbish. They possessed, however, an inherent elegance and suavity that in himself had to be acquired. The type of woman in London Society whom he preferred, refused to consider him in marriage, and he had realised quite early that his only chance was to marry quietly a girl of breeding and, if possible, a little fortune, who would do him credit and attract people by her bearing as his hostess. His circle was not enthusiastic as to his choice, Olivia seeming aloof and cold. But that other circle that he proposed to enter contained better judges. Eustace did himself quite definite good by his marriage. After that event, Olivia for some years saw very little of her relations, Eustace being convinced that they would all try to borrow money off him. Olivia speedily worked up a reputation for being smart and amusing; she contributed bright Society chat to some of the larger weeklies, with very shiny paper and a great many photographs of the right people. These generally took the form of letters beginning "Cherry sweetest," or "My darling Babs," and were described as "devastating." Eustace was proud of her ability to attract the right kind of attention and to make money on her own account. It seemed to him unusual to combine these qualities with the appearance and manners of a lady and a placid tolerance of his own uxoriousness, that was pronounced even in public, when he could not refrain from touching her shoulder or arm, or allowing his body by apparent accident to come into contact with hers.

As to Olivia's relations, Eustace thought them a poor lot. Richard was suspicious, stand-offish, and proud without any reason that Eustace could discover. Miles he affected to dislike—did, indeed, dislike, with the petty, uncomfortable jealousy of the man who senses his own inferiority. Their relations on the surface were cordial, but they met seldom. Miles, Eustace would remind himself, was younger, poorer, nothing to look at, had no ambitions worth mentioning; he had married a younger daughter and had obtained no dowry with her; Ruth Amery could not even give him sons. There were two little girls who never came down to King's Poplars, and Ruth was not a Society figure, being short and dimpled and quite unfashionably dressed. When her children were babies, she had often wheeled them out herself, because the Amerys could not afford an adequate staff; so that, all things considered, it was absurd for Eustace to feel that Miles was his superior. And, in spite of everything, that sensation persisted. Naturally they met seldom.

Brand, oddly enough, was an asset. Eustace would say casually, "That's the devil of these old families. Inter-marry with their own kin till the blood's no thicker than water. Look at that brother-in-law of mine, now. Hardly any better than a cretin. Earns about four pounds a week in some bloody little office in Kingsway, and, of course, they're the most fertile class of the community."

Olivia, fortunately, did not possess a very high standard. She could compare her home, her jewels, her clothes, her afternoons, her amusements, her car, and her children with those of other people and find them superior. She seriously matched her work against Brand's "studies" (because to her his canvases were never complete) and preen herself on her better art. She spoke of her own work as literature, with her tongue in its normal place, between her teeth. She admired the lithe, crafty, smooth sons of Eustace Moore, who were already aware of what constituted real values, and seriously debated with their father the commercial value of a University education.

"You meet a queer lot of fellows up there these days," Monty would say. "Don't know that it's worth your expense, Dad."

"They have money if they haven't breeding," said Eustace shrewdly. "You don't often find the two together. But they're both worth plucking."

East of Oxford Circus, Eustace was regarded with a certain wariness; he was the director of a number of concerns, with a probing and energetic finger in many others. His companies were in a minority in declaring large dividends shortly after their inauguration. Shareholders had the option of drawing these or of allowing them to accrue with the original capital. About eighty per cent chose the latter course; the remaining twenty took their dividends and recommended the shares as an excellent investment to their friends. Eustace contrived quite a good connection by means of that smile and generally pleasing manner, that so much appealed to women. He was not actually attracted by them, particularly by the young, who he considered on the whole lacked the decorum and good manners he had admired in a previous generation. But he was nothing if not practical, and he suffered familiarities of speech and gesture that were personally obnoxious to him, when the speaker was possessed of private means, and he saw a reasonably good hope of persuading some of these into his companies, and so into his purse. But he retained to the last all his race's strong family sense, and, apart from his wife, he shrank from physical contacts.

The crisis that had arisen this Christmastide was as unexpected as it was crucial. A nameless traveller of no significance, returning from some distant place where Eustace (and his shareholders) had interests, began to speak freely in mixed company of the impracticability of Eustace's proposals in certain connections. He chanced to do this in the presence of one of the shareholders, a truculent fellow, who instantly called him to order. The traveller, unaccustomed to being hectored or contradicted, made something in the nature of a scene. The petty disagreement spread, and other shareholders heard of the nameless man's views and were inclined to be impressed by them. As a result of letters he received from strangers, Mr. Plant wrote to certain organs of the Press, putting into forcible language his view of the morality and general character of a man who would attempt to hoodwink harmless persons and deprive them of their savings. Everyone expected Eustace to start a libel action, and when he sat tight and did nothing, a miniature panic sprang up. Each man, eager to be before his fellows, gave orders to his broker to dispose of his shares. These became a glut on the market, and fell to next to nothing. In an attempt to dispel public suspicion, Eustace ostentatiously bought up these shares as they touched bottom prices, and encouraged a report that Plant was a person well known to him and receiving handsome payments for spreading his story. He was not, however, very successful. The first man who had the temerity to go to Plant direct with this version was sent home minus a front tooth, and only Plant's inability to lay hands on evidence against Eustace, who was careful to commit nothing to writing, stopped him from bringing an action. There were more rumours, and scandal raised an ugly head. Even Eustace's boys heard of it and wrote their father urgent letters quoting little snivelling nonentities among their school-mates whose parents were being ruined by this hanky-panky, and imploring him to scotch the story before their own reputation went. Matters assumed a gravity of which Eustace in his most pessimistic moods had never dreamed. He hastily convened a board meeting of the directors of the doomed company, and, white-faced and alarmed, they consulted with one another as to what had best be done. There were not many of them, and the majority were smallish men whom Eustace had selected as likely to be sharp enough to be of use, but not sufficiently astute to work for their own ends. It was agreed that it was necessary to raise ten thousand pounds at once, if criminal proceedings were to be avoided. Eustace had no doubt at all as to the result of such a course; he would be committed and sentenced, and at best would get five years. Besides, there were his sons to think of.

It was, therefore, necessary to put the position with brutal clearness, not to say crudity, to his father-in-law, who, by a skilful manipulation of the facts, could be made to appear a partner in the dishonesty. This point of view had not occurred to Adrian. Eustace brought to the distasteful interview an air of jaunty cynicism, concealing alarm, assuming in the older man a knowledge of speculative procedure that he must have realised Gray did not possess. No man with even half the knowledge with which Eustace prepared to credit him would have allowed so large a proportion of his private means to lie within the younger man's grasp. When Gray, at length perceiving the position, broke into a paroxysm of mingled horror and rage, Eustace treated him with an impatient levity.

"Come, come, sir," he admonished him, "this kind of thing helps neither of us. It's too late now to pretend to an innocence no jury would believe you to possess. The obvious point that you were coolly drawing these high dividends at a time when men are thankful for a mere three and a half per cent would attract suspicion. And how do you suppose it will improve Richard's prospects to have a father in the dock for wilful fraud?"

There he touched Gray on his one human spot. He had never cared for any of his later children, but this first-born held such of his heart as was not occupied with his financial affairs. Nevertheless, he faced up to Eustace with commendable forcefulness.

"I'm not a child, to be scared by bogeys," he told him.

"Nor a child to be acquitted on facts that even a child would hesitate to accept," Eustace retorted. "I implore you, sir, to view the position squarely, and see your own liability, in the eyes of the public if not of the law or of your own. Who is going to believe we weren't hand in glove? Not a British jury, I assure you, and though you might, through a lack of evidence, be acquitted on the main charge, your reputation will stink in the nostrils of all honest men." Eustace could produce with the fine melodramatic flourish of his race just these high-sounding clichés that infuriated Gray, the more because he realised the truth of them.

Nevertheless, he clung stubbornly to his refusal to part with a penny to see his son-in-law through his unpleasant crisis. In vain did Eustace cajole, bully, threaten.

"Do you suppose I don't know why you want this money?" Gray was goaded into exclaiming before the wretched undignified conversation came to a close. "You want to get hold of my cash and vanish with it out of the way of the law and set up your web somewhere else."

Eustace, trembling with passion, retorted, "Very ingenious suggestion on your part, sir. And do you expect anyone to believe that a man so astute as that didn't know what he was doing when he put thirty thousand pounds into my companies?"

II

Up and down their room, in slippered feet, turning, hesitating, pacing, halting, turning again, went Eustace hour after hour through the interminable evening, until Olivia, her tact, patience, and sweetness of temper exhausted by this intolerable prowling, cried, "Oh, Eustace, for heaven's sake stop it. I shall have hysterics."

Eustace paid no attention; for the moment, she did not exist. Olivia, realising the depths of his absorption, compelled her nerves to remain calm for a little longer while she enviously watched her husband's supple figure moving like a great cat in and out of the shadows. Her own was thickening disquietingly. They said Jews were stout, gross even, particularly if they were financiers, but nothing less like the novelist's conception of a Jew than Eustace could be conceived. Only in the shrewd expression of the dark face, and the smooth black hair brushed straight off an olive-coloured forehead, did he betray his origin.

"And he doesn't have to wear corsets or endure massage. And he certainly eats and drinks far more than I do," thought Olivia resentfully.

At length, however, she was aware that, come what might, some sort of a scene was inevitable, and, sitting bolt upright in the bed and speaking very loudly, she asked, "Have you any aspirin, Eustace? My head is driving me crazy. It's watching you like this, hour after hour…"

He came to an abrupt standstill at the foot of the bed. "Olivia, you should know your father better than I do. Is there any way of compelling him to help us? I thought the threat of dishonour would be sufficient, expecially if I mentioned Richard, but apparently I miscalculated. He's our only chance now."

"He has got the money?"

"He's got fifteen thousand pounds' worth of bonds in the safe in his room. I saw them myself not two months ago, when I came down to talk over further investments in the —— Co. Ten thousand would pull us through and set us on our feet. Moneylenders can't help us; the City of London is honeycombed with spies; they'd realise at once that everything was up, even if anyone would lend us anything on our security. Well?"

Olivia said, "It isn't only us. It's Richard, too. I'm sure he's in a tight hole, and has been trying to touch father. Perhaps he's been luckier than we."

"We know Richard's in a tight hole, but not so tight as ours. He can't afford publicity any more than we can, but at least it won't mean broad arrows for him. I daresay"—he shrugged elaborately—"it won't be very pleasant to be sold up. They say his extravagances these last six months have been fantastic. But there it is. I don't for a moment believe, though, that Richard has been any luckier in getting anything out of your father than I have. I had first innings for one thing, and for another I saw Richard coming out of the library looking like murder. He'll hardly speak to anyone. Oh, he's in a mess all right. If he weren't, he might have done something. It won't be pleasant for him having all his relations in the criminal court. Besides, there's some story about a woman I've been hearing lately."

Olivia forgot her headache. "Richard—and a woman!"

Eustace laughed unguardedly. "Well, why not? He's human, isn't he? And that wife of his is a bit of a stick, or I'm mistaken."

"I was thinking it's so unlike Richard to spend money that he can save. Is she—this woman—making trouble?"

"They say so. They generally do, of course. The fellow must be a fool to let this come on him at such a critical time, but between you and me I never have considered Richard quite the brilliant chap he thinks himself."

Olivia was following up a train of thought of her own. "Then, if she's making trouble too, and he hasn't any money, he must get something out of father if he isn't to be ruined, Eustace!" She shot the words at him. "If what you say is true, that father's pretty well ruined himself, he certainly wouldn't have much to give, and anything he had would go to Richard. I'm convinced of that."

She dropped into silence. Eustace, who saw no point in wasting anything, not even words, recommenced his perambulations.

"And there's Brand," said Olivia gloomily, determined to get some kind of Russian satisfaction out of the general depression.

"Yes. I gathered he was cropping up again. Oh, I wouldn't care to be in your father's shoes. All his relations by blood or marriage, with the exception of the unambitious Miles, at his throat for cash. Is it anything new so far as Brand's concerned? Is he threatened with a writ or the police, too?"

"Oh, nothing fresh, I expect. He's been a nuisance to us ever since he was fifteen. You know, he was expelled from —— for what his headmaster called obscene caricatures of those in authority."

"Oh, I know that sort of thing," said Eustace impatiently. "Anything that detracts from the dignity of these bearded old men is obscene. I daresay he was extremely clever—there's no doubt about it, he's an artist to his finger-tips and a different type of man from your father might be rather proud to help him. It's fortunate for us that he isn't, or our final hope would be sunk."

"A charming family *débâcle*," Olivia agreed. "Well, you must acknowledge this, Eustace. We do do things thoroughly; no skulking in odd corners for the Grays, once they get started."

"Has it ever occurred to you to wonder what corners are for, except to be skulked in? And that waste of any opportunity is a crime?" For an instant he had allowed his composure to be shaken, but now he regained control of himself. "I must say I see your father's point of view. It must be extremely annoying for a man who believes in no kind of possession but the material to learn that more than half his shares are worth no more than a load of stones. That's a man who'd hold up the Last Trump to get his halfpenny change."

Olivia laughed unwillingly. "What a good subject for Brand's malicious brush. Oh, Eustace, come to bed, if you don't want me to go mad. I've had enough for one night, And do you realise it's already Christmas Day?"

Eustace said in interested tones, paying no heed to her exhausted query, "The trouble with your father is he's not a racing man. A fellow who's going to speculate as we do ought to know what it is to drop three figures on a horse.

That's the only right type for speculation. The other kind are fools—blind fools, if you like, but beyond redemption. All right, Olivia. I'm going. Good night."

He drew the dark-blue brocaded dressing-gown more closely round him, and opened his dressing-room door.

"What are you going to do?" his wife asked.

"Think out some other way of pulling us out of this mess," he returned coolly, and closed the door.

After a minute, she hid her face in the pillow with a furious groan. The house claimed to be well built, but even through the heavy door she could hear those neat pointed feet going up and down, up and down the dressing-room as for the past two hours they had gone up and down before her bed.

5. Ruth

While Richard was venting his wrath—which, if it could not vie with the mercy of the Lord and endure for ever, at least lasted for a considerable period—upon an indifferent Laura, while Eustace was driving his wife crazy by walking up and down in front of her, and Amy, sitting up by candlelight, calculated the cost per plate per person of the Christmas meals, Miles Amery sat on the foot of his wife's bed and murmured affectionately, "Darling, you're getting as plump as a partridge. How I adore fat women!"

"I'm not a bit fat," said Ruth placidly, "and if I am, it's only because I like to please you. I'm sure it gives me no satisfaction to go about looking like something out of a pudding-cloth."

"You know my opinion about things that come out of pudding-cloths. Ruth darling, not even for you will I spend another Christmas under this inhospitable roof. I'd as soon be in gaol."

"Well, they are my family," offered Ruth weakly.

"For the hundred-and-first time, I'm convinced that you were a come-by-chance. No offence and all that, of course, but you simply can't be a blood relation of this preposterous family."

"It isn't that I wanted to come. You know I hate having Christmas away from the children. But this year you did seem quite as keen as me."

"Which isn't saying very much, if you come to analyse it. And I won't bring the brats here, even if your fond sister, Amy, would have them."

"She mightn't mind," suggested Ruth, in the same indecisive voice.

"I daresay she'd be quite pleased. I'm sure she'd find excellent excuses to beat them within an hour of their arrival. Very badly brought up, our children are. It's a pity she didn't live in the days of Solomon. She might have been his thousand-and-first lady friend. She'd have carried out his precepts regarding the upbringing of children so well. No, I wouldn't have them here for any bribe. Let them at all events preserve the illusion that Christmas is the children's feast, when one's efforts are primarily directed towards their entertainment, when they do come first and can, practically speaking, demand what they like and no one will refuse them. They'd develop into infant cynics if we had them down here for twenty-four hours."

Ruth thought of her babies, aged seven and four. They would be asleep long ago, and she was jealous of Emily, Miles's sister, who would have them for the three days of the holiday. They'd be lying in their blue-and-white striped pyjamas, excited and longing for the morning, Moira a little sophisticated and less ready than formerly to believe in visions and the sudden appearances of angels, but Pat still prepared at any moment to greet them, in classic robes of pink and blue, with haloes like gold soup-plates; or even the entire Holy Family peering out of the dark. It would neither have surprised nor alarmed her; just another instance of the fun and splendour that was her present conception of life.

Both had heart-shaped faces and short bright hair and were busy throughout the day with a grave intentness that charmed their parents. The beautiful solemnity and eagerness of their bearing as they mapped out a route for a picnic or arranged a dolls' tea-party or baptism touched Miles as being extraordinarily lovely, so that he resented the more being separated from them at such an important time.

He came at length out of his brown study to observe in troubled tones, "As a fact, I only agreed to come down this year because of Brand."

"Brand?" She made no attempt to conceal her surprise. "I didn't know you were specially friendly with him."

"I'm not. But I happened to be visiting in his part of the world the other day, and I met a man who knows him in a spasmodic sort of fashion. Brand has so few friends because that wife of his makes his home life so impossible. This fellow, Day, told me that there are people round there who would like to know Brand better, but the circumstances and the character of that appalling woman he's married put anything like intimacy out of the question. I shouldn't shout it from the housetops, but I believe the average decent chap is afraid of going into Brand's house uninvited, because he isn't sure whether he may not find himself alone with Sophy, and she's up to any game. Well, there seems to be a rumour that he's declared he won't stay there any longer; he's going to clear out and the others can fend for themselves. I don't suppose he would actually do that—it would be a bit difficult, because legally they're all his children, though rumour has some very odd stories to tell about them—but I shouldn't be at all surprised to know that he came down here in the hopes of getting his father to help him to get away."

"I don't for a moment suppose father would do anything of the kind."

"And yet it might be the best thing for everyone. It would certainly be the best thing for Brand. As for that woman, she'd soon find someone else to keep her, and she'll train those children to look after themselves. The eldest, Margot, can't be more than ten years old, but she's no little innocent. She'll know her way about almost as well as her mother by the time she's fifteen. And it would unquestionably remove a very dubious acquisition from our midst. After all, I suppose all those children are your nieces."

"And if Richard gets his title and doesn't achieve a family, Ferdinand—did you ever hear such a name for a Fulham baby?—will be Lord Tomnoddy in due course. I wonder if Richard's thought of that?"

"If he hasn't, some member of your amiable family is quite certain to point it out to him. I shouldn't trouble, if I were you."

"But you, Miles, why did you say you'd come down? What can you do?"

"I daresay I can't do anything, but I don't think Brand detests me quite so much as the rest of the family, and I'm really holding a watching brief for him, to prevent, if I can, anything too frightful happening. I feel that nothing would be too fantastic, considering the atmosphere of this place, and the people gathered under its roof. Between ourselves, I shan't be at all surprised if something tragic takes place before we get away. We've all the ingredients for a first-class explosion, and if it blows the place clean out of the ground, so much the better."

Ruth said uncertainly, with the haphazard impulsiveness that marked her younger child, "I suppose, if we got up now, there wouldn't be a train we could catch? I don't know why it is, but suddenly I feel as if I couldn't stay here. I don't always believe you, but there's something prophetic in your speech to-night. I believe there will be something horrible…"

"It won't be any less horrible because we've run away from it. No, we shall have to stay here. Besides, there's Brand. There are the others, too, but I don't give a flip of the fingers for them. Their trouble is money in its most sordid aspect. Brand's different. He's paying in compound interest for a stupid mistake he made a dozen years ago. And he's got something rare which I don't believe any of you have recognised. It's burning still, through all his disillusion and despair. He's in the wrong place, and of course he's making hay of his life. If he could be got out, it might be the saving of him. There's something in Brand that's valuable, that mustn't be allowed to go to waste. If something isn't done soon, there'll be a worse tragedy than anything that happens here to-night."

"I didn't know you felt like that about him," marvelled Ruth, her dark eyes grave, her face, like her elder daughter's, perplexed and enquiring.

"It isn't Brand himself—not the individual he represents, I mean; it's something he is, something intangible—not the man but the vehicle of power that he represents. Do I make myself at all clear?"

He felt that he probably didn't, and went to stand by the window, whence he could see little groups of people bent against the black wind, making their way back from the Midnight Mass. Like pilgrims of the new age he saw them, returning from Bethlehem, walking gravely and without speech. Their dark figures against the snow were like a Lovat Fraser frieze. His heart smote him anew for his little girls.

The house was uneasy with the noises of old houses at night. Doors creaked and shadows seemed full of anonymous life; phantom steps sounded in empty corridors and on the black stairs. Once Miles thought he actually heard ghostly feet hesitate in the passage outside his door, but brusquely he drove the thought away as an absurd imagination. But that, had he known it, was Brand groping past the lighted door to his own room, his shoes in his hand.

6. Brand

Brand had been from the first a thorn in the side of his family. Destined for the Church, in place of the dead Philip, to fill the handsome family living whose incumbent was invariably a Gray, he rebelled at the age of sixteen, demanding instead his opportunity to become an artist. He was singularly unfortunate in his parentage in this connection. Since a certain deplorable incident in his own career some years earlier, Adrian had become each year more intolerant, stupid, and suspicious of the motives of other men, and was convinced that men only wanted to study art because that kind of life allowed a greater licence of morals and behaviour. Artists, he knew, did not marry the women with whom they lived, failed to provide for their children, left their quarters without settling their rent account, borrowed money they never intended to repay—were, *tout court,* a drunken, licentious, bawdy crowd, who paid nothing into the community sack in return for the board and lodging they exacted as their due.

Brand's school career had been a chequered one, and this further proof of his instability enraged his father. He treated the boy without tact, and with a complete absence of the deference due to youth by its elders. Brand retaliated by leaving home without a word; nor did anyone ever discover whence he obtained the means for flight. Some months later he was heard of in Paris. Richard travelled over to bring him back, but returned unaccompanied. Brand, he reported, had obtained work of a kind that, he declared, provided his daily bread, his candle, and his rent. His lodging, said Richard fastidiously, was highly unsatisfactory, and his mode of employment unbecoming to his birth and parentage. As to his leisure time, this he spent in the most thriftless and even perilous way. He had seen a number of sketches, of the type that young would-be artists appeared to prefer, decorating Brand's single room, and he personally considered them shocking. He spoke gravely to his father of the danger of contamination to young innocent sisters. Brand, moreover, had formed a number of quite undesirable friendships, having, it seemed, no sense of what was due to his tradition. Altogether, the whole affair was humiliating and apparently incurable. Three years later Richard made a second journey, on this occasion because Gray was seriously ill and it was thought he was unlikely to recover. By this time he discovered that he and his father and Amy had been perfectly justified in their prognostications. Brand had given up his earlier employment and now made a precarious living as an artist. He was something of an experimentalist, and whenever he felt himself master of a certain technique, would abandon that particular type of work and embark on another—the height of folly, as Richard pointed out to him, as editors and patrons appreciate stability as much as other men and prefer to know what they are buying. But all Brand's pictures were pigs in pokes, and he appeared not even to consider his brother's suggestion that he should confine himself to one definite type of work. Jack-of-all-Trades, Richard dubbed him.

But worse was to come. It transpired that, during the previous year or more, Brand had been living (promiscuously, said Richard. "You ought to buy a dictionary," retorted Brand) with a woman of dubious reputation, known to the quarter as Sophy. None of the family, at all events, ever knew

her other name. Taxed with the episode, Brand unconcernedly acknowledged its truth, adding that the association had
terminated some months since. After this Richard scarcely
tried to persuade his brother to return, and in any case Brand
had no intention of doing so.

Richard's report to his father lacked no tone or hint that
might make it effectual. But even he was alarmed at the
depths and violence of the older man's rage. It was several
hours before he could be sufficiently quieted to remain seated
for a quarter of an hour at a time in one chair.

"Such profligacy," he panted, "such depravity! And if he
is like this when he is young, what are we to expect later?"—
taking the rather illogical view that such conduct in an older
and more experienced man, who might be expected to have
learned more self-control, would be less heinous.

"He is no son of mine," he cried fiercely, "and he shall
never again enter this house." And proceeded to inveigh,
with a pronounced biblical fervour, against these "strange
women" and their partners in evil-doing.

Richard pacified him at last, and Brand's name was
dropped. Meanwhile, he himself continued to live in Paris
in strange places, and to work, when he could not sell his
pictures, at employment not commonly resorted to by men
of birth and education. It could not be urged, in defence of
his choice of a career, that either fame or money rewarded
his rather bizarre genius. He came perilously near to starva-
tion several times during those experimental years, and then,
when he seemed to have lifted himself for the moment out
of the rut of anxiety and poverty, his family was shocked
and enraged by his announcement that he had married the
woman Sophy, and that there was already a child, a boy,
born several months before the ceremony. Little news came
from him thereafter. Gray refused to speak of him or to
meet his wife. Brand never wrote, and it was by haphazard

means that they learned of the death of the little son when he was five years old. They had no details of the days and nights of agony, the travail of spirit and flesh that Brand endured as he watched the puny child struggle for his life, the twisted limbs and tortured pinched features—of all this they never knew anything. Six months later Brand and his wife and their three small daughters left Paris for London, where Brand obtained an insignificant post as draughtsman to some obscure firm, who paid him badly and worked him dishonestly. Sophy was again pregnant, though not, said malicious neighbours, on her husband's account this time. Brand paid no heed to rumour, nor appeared to care what his wife did. He took no interest in his surviving children, to whom he seldom spoke. The family settled in a shabby, artisan quarter of Fulham, where the slovenly Sophy, a shawl over her disordered hair, could be seen gossiping with her less reputable neighbours, and buying canned food for her family, while the house was thick with dust and the children went neglected and dirty to their compulsory school, where they were consistently miserable, and were jeered at for their torn frocks and broken shoes. Early in life, however, they had adopted a stoic philosophy. Since their neighbours seldom allowed their own children to play with the little Grays, the latter rapidly gravitated to the level of the unkempt urchins whom they saw playing in the roads and grubbing among dust-heaps and drawing wooden sticks with great rapidity along railings, maddening the more sensitive in the neighbourhood, nor did they suspect that Sophy was more than normally neglectful or abusive. Quarrels between their parents they accepted without comment, even among themselves; when Brand came in they were apt to scurry out of sight. Their mother possessed the vicious temper and uncertain ways of the slattern, and they were often beaten or underfed when one of her bouts of inexplicable ferocity attacked her, or when, as frequently, she was under the influence of drink. Sometimes they were pitied by neighbours, who thought them half starved and blue with the cold, and would invite them to sit by their fires, and give them thick slices of bread and dripping or crusts spattered with a peculiar red jam. It did not strike either Brand or Sophy as strange that their uncle should be a prominent Member of Parliament, living at Belgrave Square, and their grandfather a country gentleman of independent means. The children, of course, knew nothing of their relations.

On the 23rd December, 1931, Gray received a letter from his younger son to the effect that he proposed to join their party for Christmas. The embargo against his presence had been lifted some years after his marriage, although Sophy never accompanied him on his visits to King's Poplars. For this, Brand was grateful enough. His life with her in their inadequate quarters, the difficulty he experienced in escaping from her nagging tongue and her unclean ways, irked him even more than the conditions at his father's house. Besides, he enjoyed twitting Richard on his childlessness and enraging Amy by his disregard of the household's conventions. She counted every slice of bread and every ball of butter a visitor consumed, and it was amusing and at the same time satisfying to a man who was not accustomed to good food to irritate her as much as possible in this elementary fashion.

Gray had returned no answer to his son's letter, and Brand, whose finances were in a worse way than usual, went down black and fierce, and determined at all costs to put his plan into action. He could expect no sympathy from any of his relatives, since this plan involved the virtual desertion of his family in order to enable him to return to Paris and resume his work there. He proposed suggesting that Sophy and the children—the last of whom he was convinced was not his child, whatever might be said about Anne—should pay a protracted visit to King's Poplars, and so insanely bent was he upon the successful consummation of his endeavour that he contrived to persuade himself that he was putting forward a reasonable request. He found Eustace and, later, Richard in command of the field. His efforts to see his father alone were frustrated by both of these, and also by Amy; so that it was not until the party had broken up for the night—early, on account of the morrow being Christmas Day—that he found an opportunity for approaching Adrian.

From the outset the interview was stormy; Gray's tone, while remaining suave, became increasingly sneering and bitter. Brand spoke fiercely and unwisely. Gray retaliated by giving his son his views on art, and the conversation closed in the manner indicated above.

Part II

The Journal of Hildebrand Gray

1

…And the extraordinary part of it is that it was nothing
but an accident, much as if I'd smashed the milk-jug or
dropped one of the dinner-plates. Even in my moments of
panic I was able to appreciate that. It hadn't any more significance than those trivialities. The significance lay in the
consequences. And those hardly bore thinking about, in all
the circumstances.

I was so much taken aback when I saw him slip down to
my feet with so little sound it might have been a ghost falling, that at first I was incapable of realising what I'd done.
I just stood and stared. I couldn't believe that he was dead.
When at last I did, two things amazed me. The first was
the shocking swiftness of death. A minute ago he had been
standing in his favourite attitude, patronising me because
I was a failure by his standards, that have always seemed
to me intolerably contemptible and false, and now he lay
there—and he would never, never get up again.

I suppose it isn't a very ordinary situation. Not many
people can have murdered their father in a fit of rage; and
so it may be difficult for the majority to believe that I simply
couldn't understand, couldn't make my mind understand,
that is—what had occurred. I repeated over and over again,

"He's dead. I've killed him. I'm a murderer. Murderers hang." But it was no use. I couldn't believe it, and presently, through sheer repetition, the words ceased to have any meaning at all, and became as incongruous as any casual collection of letters might, if you stared at them long enough. Even the word "murderer," the word "hang," meant nothing.

And the second thing that struck me was the effect that death has on people, the instantaneous, humiliating effect. I am thirty-two, but I haven't come in contact with death much. The only other time I remember was when Hartley died in Paris, and everything was different then. He was not six years old, and he died in agony, and everything was prolonged to a nightmare extent. That wasn't like death as I had ever conceived it. That was an anguished withering of childhood into a premature decay. There was nothing peaceful or beautiful about him as he lay in his coffin, an absurd white satin affair, with lilies of the valley round that dreadful shrivelled face. That was the sole occasion when I found myself compelled to realise that there is an agony known to men that cannot merely stir, but actually wring the heart. Even now I can't bear people to talk to me about him, and one of the reasons why I left Paris was because I wanted to settle among people who had never seen him. He's the one thing, besides my work, that I have cared for in my life, and he has gone out of it. It's ironical, if you care to stop and think about it, to realise that I married Sophy solely for his sake, and now he's vanished, and I am left with her and Margot and Eleanor and Dulcie and Anne, and the baby, whose father I most probably am not, though, of course, I can't find out, and anyway now it has ceased to matter.

But here there was something so shocking, so abominable about death that I stared at my father's face in a kind of repelled fascination. I had expected something, in adult death at least, of dignity, a certain majesty and grandeur.

But there was none, not a trace of heroism. Now that the corners of the mouth were no longer kept under control by the tense jaw—and it's queer how I had never realised the desperate effort it must have cost him to preserve that aspect of nobility that made men admire him and women feel a peculiar attraction towards him—the muscles sagged to a weak peevishness; his nostrils, that had been finely modelled as a younger man, became pinched and fretful; the eyes were vacant and the whole face, in shedding its handsome scholarly asceticism, that had been so fine a mask during his life, betrayed now an astounding cupidity.

Of course, it didn't surprise me, any more than it would surprise Richard or Amy or—I fancy—Miles Amery, whom I have always credited with more than the usual amount of commonsense, that isn't without its shrewd vein of cynicism. And I don't think he was ever deceived by my father's manner. He (my father) liked to appear a philosopher, a man of tranquil moods and reflections, and if some company in which he held shares passed its dividend, or if the shares themselves went down a point or two, he'd sulk like a child, refuse food, make the most humiliating scenes about trifles in household expenditure, curtail this or that necessity, and in general behave as though he had lost thousands of pounds.

I looked up and saw the eyes of the first Hildebrand watching me. I was named for him, the famous prince of the Church of the early sixteenth century, whose portrait hangs in one of the recesses of the library. It's supposed to be immensely valuable. There was another Hildebrand, too, but he was an obscure preaching friar, who took the habit and lived in a manner that we—even I, who pig it in a squalid hole in Fulham, where the ceilings are cracked and the wallpapers speckled with damp and the sanitation unspeakable—should regard as absolutely disgusting. *Autres temps, autres modes.* It appeared to suit him very well, and shortly after his death so many miracles were reported at his nameless grave that his beatification was accelerated, and perhaps he is now in a superior position to the Cardinal. Which exemplifies the Church's teaching about the first and the last, and is therefore quite fitting.

This Hildebrand who hangs in the library has the expression of a statesman, a disillusioned statesman who knows his own power and despises it. I am never wholly comfortable when I meet his eyes. But, if it comes to that, I'm never wholly at ease in that room at all. It gives you some notion of the type of man my father was that he could sit there and brood over his financial affairs without a sense of self-abasement or even of discomfort. On second thoughts, I'm not sure it isn't the kind of room every artist should have to work in—by which I mean, should be compelled to work in. It isn't a room where such a man could produce scamped work or be satisfied with the second-rate or even with the first-rate that came easily to him. Because it is conceivable that a time comes when the work a man does becomes devoid of effort, and then, of course, he must go forward and experiment with the impossible till that becomes attainable, too, and so on. I doubt if my father had ever experienced a shred of diffidence of that kind. He could strut pompously into that amazing room and sit for hours calculating possible gains and losses, and not even understand that he was hemmed in by the greatest wisdom, beauty, and craftsmanship of the centuries. The walls are lined with the achievements of genius; there are books there crammed with a learning that must make the greatest of all artists ashamed of his own deficiencies. And in a glass-fronted case against one wall is a collection of articles in crystal, amber, and jade so beautiful in their sincerity and perfection that they take the breath away. To say nothing of the embroideries on the chairs and the long couch that half fills the window recess. My father used to have me down there years ago when there was trouble brewing, and for the life of me I could never bring out the elaborate lie I had planned before coming downstairs. But he himself never felt any embarrassment. When I was about seventeen I realised that only two kinds of men could work in such a room—the very humble and the supremely conceited. But, brooding over, and even ashamed of, his insignificance, it did occur to me, as I saw him dead at my feet, that probably he showed here to the worst possible advantage, and might look less despicable in any other room.

I found myself, indeed, saying aloud, "It would be bad luck for any ordinary man to die in here," and as I spoke I heard the words for the first time, and realised what I had done. It was no longer necessary for me to repeat my formula. The position in all its peril was suddenly quite clear. The fact that I had picked up the oblong of brass, that he used as a paper-weight, with the intention of slamming it on the table to silence him at all costs, and with no idea of striking him with it, wouldn't for an instant count in my favour. I should never make a level-headed jury understand that when a man of my father's calibre starts talking about art, and the obligations of the individual to the community (that he doesn't, of course, consider artists fulfil), he has to be stopped; he becomes intolerable. I felt myself tremble with that mad impotent rage children know when they recognise their powerlessness to insist on their own aspect of a position. A man who could seriously hold his views had no right to go on living; he was so much waste matter. And I have no respect for life *qua* life, though I have respect for any form of life that fulfils its proper function. Nor do I agree that any mass of men has the right to dictate to the individual, or to any other mass as to the nature of his or their particular function. Everything about my father was futile, his death as much as his life, and since I caused that death I share his futility. Indeed, I have never been so much ashamed of anything, without being in the least sorry. It was foolish, of course, to have married Sophy, but I can find reasons for that. There was Hartley, and I couldn't have foreseen that he would die when he was five years old. But this was the result of a fit of blind passion, the kind of feeling that insincere and ignoble people create in me. I would have minded so much less if he had had the courage of his convictions and said, "All I care about is what I possess, what belongs to me. That's my world." But he had to pretend to be something much finer and nobler than he was, and that's where he failed completely from the artistic viewpoint. But I realise as well as anyone else that you can't talk that kind of argument to a jury.

Remembering juries brought me back to a consideration of my position, and I was immediately enraged to think that my life, that has a certain value, should be forfeited on account of his, that was quite worthless. Not, of course, that anyone would agree with my scale of values. None of my family under this roof, not Sophy either. I doubt whether anything that happens to me will affect her. She at least makes no pretence, though I do not appear to like or admire her any better for that. I suspect that at bottom I am as completely illogical as she. I don't allow that either she or my father has any purpose in life, and therefore they have actually no right to life at all. She has no family pride through which she can be attacked; in all the circumstances it would be unreasonable to look for it. Her own mother had as little reputation as herself, and my family has refused to recognise her existence. With the exception of Isobel, who doesn't count and has been utterly crushed by my father and Amy, they would not have her near the house, and certainly she wouldn't be at home here. Not that I think she would be embarrassed and humble to the servants or cringing to my relations. She'd be brazen and underbred—well, I knew she was that when I married her. It is too late in the day to whine now.

My rage was chiefly on my own account. I had at length come to an unalterable decision, had determined to close this drab phase of my experience and return to my place in the only world where I am familiar and can do useful work; and precisely at this juncture a piece of crass stupidity was going to overset all my plans. It was intolerable to me that my father, who had consistently thwarted and disappointed every hope I ever cherished, should be able to continue that work after death, with my connivance. For if I'd flung that brass weight on to the table, as I had intended, instead of swinging round on him with a mad desire to wipe that smooth patronising sneer off his face, even he couldn't have prevented my putting my plan into action. Somehow I'd have compelled him to help me. He had sworn he wouldn't, but he would scarcely have allowed it to be said that his grandchildren were in guardians' homes. In fact, I believe the law could force him to make some provision for them. I told him so.

"I'm clearing out," I said crudely. "I'm going back to Paris."

"And what of Sophy and your children?" he demanded.

Some fiend in me prompted me to reply, "There's yourself, sir, if other provision falls short."

"I won't give them a penny," he shouted, and added that probably half the children weren't even mine.

I retaliated that English law makes a man responsible for all his wife's children, regardless of paternity, so long as she remains his wife, and added that he'd be liable for them all, should it come to a question of State support.

He leapt up in a towering rage, screaming abusively that he wouldn't have anything to do with the bastards, and they could all die in a workhouse for all he cared. I said I didn't suppose they knew they had a grandfather, as they'd never been allowed within a mile of the house, and my disappearance might be an advantage to them, inasmuch as it would give the whole lot of them a chance to meet one another.

He cried me down; he talked of cumberers and touts and leeches; he reminded me of the times he and Richard have helped me in the past. He orated on improvidence, dishonest improvidence.

What could I say? Of course he's helped me. He knows my circumstances, and it would be instructive to see how he or Richard could bring up a family on something under five pounds a week. My only retort, that he'd spent precious little on my education and that, without investment, you can't expect dividends, brought the rejoinder that I'd had my chance, and refused to take it, and had forfeited any further consideration. That was when my temper began to boil over, because he went on to compare the present with the roseate might-have-been—would-have-been according to him, if I'd accepted his judgment. And, of course, he couldn't leave Sophy alone. He's never met her, and he couldn't probably, at any time, understand the peculiar effect she had on me a dozen years ago. She was one of those haggard-looking women who seem a well of suppressed passion, but are really like those cardboard moulds of butter that you see in the windows of dairy-shops. At the time, however, I pictured her as Héloïse or Laura. We drifted apart for a bit, and at first I forgot her, and then went mad for her again and made frantic efforts to find her out. It was then that I discovered she had borne my child. It sobered me considerably; I was just twenty, but I felt I had a wealth of experience, uncommon in men twice my age, behind me. When I saw little Hartley (she hadn't troubled to have him christened, so I could please myself as to a name) I insisted on marrying his mother. From the first she occupied a secondary place;

what that boy meant to me I couldn't express, and, anyway, it doesn't matter any more. It didn't spring, my feeling for him, from any innate love of children. When Sophy began to breed them as thick as rabbits I ignored them as much as I could. Sophy didn't seem to care about them, either, and she never showed them much attention, beyond feeding them in a haphazard manner and threatening to skin them alive if they weren't quiet.

Each time a new baby came, I swore it should be the last, but living as we did, pigging it in small rooms on practically no money, I wearing myself out with work and anxiety that unmarried men don't experience, I fairly naturally broke through my resolutions and took from Sophy any satisfaction I could get. Presently even I had to admit we couldn't go on; I was making very little money, and one or other of the children was perpetually ill, wanting a doctor or needing medicine, or clamouring for warm clothes. Sophy's complaints got more and more on my nerves. I couldn't start work but she'd come plaintively up to the studio, whining that there was insufficient money in the house for the midday meal. I wrote home for money once or twice, and my father sent me a little of that and a great deal of advice and garnered wisdom. But life was becoming impossible for me, and at last, in a frenzy, I accepted an offer of work in a draughtsman's office in England. I earned four pounds a week, and on the strength of this we took a house in a frowsy terrace in Fulham. Hartley was dead by this time, and in his place were three little girls, and another baby on the way. My job entailed drawing houses about three times their actual scale, so that my employers' clients were deceived and swindled. I don't pretend that the ethical position affected me much. What seemed to me unpardonable was that I should be spending the best years of my life in this futile way. I was twenty-seven, and I've been at it for five years. And a month ago I made up my mind that, at all costs, I would get out and get back to my own job.

And just as I didn't concern myself with the men who were cheated by my drawings, so I refused to consider Sophy and her children. I was, by this time, sufficiently cynical to believe that if people chose to allow themselves to be cheated, that was their affair. And I regarded myself among those who had been hoodwinked. I despised myself utterly.

During those five years I worked—in my sense of the word—whenever I could. At first Sophy encouraged me, till she realised it wouldn't mean more grist to the mill. She would follow me to the studio, saying, "But, Brand, why not do a pretty picture of the bridge? There are always men painting that bridge, and they sell them and come back and do more."

"And sell those and come back again," I suggested.

She nodded.

"And that's your idea for me?"

She became, as usual, abusive, tart, and vulgar. "My idea is that the children shall have shoes and I shall have under-clothes that I would not be utterly ashamed to be found in in an accident," she shrilled.

One becomes accustomed to this outlook at last—that practically everyone really professes and believes it to be more important to earn a living than to do your own job. No doubt I was to blame in getting married, but I wasn't going to waste my precious leisure painting bloody little pictures of the Battersea Bridge or the view from Hammersmith down to Putney.

My sister, Olivia, was another person who could not leave me alone. I daresay Sophy went to her asking for money, probably taking a child in a ragged frock. I have always detested Olivia, and particularly since she married that smooth-faced double-dealing Jew financier, Eustace Moore.

He's tremendously proud of her; they go about "simply everywhere, my dear," and she writes damnable bright letters in the Illustrated Weeklies—"Cherry, darling, I simply must tell you of a hat I saw on the boulevard this morning," and "They do say the most extraordinary thing happened at the Monroe-Phillips' last night..." Eustace thinks the earth of her because she can look like a lady (his conception of a lady anyhow) and yet makes money like a business woman. They have two sons, called Montague and Arnold, and a car whose photograph gets into the papers. Every now and again Olivia writes to me, or even comes down to Fulham ("Pray for me, darling, I'm going slumming. Yes, my poor relations. Too revolting, isn't it?"—I can hear her say that to her fashionable friends).

"You mustn't think me unsympathetic, Brand," she says in what I believe is known as a liquid voice, "it isn't that I don't feel for you. But life is even greater than art, and you have your children to think of. It isn't as if I couldn't see your point of view. But Eustace would feel himself dreadfully badly used, and so would the boys, if I didn't tear myself away when they need me. And yet I'm sure when I'm in the mood I scarcely feel as if any other world existed. It's all a question of discipline, and even if I do resent Eustace sometimes interrupting me, I comfort myself by thinking that discipline is as necessary in the study—or the studio—as in the nursery."

"And all this bloody stuff I do at Higginsons is good discipline for me?" I suggested.

She beamed and said yes, it was. For years now, whenever I've thought of her or seen her, I have dreamed of getting my own back. Between her and Sophy and my father, things have been almost intolerable. I reminded him of that to-night. You know how it is sometimes, when the dignity of life holds you and you instinctively respond, feeling a kind of nobility in yourself simply for being linked to life. And then there are other days—and this evening was one—when dignity is a word without a meaning, and you feel yourself cheap and vulgar and uncontrolled. That's called a nervous outburst or hysteria, I believe. It really means a stage when you've endured all that's possible. After the past seven weeks at Fulham this evening's scene with my father was the last straw. I had known when I came down to King's Poplars that I wasn't really ready for the interview; I wanted a little time to get my second wind. But when I saw Richard and Eustace hovering like vultures over a corpse not quite dead enough for them, but prepared with beak and talons to defend their carrion, I knew I dared not wait. My brooding on the kind of life I henceforth proposed to live had given me a quite unfounded optimism, and when I went down to my father I give you my word, though no one will believe me, I did so with an assurance that this time I should make him appreciate my point of view and fall in with my suggestions. Within five minutes I realised the kind of fool I had been. Anticipations and hope might have changed me, but he was the same as ever. I could repeat his strictures for him. Always the same stuff about responsibility and the family name and the value of honourable work. I tried to make him see that it wasn't honourable, either in essence or in fact, and that for a man of my potentialities to remain there was as bad as theft. Of course, he dismissed all this in the most slighting manner—Fulham oratory he called it—and both our tempers began to split. He was quietly, futilely, impertinently humorous at the expense of men whose shoes he is not fit to black. The scene became increasingly violent; having lost my head, I was soon at the end of my tether. It was then that I seized the paper-weight.

He laughed. "You're quite right," he said; "arguments like yours need solid reinforcements."

And then I struck him, with no more notion of what I was doing in the moment of performance than the weight itself. The moment he dropped, so quietly and without a groan, I felt all passion die out of me. I was small and light and empty. Also I realised that the room was very cold. I looked at the fireplace; the fire had gone out some time ago.

2

For some time after I came to my senses and saw the position as it actually was, I walked aimlessly round the room, accomplishing nothing. I knew vaguely there were things to be done, but I could not recognise what they were. For a minute I think I expected the door to burst open and all the family to come rushing in pell-mell, in their dressing-gowns, their hair wild, their faces creased with suspicion. Indeed, I even had a vision of them, like a tail-piece to some child's story. But nothing happened, and I forgot them again. I began to shiver, but that, I think, was only because of the fierce wind raging outside. The Manor at King's Poplars is built on the side of a steep slope, and is quite unprotected from any rough weather. In the mornings the grass in the pasture is like glass when the sun catches it, and the streams are all frozen over. This Christmas night the earth was as hard and rugged as Christina Rossetti pictures it in her carol. "Wind made moan, Earth was hard as iron, Water like a stone." There were no cattle in the fields now (they'd have been frozen, I think), and no fowl on the ice-bound lakes and streams. The whole aspect was peculiarly desolate. A good many of the neighbouring houses are farms, and here there has been any amount of distress during the hard winter. The land is a tricky employer at the best of times, and this black season had followed a bad harvest; the valleys beneath our windows were full of unemployed men, and there had been ugly stories of rioting near by. For the past twenty-four hours a fierce gale had raged. If you stood still for a moment and listened, it seemed as if the house must come down about your ears; there was so much noise and confusion beyond the window, where the shrubs and trees creaked and groaned in the wind. Indeed, when at last I came back to the body by the window, I had very distinctly the impression of being the only living thing in the place. At that thought, there came to me the curious impression everyone knows, that someone was actually in the room with me, and, lifting my head with a jerk, I saw, with a shock of horror, another face staring into mine. I did not recognise it at first, that dark-skinned face with the head flung back, the lips curled and set, the dark hair swept back with a clean hard decision, the dominant chin, the eyes dark and blazing, the whole countenance irradiated with a vitality that held me dumb. Then I knew who it was. Since my last visit here my father had acquired a French mirror of very beautiful workmanship, that now hung on the opposite wall. And the face that I saw was my own, flashing back at me. I was so much fascinated to know what I looked like when I was off my guard, unconscious and alert, that I stepped over the body and went closer, moved by a curiosity that was even greater than my admiration. So this was the personality I habitually concealed beneath the shabby dress and bearing of a clerk at four pounds ten a week. This was the essential man I had intended to be, who was intended to be myself (I kept twisting the words round to hammer the fact into my startled consciousness), and who had, it seemed, not been entirely conquered by the circumstances of my personal life.

When I saw that keen thrusting face, I thought immediately, "It's infamous that such a man should spend his life drawing faked plans for Higginsons." Already, so powerful was the force of the revelation, I was eager to be out and

doing my own work. I thought I could detect a new supple-
ness of wrist, an enlarging of vision, a greater ease of imagination, a more swiftly thronged brain. I foresaw my future,
thick, not with success—I anticipated neither that nor the
money that accompanies it—but with new conceptions, with
experiments, with colossal ideas. As if a dam had burst, or
some gate been flung down, I felt these new forces filling me,
submerging my timidities and anxieties. I owed it to the self
that mirror had revealed to give that man his opportunity.
Instinctively I determined to preserve his expression and
purpose, to strengthen my own resolution in the days ahead.
I always carry about with me a sketch-book and pencil, and
this pencil I lend to no one. I'm not precisely superstitious
about it, but I don't lend it for ordinary note-taking. In fact,
I don't lend it at all.

My brain seemed on fire. My hand had a new assurance
and zest. I soon transferred to paper that memorable face,
and when I had finished I stood admiring my own work,
the bold economy of line, the clean strength, the neatness of
detail, the sense of vigorous personality the sketch conveyed.

I signed it as usual, with what Sophy calls my melodramatic monogram, and glanced at the calendar for the date.
It has always been an idiosyncrasy of mine to sign and date
even quite insignificant studies. When I saw the figures "24"
on the calendar I remembered that this was Christmas Eve,
would soon be Christmas Day. And, looking at the clock, I
saw with surprise that the hands pointed to half-past one,
and that Christmas Day had actually dawned. I began to
scribble 25.12... when I was startled by a sudden tremendous commotion behind me. I turned, dropping the pencil,
prepared to face some terrific onslaught. But it was only the
wind, that had torn open one of the casement windows, sent
the curtains billowing into the room, and swept a blue bowl
on to the floor. The room was full of uproar, a succession of

blasts and whistles and the peculiar heavy thrashing sound made by tapestry curtains in a storm. I stood aghast. Now, I thought, the whole household will descend, and take me like the proverbial rat. And with the instant death of hope I found I was, surprisingly, not afraid. I stiffened involuntarily, certainly, but I think any man might have done as much; but I neither trembled nor sweated. I still had the sketch in my hand, and I seemed to derive a certain derisive strength from that. I had dropped my pencil when the vase went over, and now, as I stooped to retrieve it, I found to my annoyance that the lead had broken off short. I looked round for a knife, but there was none, and in any case, I reflected an instant later, I didn't need one now.

Mirabile dictu, no one came. Yet the house was full of people. I thought of them as I had seen them at dinner, so correct and well established, in their fine well-cut clothes, with their perfect manners, their polite meaningless gestures, their aimless chit-chat, their complete ignoring of reality. And yet I daresay that was merely the surface; underneath, Richard and Eustace at all events were agog with eagerness and suspense. But they concealed it well. Still, even in their politeness they managed to make it abundantly clear that I wasn't of their world, but was here, not even on sufferance, since I hadn't been invited, but because I had thrust myself upon them. I remembered particularly Olivia in white satin, that her complexion can't really stand well, and that woman Richard married looking absolutely magnificent in sea-green brocade. It was much too fine a dress to wear in a place like this, but it made her stand out like some figure in a canvas. I don't care much about portrait-painting myself, but I should appreciate an opportunity of painting her as one of the great symbolic or legendary figures. I have never seen how she could care for Richard, but like the rest of them she puts up a fine bluff.

Thinking of them all, and of my own ambitions, that were never for more than a moment out of my thoughts, I visualised them as a pack of hounds on my trail, and immediately I determined not to be taken. Somehow I must contrive to put them off the scent, lay a false trail, deny having been here. Immediately I began to examine the room, to see what traces of my visit were obvious. The first thing I set eyes on was the paper-weight, lying on the edge of the writing-table where I had put it in that first moment of blank confusion. There was a dark stain on it—blood, of course—and a sliver of bloodstained skin. I turned to my father and saw that where I had struck him the skin of the temple had swelled and become a bluish-purple in colour. There was a long, clearly defined cut just above the eyebrow level. My first hopes of suggesting an accident were dashed. It would be obvious that he had not fallen, but had been struck down. I brooded for a minute on suicide, but that was equally out of the question. A man could scarcely take his own life in that fantastic manner. There remained only one solution, the truth; and that I must twist to make it appear that someone else was guilty. I pulled a handkerchief out of my pocket and polished up the weight. I couldn't afford to leave tell-tale marks on anything that might be connected with the crime. And, since the handkerchief was now stained, I decided to destroy that before leaving the room. I was sorry, because it was a good handkerchief, of fine silk. I had not held such a handkerchief in my hand since I married. Sophy gives me cheap cotton squares, that I sometimes suspect her of making out of disused sheets; at all events, they never wash satisfactorily, and are generally impounded for one or other of the children, whichever of them at the moment has the inevitable cold in the head. I saw Olivia staring disdainfully at my handkerchief the day before, at lunch, so when, coming down to dinner, I saw that Eustace had dropped one of his silk ones in the doorway of his room, I appropriated it without a twinge of conscience. Isobel teased me about it. Going up in the world, she said I was.

Olivia has a habit that I have always loathed, but that now I might turn to good account. As a child she always knew the extent of her possessions, and ferocious battles were waged as to the ownership of some paltry plaything or scrap of material. I make no doubt that at any moment during her married life she could have reeled off a list of Eustace's wardrobe and her own, recalling where every article was bought. And if he lost a handkerchief she certainly wouldn't allow that to be overlooked. I hoped for my own sake that she would discover her loss before anyone raised a hue and cry, for then all that was left of it would be found in the same room as the dead man, and obvious conclusions would be drawn. The fire, unfortunately, was out, and I had to burn the handkerchief by means of lighted matches. It took a good many, for one of Sophy's economies is to buy cheap foreign matches, whose sticks are often no more than a splinter and snap at the slightest contact. When I'd burnt it completely, holding it down among the ashes with a poker to make sure it remained as evidence, I looked round wondering what next to do. Then a frightful thing happened. All my life, since very early childhood, I've been subject to sudden panics, due as a rule to overstrained imagination. As a small boy, for me, also, the hag sat nightly by my pillow; and in moments of panic I suffer a return of these delusions. For instance, at this moment I perceived an exceedingly tall man lounging against the bookcase in the shadow, watching me sardonically. Turning my eyes thence, I discovered a small hunched dwarf among the hangings and draperies of the couch; faces gibbered from the folds of the curtains, and steps sounded in the shadowy corners. The horrid thought came to me that these apparitions had not been apparent until I had closed the window, and the fancy attacked me that I had thus shut myself in with these creatures of fable and imagery. Absurd though it must seem, it was some minutes before I could persuade my overwrought brain to accept the obvious facts, namely that I was allowing myself to be terrified by an accumulation of shadows, echoes, and the effects of a chance draping of hangings and tapestries.

It is astounding how slowly the mind works in times of crisis, when you might suppose it would be more than normally alert. I found myself staring aimlessly round the room with no fixed idea in my mind, except a rigid intention to escape somehow the consequences of what I had done. Not that I underrate murder as a crime; I am even prepared to admit it is the worst of all crimes, since it involves robbing your neighbour of the one thing worth possessing—physical life. Though what value life could have had to such a man as my father I don't know, particularly as, if accounts are true, he was on the verge of losing even the wretched things he did care for. It was then that I saw the cheque-book lying among the other papers on his desk.

3

There is a great deal of nonsense talked by men who are neither artists nor poor about the advantages of poverty, of the freedom engendered by small incomes and a corresponding lack of responsibility. Poets who don't have to earn a weekly wage, but write as they will, sing blithely in praise of our Lady Poverty, and hark back to St. Francis and various other saints, who don't appear to have had families to support. In any case, they'd be the first to blame us if we tried to shift our burdens and live on the community. And begging wasn't an offence in those old days. Besides, it's all wrong. I only wish these lunatics could experience poverty for themselves, real poverty, that would teach them what responsibilities mean when there are insufficient means to cope with them. Life doesn't send the greatest responsibilities to the men with the most comfortable incomes. They get visited on rich and poor alike. And poverty in the twentieth century means, as I have ample reason to know, cracked ceilings, undignified shifts and excuses, damp-speckled walls, peeling paper, inferior food, the persistent whine of dissatisfied or sickly children, a general crowding together and lack of leisure and privacy both, and all the kindred humiliations of the dispirited poor. I don't pretend that everyone else feels the lack of space both to move and think and create that I do. I know my father and brother call them luxury, but to me they're as essential as bread. And so, when I saw the cheque-book, I thought I saw also my opportunity.

Since I had killed a man, I might surely take full advantage of the fact. Later it might return to haunt me; but at least it should not deride my futility, cowardice, lack of enterprise, call it what you like, as well as my crime. I knew my father well enough to realise that, of his estate, not a penny would come to me; nor could I appeal to any of my relatives. But from childhood I have had a certain dexterity in copying signatures. I tried it seriously for the first time when I was a schoolboy of thirteen, and wished to be excused certain work I had decided was useless to me. I forged a letter in my father's hand, signing it with his usual crabbed scrawl, and handed it in. By pure ill-luck I was found out, some weeks later, by my father encountering the master in question, who raised the point with him. My father's rage was indescribable. He had a criminal for a son, he declared, a base, prospective (no, actual) felon. I was unfit to mix with decent people, and certainly not with my own family. I had my meals apart, and in addition was thrashed till I could hardly stand. He even suggested that Green should repeat the performance. Luckily the fellow had some sense of humour, and he mildly suggested that the affair had probably begun as a joke, and he was convinced I had had a sufficiently serious lesson. He was right, in so far as I didn't repeat the experiment while I remained at home, but some months ago, at Higginsons, I became a forger for the second time. There was an older man in our department, a fellow called Wright, a pursy, strutting nonentity, with a great conceit of himself and an intolerable manner. At length he became so disagreeable that a number of us got together and drew up a letter, that I signed with the name of the head of the firm, warning Wright that disquieting rumours had been received concerning his work, and also his attitude towards his juniors. Unless he showed considerable improvement in both respects, the letter continued, he could seek employment elsewhere. There was no need to mention this letter, which was intended for a confidential warning.

The results were stupefying. Wright took the letter in dead earnest; his nerve, his conceit, the foundations of his security were shaken. He had a wife and several children and no private means. Within twenty-four hours his manner had completely changed. He was no longer officious and arrogant; on the contrary, he asked opinions, even cringed, was apologetic, and submissive. It was so simple we were tempted to make a second experiment; but the more sober spirits urged that we had gone far enough, and it would be tempting providence to try again, so we left it at that.

I had these two successes in mind as I drew the cheque-book towards me. At last the possibility of attaining leisure and security lay under my hand. It was dishonest, of course, but my whole life has been stamped with dishonesty. The work I do, my relations with Sophy, my deliberate blindness as to her probable relations with other men—this seemed no worse, and at least it had some purpose. Of course, it was dangerous. It was borne in on me, as I stood wondering how much I dare put myself down for, how dangerous. No one would believe that my father would willingly give me a halfpenny. I should have to contrive some story that would satisfy or at all events silence Richard and Amy and Eustace, who'd be on my heels like a pack of dogs after a fox. But since my present way of living was intolerable, and my life had been trapped in a cul-de-sac whence I saw no other possible escape, I determined to run the risk. I had suffered so much from the humiliations of poverty that anything seemed preferable.

I began, this decision once taken, to find excellent reasons for the forgery. It would, I argued, actually strengthen my hand to produce the cheque, for what earthly motive should I have for murder in that event? This was so subtle an argument that I promptly took a pen from the rack on the table and began to test my skill on a writing-pad lying near at hand. I found I retained the art as skilfully as ever. Any one of those specimens, I think, would have been passed by my father's bank. So I took up the cheque and in a moment of fine, reckless frenzy filled in a sum of two thousand pounds. Colossal, of course, but I had to make provision for Sophy and the children, and I couldn't go abroad without a penny in my pocket. In any case, the temptation was too great. I might easily be detected, and, if so, it would be humiliating to have lost freedom for a beggarly five hundred pounds. But when I had signed the cheque and torn it out and filled in the counterfoil, with my father's customary meticulous detail, I stood there, rather at a loss, feeling I should do something to safeguard myself. For, considering the position, it now seemed obvious to me that the simplest intelligence would realise that I had been the last person to see my father alive. It was unlikely that anyone else would come down to-night. Yet, to save my own skin, I must make it appear that he had

had a later visitor than myself. The solution was, of course, a simple one, though it was some time before I hit upon it. I tore out a blank cheque, that I destroyed, filled in the second counterfoil with Eustace's name, and an amount of ten thousand pounds, and dated that the 25th December. The plan was simplicity itself; anyone turning over the leaves of the cheque-book would leap to the obvious conclusion that Eustace had visited the library after my departure. It being now Christmas Day, there would be no possibility of his arguing that he had received the cheque before the evening.

It seemed to me that I had laid the perfect trap; in addition, there was his handkerchief lying destroyed in the grate. It might, of course, be shown that some other member of the family used silk handkerchiefs, but the association of facts seemed to me invincible. As for the amount, I was aware that Eustace had mentioned a sum of ten thousand pounds as being requisite for the settlement of his affairs.

I chose him instinctively as my victim, because he suited my plan better than anyone else in the house. He needed the money desperately, for one thing. Again, it would be difficult to imagine Richard using violence against his father, whatever his provocation, whereas, I argued, Eustace might easily lose his head. (I think now that I was wrong, but at the time I really did believe in my own argument.) And when I came to consider the position, I realised that, if I had had time for a mature judgment, I should have come to a similar conclusion. Eustace was Olivia's husband, and I owed her and him and their supercilious young sons a long reckoning. And beyond all these facts, I revelled in the notion of watching that crooked dealer squirm and writhe in an attempt to extricate himself, as his dupes must often have squirmed and wriggled, without an iota of sympathy from him.

My sole desire now was to leave the library before my presence here was discovered. By filling in the second counterfoil I had intensified my peril a hundred times. Moreover, panic was beginning to assail me. To my troubled ears, the house now seemed full of turmoil. I was continually jerking up my head to observe the door, that at every instant seemed about to open. It was all I could do to refrain from crossing the room and flinging it wide to reassure myself that no malevolent presence lurked in the shadows of the hall. Odd shapes, like mysterious birds, flashed across the ceiling. The thunder of the gale at the windows and the chimney were heavy with voices. There were steps on the stairs and faces at the pane. Nevertheless, I beat down the approaching storm of terror, and compelled my imagination to work for my release. Before I left the room, I must evolve some kind of story to account for the magnitude of the cheque; indeed, for its very existence. For the life of me—literally for the life of me—I could not for some time strike any plausible explanation. The only answer to my problem that occurred to me was blackmail, and I knew too little, and Richard probably too much, of my father's life to be able to play such a card. In my mind I carefully recollected the heated conversation that had preceded the blow that killed him. There had been his comments on art and artists, and his insulting references to my wife. Next, I remembered that I had promised—had even offered to give him a statement in writing—that if he would help me now, I would see to it that neither I nor Sophy nor our children should ever appeal to him again. He had merely laughed in an offensive manner, saying, "Likely story, my dear Brand!" But suppose, my imagination urged, he had not laughed? Suppose he had accepted my undertaking, surely then he might have bought me off handsomely?

I brooded. I had offered him a signed undertaking. And he hadn't accepted it. But who was to know that? Here were pens, ink, and paper to my hand. I had already proved my ability as a forger. In any case, my blood was warm and my spirit intrepid. I had forgotten to be afraid lest this fresh venture betray me, and in a fine frenzy of excitement I began to write.

What I wrote was something like this:

> I, Hildebrand Gray, do hereby agree that in consideration of the sum of two thousand pounds paid to me this day by my father Adrian Gray of the Manor House, King's Poplars, Grebeshire, I will never again appeal to the said Adrian Gray for assistance in money or otherwise, never permit my wife, Sophy Gray, or any of her children, Margot, Eleanor, Dulcie, Anne, or Ferdinand Gray to approach him for any reason whatsoever. And I voluntarily abandon any claims I may ever have put forward against the said Adrian Gray both for myself and for them. In addition, I agree never to give the said Adrian Gray's name as a reference in any circumstances whatever or proclaim the relationship except where this is unavoidable.

It seemed to me that, having signed this preposterous declaration, I had now done everything possible to mislead the authorities. Richard and probably Eustace would recognise in its pretentiousness the authentic note of pomposity and inhumanity that had marked my father's relations with myself. I had written the paper with a pen that lay on the inlaid lacquer inkstand, but I signed it with a cheap one I took from my pocket, pausing to admire my own enterprise. I had allowed my instinct to guide me as to the precise formation of my father's writing, for it was long since I had heard from him, long enough for me to forget his personal idiosyncrasies. Yet when I re-read my masterpiece I was convinced that, had I not been in the secret, I should not have questioned the genuineness of the paper.

There was nothing more for me to do but contrive to reach my room unperceived. The construction that I hoped everyone would put on the position was that Eustace, in dire straits, had come down in the early hours of the morning to put the position more clearly yet to my father. For I knew, though possibly the old man did not, that Eustace had been sailing very near the wind, and might even find himself involved in criminal proceedings. By leaving my document in a prominent position on the table, I might suggest that he had inadvertently read it, and his anger would at once be roused at the thought of such a wastrel as myself being presented, in any conceivable circumstances, with so large a sum, while he was denied a penny. After that, the interview might become heated; Eustace might confess the desperation of the position, practically compelling my father to part with the ten thousand pounds. Presumably, however, he would only do so on certain conditions, and these might prove not merely humiliating to Eustace, but positively dangerous. My father had a very vitriolic tongue, and Eustace was in a state of considerable nervous tension. Moreover, it would obviously be unsafe to let such a man as Adrian Gray retain a document that might, if produced, involve Eustace in some very difficult explanations, and I doubted whether my father was the type of man to let an advantage of this nature slip. Eustace would, of course, realise that. Possibly my father would gloat openly. The paper-weight lay close at hand. The conclusions the police—I presumed, of course, that this would be an affair for the police—and the family would arrive at would, I hoped, be too obvious to admit of discussion.

On my way to the door I detached the leaf of the calendar for Christmas Eve. The quotation was "Wealth is of the mind, not of the pocket." The new quotation said, "Peace on earth, goodwill towards men." I looked round for a final glance to see if there was anything I had left undone. This was my last chance. Amateur criminals, they say, usually leave some glaring piece of evidence behind them, and their careful work is seldom appreciated. Anything I left now would betray me to the experts. Probably I should not enter this room again till all the formalities were over. I felt extraordinarily sleepy and foolish, and, to keep myself awake, I took up a round black ruler and twisted it in my fingers. When I put it down, I did not attempt to rub it clean of finger-prints. It would be less suspicious to leave some trace of my presence in the room, since I had no intention of denying the interview. The whole family is aware of my trick of taking up any convenient object and handling it while I talk. It is one of the pegs on which they hang their various objections to my character. Indicative of the restless temperament that is never satisfied, they tell one another; no self-control. Then it occurred to me that I might add a little to the general mystification by opening one of the windows; that might suggest the alternative of a criminal from outside. Moreover, it is precisely the type of thing Eustace would do, in such circumstances.

I was surprised to find that it was snowing heavily. And with the snowfall the wind had dropped. Outside, everything was deathly still. There were no lights to be seen; even the snow looked dim. Nor was there a sound inside the house or beyond it.

I decided to switch off the light. If I left it on, it would be discovered by some officious servant, descending early, and the story that was already maturing in my mind depended on my seeing some of the family before the discovery was made. Besides, I was sure Eustace would switch it off. It has always struck me as strange that a man who launches out into his dangerous schemes should have so narrow an imagination. I've tested it more than once, and never without a fresh stab of surprise that an ingenuity—I won't call it a mind—that can evolve these fantastic plans for picking other men's pockets should be practically blindfolded most of the time.

4

I was fortunate in meeting no one as I crept upstairs. My room was at the end of a corridor. This is an oddly built house, low and L-shaped, the short arm of the L comprising the servants' quarters and store and box rooms. As I shut my bedroom door, I seemed to shut all my alarm and terrors outside. I put the thought of what I had done behind me. Whatever mistakes I had made, it was too late to rectify them now. I have the same sensation when I finish a picture. I've never messed about with a canvas. When it's done I let it go. If I want to do something better, I start afresh.

Switching on my light, I saw that against the blind in one of the servants' rooms a light still burned. I took it for a feeble gas-jet, though it might have been a candle. (It's indicative of the position of the servants in my father's house that, when electricity was installed, their rooms retained the old-fashioned gas.) I began to wonder why she stayed up so late, considering that to-morrow would be a heavy day. And what she was doing sitting there so quietly at the window when the rest of the house was abed.

This problem, trifling though it was, intrigued me. I walked across to my own window, that I flung open, dislodging a soft shower of snow. The shadow on the blind moved, the blind was shifted, and I saw a white figure lean forward a little. She had no interest in me—I was sure of that. But "She can't have a lover in this joyless house" I marvelled, and then some quite material explanation occurred to me, such as tooth-ache, or perhaps she was mending clothes, or even, possibly, she was devout, though I found it hard to believe that such devotion would keep her awake until two o'clock.

She pushed aside the blind and stared out at the snow, but it was too dark for me to distinguish her face. On my rare visits here the servants are always new, and I never pay any heed to them—except Moulton, of course, who has been here for twenty years. I could see that the girl had something in her hand, which by its shape I took to be a book. Her dark shadow, the straight lines of her dress, her artless pose, gave her the appearance of some mediæval figure—say, the Spirit of Christmas. She stood there without stirring for some minutes. Then something startled her. Perhaps she caught sight of my light. Anyway the blind dropped back into place, and she disappeared. A moment later the light was extinguished.

The sight of her had excited and stimulated me, not in any physical way, but in my mind. She seemed the antithesis of the body downstairs, even when that body was quick with life. She was young and vigorous, and, if she had been reading, she was sufficiently steeped in life to lay aside all those tiresome duties that held her during the day, and enter into the new world that books do open for one, even the silliest and most dangerous. So that I continued to stand there, forgetting I had been tired and had meant to collapse immediately on to the bed, thinking of her, not as an individual, but as the symbol of a new hope. I was sorry she had gone, but the memory of her pleased and invigorated me.

Then, for a time, I watched the snow. It had already obliterated landmarks that had been familiar to me since childhood, piling itself softly on my sill; I went to the bed presently and lay down, still watching it fall. It fascinated me in its beauty, its silence, and its persistence. There was no light in my room now—I had switched off the electricity—but the reflection of the snow, and by this I could just distinguish the outlines of the severe ramshackle furniture. The events of the evening, though chiefly, I think, the sight of that girl at the window, had kindled the creative flame in me, and I fell to wondering about the furniture—the carved mahogany dressing-table, with its haughty mirror, its curled claw-feet. How much had that glass reflected, what had the drawers held? I pictured to myself all the scenes that had perhaps occurred in this room, the whole gamut of the emotions the walls had witnessed—passion, despair, misery, patience, joy. A procession of dead and gone Grays and all the nameless guests this room had housed, and who would never forget it because of some occasion of heartbreak or ecstasy it represented, filed past me. And at the end of the procession, perhaps, myself. The murderer. One of them might have been a murderer too, for all I could tell. And I wondered if a member of a later generation, lying wakeful on some crucial night, as I lay wakeful now, would have any conception of the emotions that racked me. I turned over and traced the faded blossoms on the wallpaper with a critical finger. I thought, "These I shall never forget, these lilac roses that never grew on bush or spray, gathered in baskets and tied with true lovers' knots, never forget their moulding, the fantastic shape that would give a botanist nightmare." To-night they had a certain life of their own. My own vitality possessed them. I knew it would be hours before I should sleep. Nevertheless I began to undress slowly in the dark. To a man who knows no privacy these minutes of solitude were exquisite. At home there was always Sophy and often a sickly child whose cot was dragged in and put in the inadequate space at the foot of our bed. I thought, if I were a rich man I would often spend nights in hotels for the joy of knowing myself immune from disturbance. To sleep under the same roof as even those to whom you are inescapably tied destroys the charm, though you have a whole private suite. There is always the possibility of invasion by those who have the right to interrupt your privacy. Now for a few hours I was free. When I had undressed I returned to the window; there were trees beyond the glass soughing a little in the subdued wind, and I reflected that there were also trees within, trees that had been carved, hacked, disciplined into unnatural shapes for the service of men, who would shape to their own pleasure everything they touch, including their own kind. So powerfully enticed was my imagination that it seemed to me the noise of the branches came from within rather than without. It would scarcely have surprised me if the tallboy had blossomed into green buds and the chairs burst into leaf. My imagination does this to me sometimes, transporting me into a sphere of pure delight, when the sense of beauty ceases to have any shape or even to pronounce itself as beauty at all, but is a natural environment. But naturally one remains outwardly cold, savage, and morose, in case that treasure, too, is looted.

Out in the darkness, prowling through the snow, I caught a glimpse of twin sparks of green light, the eyes of a wandering cat. I loved it as it moved silently through the dark, disdaining that security that humans and dogs crave, and roaming fearlessly as it would. A line I had read somewhere returned to my mind: "Plundering the secret richness of the night"; a type, I thought, watching those eyes flame at me, and conscious of their heat, of all the unhoused adventurers of the earth—Cyrano, Traherne, a nameless host, men and women who didn't want the security my family holds so dear, preferring the unattainable and the unknown.

The cat vanished, seeking its adventure, leaving me to brood on its strange silent appearance. My thoughts slipped irrelevantly from one thing to another, touching different levels, like water dropping from shelf to shelf of rock. I thought about cats. Black ones were popular emblems for Christmas cards. One saw them in ridiculous postures, conveying good wishes in every conceivable manner, from the merely absurd to the insipid and vulgar. There was an enormous grey Persian cat, I remember, that used to fill the window of an undertaker's establishment in Paris. There was a thin dirty little tabby that howled outside our Fulham windows every night, until in desperation we took it in, and it promptly loosed its fleas on the children. There was the legend of the Cat that walked alone; and that carried me on to the Christmas stories of Michael Fairless, and brought keenly back to recollection a Christmas I spent when I was fifteen in Germany (one of those exchange arrangements by which the youth of both nations are supposed to learn the other's language). It had been like a fairy story, all of a piece with the painted waxen angels on bright Christmas-trees, the effigies of the Holy Child in innumerable neat mangers, the glittering balls; the donkeys, oxen, and shepherds; windows full of strange-shaped cakes, decorated with gilt bells, Santa Klaus in red and gold and green cloaks, trimmed with fur, a model of a reindeer sleigh loaded with presents, crackers and bonbons, round smiling faces and tight flaxen plaits. It was a long cry from the joyous innocence of that festival to the cynical show we made of it at King's Poplars, where it became a day of suppressed jealousy and gluttony and criticism, of secret valuations of presents and calculations as to what one had made or lost on one's personal expenditure.

My thoughts now seemed to move simultaneously in both directions, back to the ardent past, forward to the hopeful future. The snow drifted through the window on to the clothes I had flung on to a chair. I saw this and smiled. So much at ease did I feel, I was like an athlete at the end of a hard race. Already I had achieved. That was the effect of my first murder on me.

5

Presently I heard the clock strike four. Then I fell asleep. It was Christmas Day, I had my plan in readiness, and I was full of hope.

Part III

Christmas Day

1

The snow had ceased some hours when Brand awoke. It was very early and he could detect no sound in the darkened house. His watch, that he had forgotten to wind, stood at three o'clock. The surface of the snow, that lay thickly on every object visible from the window, had been frozen by the wind, and glittered brilliantly in the sharp white light that to-day preceded the sun. The road, hedges, and the steep slope of the hill were dazzling in their untrodden whiteness as, standing at the window where he had stood some hours earlier, he stared at the silent world. At his elbow lay a branch bowed down with snow. On the sill itself it was three inches deep; even the telegraph wires were white this Christmas morning.

The sky was very clear and pale and sparkled with light. As yet no one had trodden the great white bank that ran up from the road to the horizon. As Brand watched, a robin completed the Christmas-card effect by perching delicately on the snow that lay heaped on the sill. It was a young bird, its feathers puffed out because of the cold. In this simple romantic setting, the happenings of the night became fantastic. He could scarcely persuade himself they were true. At length, however, he was definitely aroused by a sound of voices under his windows; standing with bare feet on the chill oilcloth, he saw the women of the family in a little group by the gate, setting off for the early celebration. Most noticeable was his grandmother, an ancient aristocrat in weedy black; she was, as usual, absurdly ill dressed for the occasion. She wore a thin black gown and a black silk coat. As Brand watched, he saw her imposingly flap away the obsequious maid who came forward with shawls and furs. The woman persisted; old Mrs. Gray became haughty and remote. The maid, submissive and unmoved, sank into the background, burdened with prayer-books, umbrellas, a black shawl, and a heavy cloak for emergencies.

"I suppose if she didn't make that protest, my grand-mother would dismiss her instantly. It's just a ritual, like two-thirds of life."

Olivia had observed to her husband, "I suppose I may as well go. If I don't, father will make a personal triumph of it. And you can never tell. Ten thousand pounds is a mere flea-bite compared with the miracle we're supposed to be celebrating."

Ruth had not been with this contingent—with wary suspicious Amy, with her neat sturdy figure and sharp eyes that noticed who ate most ham and was most extravagant with butter; Isobel, still young, with her pale unhappy face, her coronet of pale gold plaits, her lovely hands, the air of remoteness that had clung to her since her little girl died; Laura in a fur coat that would have attracted attention in a far more sophisticated neighbourhood. But as the maid, hampered by her burdens, struggled with the catch of the gate, finally opening it with a vigour that shook a shower of soft dry snow on to Amy, and brought down a curt rebuke for her carelessness, the front door opened again and Ruth and Miles came out. The lawyer, looking up, saw his brother-in-law at the window, and waved a friendly hand. Ruth's lips shaped the words "Merry Christmas."

Brand smiled back. He felt serene and light-hearted. The old English word jocund came back to him. He supposed his sense of continuity was broken. He simply could not link up that tumbled body under the library window with his own future. He put it behind him, like some disagreeable experience on which he preferred not to brood, and that had become a part of his past. He experienced a sense of liberty as he had done last night, of anticipation even. He could scarcely wait for the opening of this new phase of his existence, so fraught with hope, so powerful with intent.

To strengthen that conviction, he took up the sketch he had made in the library a few hours earlier, and examined it critically. He had been prepared to discount the artist's enthusiasm of the previous night, and discover the thing to be a hotch-potch of blemishes and false values. But, to his delight, he found that morning sustained the earlier judgment. More, it added to his satisfaction. The picture enthralled him in its clean economy of detail, its strength and assurance, its purity of line, its massive simplicity. It was ridiculous, it was pathetic, it was abominably wrong that a man capable of such work should be grinding out his life in a draughtsman's office. The buoyancy in the atmosphere, the sharp clean air, and the sense of fresh beginnings found its counterpart in his responsive breast. He was aware of hope and of unbounded horizons. Poverty and the obligations of his wretched domestic life had crippled but not wholly deformed him. Already he recognised a new power in his brain and hand; the challenge, to which he had been compelled to stop his ears for so long, tantalised him anew. Space, leisure, opportunity—he saw all these at length within his grasp. He would make his home among the hard, resolute, one-idea'd men with whom he had lived for a time before his crazy marriage.

Dreaming thus, he was amazed to discover, by the sound of voices outside, that he had brooded an hour away. Hastily he examined his position in the family's regard. And at once the composure on which he plumed himself fell apart like a pack of cards, disclosing excitement, alarm, the realisation (at last) of the alternative to the life he had been occupied in picturing to himself. Now that the moment was upon him, it found him dry-mouthed and bright-eyed, repeating over and over again the story he had to tell. Fortunately it was very short and involved him in no admission of any importance, so far as he could see. Even his family would probably believe it, delighted though they might be to see him taken for the crime. His passion for detail in his own work helped him, and he became quite cool-headed as he memorised the story, experiencing even a kind of pleasure in allotting to each occurrence its true share of significance. His imagination, indeed, suggested to him problems so fantastic that even a fictional detective would scarcely put them to him, yet even to these he had subtle replies ready.

Opening the door, he came out on to the landing as the party from church ascended the stairs. There was a hurried interchange of greetings. Eustace emerged from his room while they were talking, said, "Cold, what?" in an abstracted sort of voice. "I suppose the post isn't in yet. Morning, Amy. Happy Christmas, Ruth." He ignored Brand, who whispered to his eldest sister. "He had no luck, I suppose. That would account for his sour temper. It must be galling to a professional shark to find a tenderfoot has jumped his claim."

Amy stared. "What are you talking about?"

"Ask Eustace. But not till after breakfast. After all, it is Christmas Day." And, laughing, he ran down the stairs.

The Grays, with embarrassed comments and averted eyes, handed parcels to one another in a shamefaced sort of way, secretly pricing both what they received and the gifts each donor gave to other members of the family. Brand's share was a collar-box, some cuff-links, an account book, some handkerchiefs from Olivia (he was sure these had been sent to Eustace and been discarded as unsuitable for him), a leather stamp-book, a bookmarker, two comic golfing calendars (he didn't play golf), and an illustrated Christmas legend. He kept the cuff-links and left everything else behind him when he went. The handkerchiefs he gave to Moulton.

Everyone except Adrian came down to breakfast, though no one except Ruth and her husband looked very festive. And even they sighed from time to time, thinking of Christmas as it should be when one has young daughters to come battering on the door at five in the morning with demands to be allowed to examine the contents of their stockings, and, permission obtained, to come scuffling into bed, to exult over everything, small or great, concealed therein.

Old Mrs. Gray was occupied with letters and cards from the survivors of her own youth. Eustace was clearly nervous; he had received a letter with a City postmark, and, after reading this through, he thrust it into his pocket, and started eating ham in a hurried and abstracted manner. Olivia caught the infection and talked a great deal, very brightly and smartly, after the manner of Dot and Lalage in her letters. Laura surveyed Brand and Eustace with a cool amusement and reflected on the peculiarity of her husband's relations. But possibly all in-laws were like this. It was like being one kind of an animal and being penned in the Zoo with another kind. Presumably one might get a certain amusement of a cynical kind from observing their qualities. She knew well enough what they thought of her—a bad bargain. Oh, well, it mattered very little, she supposed. Those early ideas, when she had thought of life as a crusade, a challenge, an affair of flame and endeavour, those died when you had been married to Richard Gray for some years. She smiled and passed her cup for tea.

Richard meanwhile was exclaiming at the absurdity of the non-appearance of the daily paper, simply because it was Christmas Day, and, being started, delivered himself of a trenchant though mercifully brief lecture on idleness in industry and its effect on our export trade, with special reference to German pianos.

Isobel sat pale and silent, eating toast. A chance reference by Ruth to Pat set her nerves quivering for the little dead Honor. Unlike Laura, she couldn't steel her heart to memory or to hope, and life seemed to her unpardonable and intolerable.

Amy said acidly, "You seem very gay this morning, Brand." And Eustace remarked in sour tones that perhaps he'd been fortunate in his presents.

Brand laughed. "Oh, very fortunate. You know, I suppose?" He lifted his eyebrows and indicated the mystified expressions on the faces of the rest of the party.

Eustace said blankly, "Know? What? I've no idea what you're talking about. But then," he added with a peevish malice that drew the attention of the whole table towards him, "I never do understand your motives, except, of course, a visit like this."

Brand, who could normally be trusted to fire up at so discourteous a rejoinder, only said pleasantly, "A touch of nature—you know the rest, I expect," at which even his grandmother was sufficiently surprised to rouse herself and say, "Really, Brand, you seem to have changed your spots completely since yesterday."

Brand said sincerely, "It's quite true, I don't feel the same man. You know—hope lost, all lost. That's how I was when

I came down here. To-day, of course, I've something to look forward to. It's the first time—no, the second—in my life I remember experiencing the legendary Christmas feeling. Amy, you've no marmalade."

As the meal drew on, the continued absence of Adrian began to attract comment and conjecture. "It's very unlike him not to be here on Christmas morning," complained Olivia, as though his non-appearance pointed a particular insult to herself.

"Perhaps he feels he saw enough of his family yesterday," countered Laura in her gay sarcastic voice.

Amy refused to smile. She only said, with an ominous folding of her lips, "I shouldn't be surprised if he is tired. He's had enough to make him." She rang a bell, and, when the servant appeared, said, "Moulton, will you see if Mr. Gray is all right, and tell him that we have been at breakfast for some time?"

On an impulse Brand got up and went to the sideboard to cut some ham he didn't want. The sideboard was a huge old-fashioned affair, with panels of glass let into the back. Brand, aware that the moment of discovery was upon them, wished to observe their faces without himself being noticed. He cut the ham slowly, half turning to ask if he could help anyone else.

"We've all finished, I think," said Amy, with her false smile.

Brand returned smoothly, "You forget, my dear, ham for breakfast is quite a treat for me." Then warned himself, "Careful, you can't afford to give yourself away now by quarrelling with that bitch. They're all against you as it is."

Moulton came back while he was still at the sideboard to say that Mr. Gray's bed had not been slept in. Brand, watching like a hawk, anticipated immediate confusion. But, to his surprise, Amy only remarked in a vexed tone, "How very provoking! He's never fit for anything when he's dropped off in the library. I broke up cards early last night on purpose that he should be fresh this morning. He's got to read the lessons. He always does on Christmas Day."

Brand suppressed a spasm of grotesque laughter at the notion of a meek congregation waiting for that dead thing to enter the church and instruct them in their duties. Gray could read a lesson as other men preached sermons, as if he took to himself all the credit for the subject-matter and severely enjoined his hearers to obey him. There was no object in remaining at the sideboard any longer; clearly the panic was, at all events, postponed, and he could watch better by resuming his place at the table. Besides, it looked less marked. So he came back, carrying his plate, and said seriously, "I'm afraid some of us combined, quite unconsciously, to frustrate your good intentions. I had a fairly long session with him myself last night, and then there was Eustace. Of course, I don't know how long that went on."

Eustace flung up his head. "You're crazy, Brand," he cried in sharp tones. "I don't suppose you know what you're saying, and certainly I don't. I didn't see your father, Amy, last night after cards broke up. Olivia and I were tired, and had one or two things to talk over, and we went up to bed early. I don't understand what your brother's hinting at."

He looked across the table to Brand, ruffled and flushed. Brand looked embarrassed. "Well, I beg your pardon, then," he burst out with averted eyes. "Only—it was a pardonable mistake, I think. The library is about the only room we use down that corridor, so I supposed, naturally, you were going to talk to father. He'd let fall something about it while we were discussing my affairs. But I don't suppose it's of any consequence. It was really father who put the idea into my head."

"What idea?"

"That he wouldn't be exactly surprised to see you again before morning."

Eustace said touchily, "I fail to see why you should discuss my affairs with your father at all."

"They came up quite naturally in the course of conversation."

"Money, I suppose?"

"Yes. We seem remarkably unanimous for once."

Old Mrs. Gray thumped the table with a triangular-shaped napkin-holder of Indian silver, heavily embossed with elephants. "Can't you for heaven's sake keep the peace this one day of the year?" she cried. "You scarcely ever meet, and when you do you're at one another's throats like a pack of dogs. It's very unpleasant for Amy and myself, who never see you at any other time. If you must be unmannerly, can't you meet at one another's houses for that purpose?"

It was characteristic that she paid no heed to the servant standing by, who now enquired respectfully whether he should rouse his master.

Richard stood up quickly. "No, I'll go. He may be asleep."

The general conversation was resumed in a desultory manner. Olivia raised the point of the advantages of Capri over Mallorca, as a holiday resort, with Miles, who had been to neither, but talked so deftly that Olivia presently said, "Dear me, you seem to have been quite a traveller. In your bachelor days, I suppose? Not much chance of going abroad now." Ruth asked Eustace about his sons. Isobel murmured something about a Christmas-card Christmas, with all the snow and robins about, to Brand, who countered grimly, "And ghosts. You can't leave them out of your old-fashioned Christmas. I wonder how many there are stalking round this house to-day."

Brand found himself quite composed now, and spread butter on his toast very thickly, because he knew Amy was watching him, and put marmalade on the top of that. His sister made an involuntary movement to stop him; then her hand dropped, though her eyebrows twitched with irritation.

2

Richard came in, very pale and grave. Holding the door in his hand, he said, with a quietness that held everyone's attention, "Eustace, did you say you didn't see my father last night?"

"No," said Eustace violently, "I didn't. Oh, I admit, I wanted to see him, but I decided to put off the discussion until after to-day."

"And what time did you leave him, Brand?"

"Shortly before midnight."

"I wonder how you can be so sure," murmured Amy unpleasantly.

"Quite simple. When I saw Eustace—not going down to the library, as he didn't go there, but just saw him—it was in my mind to hail him with an appropriate greeting—'Merry Christmas' or something of that sort—but glancing at my wrist-watch I saw it wasn't actually midnight, and, not wishing to invite a snub, I let the opportunity pass. In any case, it might possibly have looked like a taunt—the successful mendicant compassionating his less fortunate rival."

There was a minute of startled silence. Only Miles immediately realised the meaning of Brand's words, and he was too well trained at his work to exhibit any trace of feeling. Isobel scarcely seemed to have heard what he said; Olivia was troubled over Eustace. But Eustace's eyes were all for this hangdog brother-in-law, who spoke to-day with so debonair an assurance and gaiety. Amy, too, had realised what he meant, and she was the first to put her suspicion into words.

"Are you trying to tell us that you made father give you money—you—when he hadn't a penny to spare?"

"I gathered things weren't going too well with him. He seemed to have been pressed in various directions, but all the same…" He glanced uncertainly at Richard, then continued doubtfully, "I suppose he'll be sure to tell you. He didn't enjoin secrecy on me, so presumably he meant it to be quite open—but he did give me money. In fact"—the words broke quickly from him—"I'd never expected him to be half so generous."

"Why you?" demanded Eustace thickly. "In heaven's name, why you?"

Brand, who had kept himself in control under considerable provocation during the morning, broke out at that. "Why the devil not? I'm not his clever financier of a son-in-law, who gets him into a mess, and I'm not the son who wants him to buy me a title. All I wanted was a chance, and now, thanks to him, I've got it. He knew my position was more hopeless than either of yours. I've no money and no influential friends. I've no prospects at all, except of crawling along in Higginsons, with no hope of advancement that I can see. I didn't marry a wife with useful relations or money of her own"—his bitter sneer embraced them all—"and I have five children…"

"That's your affair," retorted Amy icily.

"And if it comes to that, there's no real reason why my father shouldn't be as ready to help one relative as another. He's used his influence to do what you two"—he looked from Richard to Eustace—"have wanted ever since you married. You come down here when you like, and sound him for anything he may be good for. Sophy's never so much as been in the place. She's never had an hour's hospitality from any of you. I work like some damned galley-slave eight hours a day for two shillings an hour, and you grudge me anything I can pull out of the pie. You're the last person, Eustace…"

Richard broke in, "There's nothing to be gained by a scene, Eustace; we must agree that it's quite out of the question to cross-examine Brand like this. If my father chose to help him, it was my father's money. It's not that, as a matter of fact, that I'm interested in at the moment. I want to know how he seemed when you were with him last night, Brand."

"It was a stormy interview," Brand admitted honestly. "You know he and I were scarcely likely to meet on mutual ground. He told me that he had practically every member of the family holding out their hands for money. He asked, as Eustace did just now, what I had ever done to deserve help from him, and reminded me of every farthing he'd ever disbursed to me. He had all the sum, down to car-fare, entered in a little black note-book. However, in the end he capitulated. But he was greatly excited."

Amy said passionately, "Richard, what is it? We have a right to know."

He nipped that attempt at melodrama instantly in the bud. "I'm keeping no secrets. He appears to have had some kind of a stroke, I should be inclined to say."

The grandmother pulled herself to her feet, a short, stout figure, her manner full of generalship and determination.

"Where is he? How is he?"

"He's in the library still. There seemed little sense in having him carried upstairs—not, at all events, until the doctor had seen him."

Old Mrs. Gray experienced that sense that comes to the least affectionate mother when she hears of the loss of a child she has borne. "You mean…"

"He's very cold," said Richard simply.

She came swiftly up the room, her head bent forward, her new black dress framing her generous throat. Like a little bull she seemed, thought Ruth, charging with that cool determination, that sense of futility known only to the very old and the very young.

"Why didn't you tell me at once?" she asked gently, as with reluctance he opened the door. "Have you done anything about a doctor?"

"I've telephoned Romford. He'll be along in a few minutes."

She swept out, and Amy, small, freckled, her smooth, lustreless, carroty hair drawn tightly back from a pale forehead, followed her with the persistent obstinacy of a seeking hen.

"There's nothing any of us can do," expostulated Richard unhappily, closing the door behind them. "He'd opened the window; last night's wind was bitter. It may have touched his weak heart."

The words were a wretched kind of apology for his action. Having said them, he stood silent, with an air of profound gloom, watching the six people who remained at the table. These betrayed signs of an exquisite embarrassment. Eustace spread a piece of toast with a butterless knife, and ate it in spasmodic bites. Isobel was whispering dazedly, "Dead—but he can't. And only last night…" Brand put his hand on her arm to strengthen her. "Pull yourself together," he implored her. "After all," he hesitated, then finished defiantly, "it isn't as if we were Saul and Jonathan or any of those fancy men. There wasn't such a lot of love lost between us."

Isobel's reply shocked him so much that for a time he was rendered speechless. "That's it. It's too late. It doesn't matter now."

No one else appeared to have heard her. Ruth and her husband were conferring at one end of the table; Richard's own wife sat proud and stately, without evincing a scrap of feeling, a little further off. Eustace exclaimed, "I never heard anything about his heart before. Is it a new thing? And if it's so bad that a gust would kill it, how is it that a company would insure him?"

Richard said coldly, "You asked me yesterday if I knew anything of his having heart trouble."

"Because he'd been dropping hints about its condition. I thought he was developing into one of these faddists who always imagine they have something wrong. You must admit he was absurdly nervous about his health."

"He didn't say much about it to me," returned Richard in the same tones, and looked enquiringly at Miles. Miles said he really had never known his father-in-law intimately, and anyway he probably wouldn't have remembered about the heart. Richard went away, and after a moment Laura followed him. Eustace, unable to let the subject alone for an instant, began once again to cross-examine his brother-in-law as to the dead man's exact words the previous night.

"He told me he had nothing to spare for wastrels," he added viciously.

"And you actually stayed on after that? You must have been in a tight place. I admit I should have done so in any circumstances. There's a creature called a badger that holds on till death." He could no longer restrain himself; he felt the blood burn and thicken in his veins; like a man making desperate headway against a wind that deprives him of sight, breath, and speech, he could not pause to take his bearings. He must rush headlong into debate; his period of control was over. Miles, with a despairing glance at his wife, accepted the position. The instinctive loathing between these two was coming to a head; within the next few moments almost any startling occurrence might take place. A wild battle of wits—and possibly not of wits alone—would be engaged upon, whose story would be gleefully repeated in every village kitchen so long as interest in Gray's death served the people for gossip.

Eustace also was breathing hard, showing all the signs of ungovernable rage. "The badger, I believe works underground," he commented, trembling as Brand also did.

Brand laughed fiercely. "If it so much as showed its nose above the surface it would be hit on the head without mercy."

"Quite right, too. There's only one treatment for badgers, and that is, root them out. They're no good."

"They eat wasps," Brand defended them wildly.

Olivia cut in coldly, "Brand, you might at least have the decency to keep quiet when you remember that father's dead and you most likely are to blame."

"Dead?" exclaimed Brand. "How do you know that?"

"I think it would be difficult to misunderstand Richard," observed Miles dispassionately. "Besides, he would scarcely have remained talking and asking questions if there had been any possibility of anything else."

Isobel broke in colourlessly, "He's been dreadfully worried lately. I don't know if that could have brought on a stroke."

"Of course he was worried," said Olivia. "Aren't we all worried to death with the state of the country and Government stupidity and shares drawing no dividends, without having a son who won't work on your hands?"

Brand looked up in genuine surprise, not, at first, understanding her implication. "But Richard," he began; then stopped. "Did you mean me? Me? My God, I like that. I not work? And what work do any of you do? What does Eustace do? Bluffing money out of other people's pockets isn't work. And Richard. Look at his hands. Are they the hands of a man who works? Sitting about in the House, and giving parties and getting into debt in the hope of attracting the attention of more significant vermin than himself. But real work, the kind of thing that doesn't take account of the money it'll win you or fame it brings—what do any of you know of that?"

Miles said, generously associating himself with the rest of them, though he had never asked a man for help in his life, "If Romford says that death is due to a stroke or some shock brought on by anxiety, we shall none of us be quite able to absolve ourselves. It's not an enviable position, look at it how you will. For our own sakes, let's keep cool about it."

"I think we're all cool enough, except Brand," remarked Olivia. "I daresay he has more on his conscience than the rest of us."

Eustace, however, could not summon sufficient control to save his dignity. "Do you mean you got money out of him?" he exclaimed. "But how could you? He had none."

Miles permitted himself for an instant to betray his disgust at this deplorable scene, and Eustace added hurriedly, "I have the honour, you see, to be in his confidence regarding his finances. And, as Olivia says, times were never worse."

"And I suppose that, being his adviser, you resent his making an investment without consulting you. But I daresay he was wise. He wouldn't have liked poor law officers writing to him, or asking for assistance in keeping my wife and children."

Eustace said briefly and inaccurately, "No pressure could be brought to bear upon him."

"Perhaps not. But in a village like this, where people can find food for gossip if two bees choose the same flower at the same time, it would have been very unpleasant."

"And how often was this—er—grant to be renewed?"

"It was a final payment. We had it all very formal. Really, Miles, you should have been there. We drew up the most humorous document. I doubt if you could have improved upon it. It was extremely legal for a layman. I signed like a bird. No witnesses, though. Does that invalidate it?"

"How thankful father must be that his other children can keep their families," sneered Olivia.

"And I," countered Brand politely. "If he had had to keep young Moores and young Amerys as well as young Grays he would, indeed, have been unfortunate. Though as to the

Moores, I daresay he's contributed more to their support than he is aware."

3

The doctor arrived, shouldering his way through the hall as he had shouldered it through the snow outside. He had no car, and tramped over this hilly country, day and night, in all weathers.

Richard met him in the hall, apologised formally for calling him in, and began to explain the position.

Romford thought, "Weedy chap! Too narrow in the shoulders and the forehead. Not much room for good brain there—all cramped together like a Victorian lady's stomach. And why apologise for bringing me out? Does he suppose that people are considerate enough to keep well on Christmas Day?" Besides, he really preferred his Christmas visits to any others; usually he was offered something to drink and picked up some titbit of local scandal, for he was an inveterate gossip. He was a large stout man, with a rough reddish-grey beard and long thick hair; his hobby was fish photography. He was a bachelor, cared for by a housekeeper whom he did not recognise when they met in the streets. He said he would have married long ago if he could be certain of recollecting his wife's features, but it would be equally inconvenient were he to return to find a woman patient awaiting him and embrace her heartily, and find himself cited as a co-respondent, or mistake his wife for one of those patient, garrulous women whom he saw between nine and ten in the morning and six and seven at night.

He passed into the library in front of Richard and bent over the body. He had not uttered a single word of sympathy or shock since his arrival. Richard, embarrassed and inwardly alarmed, since it seemed possible that the story of his father's interviews with his family the previous day would be made public, stood by the table, feigning an attitude of ease. On the table lay the preposterous paper bearing Brand's signature, and without taking it up he read it through for the first time.

"Brand must have been able to advance a very strong case to persuade my father to help him to that extent," he brooded. "I must see him before anyone else does."

Romford straightened himself and said, "Where did you find him?"

"On the floor by the window. It was open, by the way."

"Why didn't you say that before? It makes a lot of difference."

"Do you mean, if it hadn't been open, he might have pulled through?"

"No. He must have been killed, if not instantaneously, almost at once."

Richard said, in a dazed voice, "Been killed?"

"Well, what did you suppose?"

"I thought a stroke, a fall…"

"You have seen your father, I suppose? Who found him?"

"I did. Moulton and I lifted him on to that chair."

"Which way was he lying? His head towards the window?"

"He was facing towards that wall."

"Then you couldn't have missed this mark on his left temple. It's as clear as—we're promised—the mark of the beast shall be in the foreheads of the damned. Do you suppose a stroke accounts for that?"

"He—he fell."

"He fell on his right side. And, even if he hadn't, there's carpet right up to the window. He couldn't have bruised his skull and actually cut the skin in any sort of fall. Even the edges of this table, had he fallen against that, are rounded. Who saw him last?"

"My brother is the last person who admits to seeing him." Brand's statement and Eustace's swift denial seemed reasonable enough now. Brand, of course, wanted to establish a later visitor than himself; Eustace didn't want anyone to know he had been stirring in the night.

"That young hothead who came to grief in Paris? I should ask him what explanation he can offer. I daresay he could throw a lot of light on the position. I suppose it was pretty late when he was here?"

"A little before midnight, I think he said."

"Or a little after. Who's to tell? Your father wasn't killed before one, I should say, and the open window would account for *rigor mortis* setting in early. So it may have been as late as three or four o'clock. Well, I should ask him what he's got to say, and get the police. There's nothing I can do."

"The police?" There was such genuine shock in Richard's voice that Romford felt a stab of compassion.

"Of course. What did you suppose?"

"But surely—it might have been an accident."

"Oh, quite easily. More murders are committed by accident than anyone except doctors and lawyers guess. Though the consequences are generally the same in both cases—violent death for both parties."

"His heart?" suggested Richard weakly. "That might account for his collapsing under very little provocation."

"Well, I shouldn't call half a brick very little provocation myself. As a matter of fact, your father's heart was sounder than mine, only, as he hadn't got to get a living, he could afford luxuries I can't. My heart daren't go back on me—it knows what I should say to it if it did. Treat 'em hard, that's the best cure for these impertinent maladies. What's a heart to go on strike? When mine threatens me with mutiny, I work it twice as hard for forty-eight hours. I soon have the proud creature under. You'd better get the police. I shall have to give evidence, I suppose. It's a pity you didn't realise the facts and get them here first."

Richard exclaimed, "How could we imagine…? I still feel convinced there's some explanation of this."

"Of course there is. Whether it's the one you'll get hold of eventually or not, I don't know. As I say, it's a pity you weren't a shade more observant. Then the police surgeon would have had to waste his time at the inquest instead of me."

4

Richard put the receiver back and leaned against the table. His face was stupid with incredulity, anger, and shock. He had for many years regarded Brand as a throw-back, one of those creatures, worthless and expensive, who are to be found even in families as ancient and mannered as his own. One came across them again and again; they were shipped abroad to plant rubber, tea, or coffee; they became remittance men in nameless corners of the earth, where they could soak themselves blind without any of their more fastidious relations' friends discovering them; many of them dropped not only their caste but their nationality. They mingled with a degrading familiarity with coloured races; they were a drag and a disgrace. And all these, he considered, Brand was, with his excesses as a young student, his disreputable marriage to a woman of no virtue, his mean home and lowly employment, his periodical appearances at King's Poplars, flushed, bitter, and resolute, to demand assistance. He had always believed that his younger brother would stop short of nothing, but in his own mind the idea that he could murder his own father had appeared incredible. Even men like Brand drew the line at that. And now it appeared that precisely such a crime had been committed, a crime that would blossom into one of those hideous affairs favoured by the evening papers and the Sunday Press. Snapshots would be taken of the family; his own history and his father's would be raked up and presented in its most enticing form to the masses. There would be an inquest, a trial, his own position would be jeopardised; he would be the son of that fellow who was murdered down at King's Poplars and the brother of the chap that did it. And it was Brand, the insignificant waster, who was responsible for all this.

He went into the dining-room, where the remainder of the family was still assembled. The grandmother had gone upstairs, but Amy was here, her mouth set in a hard line, her barest gestures accusing them all of combining to slay their father. They turned with a wave of eagerness as the door opened. Richard said, holding the knob in his hand, "Brand, I want you a minute," and Brand, suddenly icy cold, then sweating as he did when sea-sick, followed him.

"I suppose he's found out something. I made a blunder, after all."

Richard took him into a small room behind the library, and, shutting the door, said, "I'm not questioning you about the upshot of your interview with our father yesterday. As I told Eustace at breakfast, he had as much right to make provision for you and your children as for any of the rest of us. But did he let fall anything that gave you the impression he was highly nervous of any development?"

"What kind of development?"

"Well, was he particularly troubled over anything or any person? Did he say anything?"

"He said a lot, most of it uncomplimentary."

"To you, or did he refer to anyone else? Or the whole family collectively?"

"He thought of all of us as leeches. I fancy Eustace has stung him pretty badly."

Richard frowned. "He never would listen to reason. Speculating may be all right for the rich man on the spot, but a man with limited means should eschew it like the devil."

"Especially with a family like ours," Brand agreed. "But why all these questions?"

Richard looked away. "He didn't give any hint of taking his own life, I suppose?"

Thoughts fled through Brand's mind. Was it possible? The open window, the fallen figure... But his reason rejected such a theory.

"No. And I'm sure he wouldn't. A man who held on to the least of his possessions, as our father did, would never, I'm convinced, throw away anything he regarded as so valuable."

"For heaven's sake, Brand, be a little less cold-blooded. He's our father, and he's dead."

"I know. And for his sake, supposing his life to have been worth anything to himself, I'm sorry. I'd rather be alive than dead in any circumstances. But I can't pretend now to an affection I never felt. These death-bed hypocrisies sicken me."

"Tell me one other thing," said Richard. "I'm not asking for particulars of your conversation, as I said before. But—he gave you money, we know, and he's literally not in a position to part with a sovereign—what inducement did you offer him?"

"Only what I've told you."

Richard struck his hands together. "That isn't sense, Brand. I knew my father better than you did. I know something of the position in which his faith in Eustace has placed him. He had to hold on to every penny to—well, to save himself from public disgrace."

"You think he may have taken his life to prevent that? But I thought first it was a stroke, and next that it was violence."

"That's what Romford says."

"What exactly has happened?"

"A blow—a violent blow on the temple."

Brand looked sceptical. "It sounds a crazy way of committing suicide. Revolvers I can understand, and poison—I suppose both of them take some getting hold of, though. Or presumably one can cut one's throat or drop out of a window. Are there any other ways of taking one's own life, assuming that it must be at home? Outside, of course, opportunities multiply. Taxis, trains, rivers…"

Richard made a motion of intolerable disgust. "Brand, so long as you are in his house, I must beg of you to speak of our father with reasonable decency. Outside is your own affair. In any case, we are not likely to have mutual acquaintances."

"And so I can't smudge your estimable career. I wasn't, let me point out, speaking of our father at all. It was a quite impersonal comment on the difficulties of suicide at home."

"And you haven't answered my question. I realise that I can't, of course, compel you, but all the same—what could you say that induced him to part with so much money?"

"Oh, I fancy that was as much on your account as his own. I told him I proposed to put into practice a plan I had been considering for a long time. That bloody office is wearing me down. I've got to get out from it. And I must go now before it's too late. I can't, of course, take Sophy or the children with me, and it's quite probable that I shan't for some time be able to support two establishments. I asked my father to give me a chance, to let me have some money to keep them on their feet while I was working. He refused, as I'd anticipated. He was, moreover, unnecessarily abusive. But then he had no feeling for art, and so, I suppose, he isn't precisely to be blamed."

"Perhaps he felt he'd no reason to feel generous towards artists."

"Think of the narrowness of the intellect that can judge art by some unsatisfactory artist—and not unsatisfactory in the artistic sense, mark you, but in the material. He knows or hears of a man who paints pictures, and also keeps a mistress or drinks, and immediately he decides that art is no use. In this case, I take it you mean he might have found it a little uncomfortable to his own pocket. However, you can't compel a man to behave intelligently about art, but I may say here that what offends you in my behaviour can't be more distressing than our father's attitude towards everything that seems to me to give life its value. However, we shall never meet on mutual ground there, so let it pass. When he refused, I told him my mind was made up. I was going, and I should advise Sophy to apply to the parish relieving office, telling them that her children were the nephew and nieces of the Member for H—— and grandchildren of a country gentleman. That fetched him. He realised that I meant what I said, and knew that it would get into the papers. These things do. And at your very critical stage in politics that would be nothing less than disastrous."

"So he gave you two thousand pounds? Why, it's fantastic. You couldn't have expected as much as five hundred."

"I didn't. But he gave himself away badly. He was so shaken that I realised I was in a stronger position than I had supposed. So I increased my price. I believe if I'd asked for five thousand I'd have got it. I gave him, of course, the guarantee, that doubtless you've read, that this should be a final payment, and indeed a final interview. I had intended to go back this afternoon. Indeed, I see no reason why I shouldn't."

"If the police allow you, we shall raise no objection."

Brand whistled. "The police? So it's come to that."

"If he didn't commit suicide and it wasn't a stroke, what other alternative is there? Besides, as you remarked, it isn't easy for a man to kill himself with a blow on the head. No, what was in my mind was that perhaps you had stumbled on some bit of information that let you into some secret he was anxious should not be divulged. Had that been the case, I should have asked you to let me share the story..."

"And I should promptly have refused. The sentences for blackmail in this country of late years have been appalling. I'd rather be taken for breaking a bank—anything, in short, except murder."

"Murder," repeated Richard. "Perhaps you will."

Brand left the edge of the table, where he had seated himself at the beginning of the conversation, and said, "Murder? I? Is that what you mean? They'll think I did it? What a fool I am. Of course they will. I'm the last person who admits to seeing him. I'd got that money out of him. Why should I murder him if I'd got the cheque? Because I was afraid he'd try and cancel it, or that, when you heard, the rest of you would urge him to do so? Not very good reasons, surely. And if I killed him, after I got it, why didn't I destroy the agreement? I admit there wasn't much likelihood of my ever touching anything, but if he had mentioned me or any of my children in his will, I daresay that agreement would invalidate it. At all events, I'm sure Eustace would make as much trouble as he could. Possibly Miles would help him. As a matter of fact, I've never been able to gauge Miles's attitude to Ruth's family. I think collectively he thinks us deplorable, with nothing but our birth to commend us, and he, being the kind of fellow he is, wouldn't give a locust for that."

Richard said coldly, "I must say, Brand, these asides are in the very worst possible taste."

"I don't know that I should call it the best of taste to ask a man if he's murdered his father."

"I merely wished to warn you of what conceivably may be suggested."

"So that I could think up my defence? Kind of you. As a matter of fact, I'm no author. I paint and I do draughtsman's work and I can get drunk and make a beast of myself, but none of those qualifications would make me capable of telling a really good story, that would get me past the police." He commenced to walk up and down the room, with long lunging strides. "I know you're thinking all the worst possible things about me, Richard, and in a way I'm sorry. But I haven't any unmentionable secrets that I could hold over our father's head, and I'm not hypocritical enough to pretend that his death makes much difference to me. My thoughts of him have always been pretty hard, and I daresay they were mutual. He was, literally, in a position to make my life. And he wouldn't. I've no patience with these bloody little poets, who go into all the magazines that charge the public half a crown and don't pay the contributors a stiver, who sing the praises of poverty, queen of the saints and all that kind of thing. Poverty's damnable; it's bad enough when one's alone, but when there are five or six other people anxious to share the crust that isn't sufficient for you, then it becomes degrading. I've pointed that out to my father time after time; and he didn't believe me. He didn't care either, of course. And so I've been in the treadmill till I was half mad. You don't know—and nor did he—what it is to walk up and down blank streets all night, because you daren't go home; you're afraid of what you might do. Oh, I don't say you never lie awake, too, but that's because someone may get a better job than you, or have a bigger house or create a bigger stir. But to know your work isn't being done—it's no use telling me there are plenty of men in the world who spend their lives unprofitably daubing canvas; the point is that it's my job, and I've been out of my mind sometimes because I couldn't get at it. You remember that torture of the ancients—how they tied up a man in the blazing sun with water out of reach? Well, we torture quite as well as that in these civilised days, and get esteemed for it. And at least that chap died comparatively quickly. He didn't eat his heart out—there were vultures to do that, presumably, and though, no doubt, he cursed them like hell, it was merciful really—hastened things, you see…"

Richard walked to the door and flung it open. "I've always thought you barely responsible for your actions. Now I know you're crazy. To talk like this—they aren't the words of a sane man—and at such a time. I expect that's the police. I'd better see them, and for God's sake pull yourself together and put some kind of a face on it. All the countryside knows you for a byword already…"

Brand began to laugh. Having begun, he could not stop. He held on to the table shaking with mirth; the tears ran down his cheeks, his body trembled. "Oh, Richard," he sobbed, between his gasps. "Oh, Richard. A byword! Because I wanted to paint, and because I haven't much money, and got fooled by a harlot? Oh, don't be so damned squeamish. Haven't you ever heard the word before? Or met one? Or known one? If you're so innocent, read your Bible. It would be a good excuse anyway. A byword! Yes, I might be that in a family like mine, that spends its time scheming for tinsel wreaths and empty honours…" His laughter ceased as abruptly as it came. "I beg your pardon. I think I'm a little hysterical. But you must make allowances. When a man is expecting momentarily to be arrested for murdering his father he is apt to be a little incoherent. At least, that's my experience. If those are the police, you'd better have the first innings. They should have a good impression of the family, or they won't conduct themselves suitably. You know, it's abominable that these things can happen to exclusive folk like ourselves. Murder shouldn't be allowed in the upper classes—so vulgar."

His violent reactions shocked Richard, who said hastily, "All this has upset you, Brand. I apologise for it. It's my fault for making such a suggestion. The fact is, I'm almost beside myself. It's true we disagreed fiercely yesterday, but he was my father, a root; I don't know if you can understand, but something definite has been cut out of my life. It can't be the same again, though it might be more triumphant, better in another way. I don't know about that. There are things one wants I've never been able so far to get. Those may all be added unto me. But this, precisely as it was twenty-four hours ago, that's gone. It affects me, Brand. Because, however strange it may seem to you, it was a relationship that touched the affections. You probably think it's my turn to exhibit hysteria."

The unexpectedness of this outbreak, this sudden revealing of a cold man's heart, touched and awed Brand. All desire to scoff left him; he knew, instead, the intense loneliness of a man who has always been a stranger to his kin. And this man whom he had openly derided and pitied had tasted an experience he himself would never know. More, it was an experience that enriched and softened. A partial realisation of the distress that this loss must occasion a man who, however peculiar it appeared, had actually loved the dead, sobered him almost to grief. But the grief was impersonal. As he had not cared for Adrian Gray, so he was indifferent to Richard; but his heart was wrung by the ineffectual misery of men for the passing, the intangible thing. He wrenched his thoughts back to his dream of the future. That held, was solid, reliable. A man's work could not be measured by any known rule; and immediately his heart lifted, his eyes brightened in anticipation. Yet, turning to leave the room, he saw again those melancholy eyes, the worn resignation of the thin face, and the dignity and hopelessness of them smote him to an intense dejection.

5

He went into the morning-room, where the family was now assembled. They all started at the sight of him, and Amy cried, "What is it, Brand?"

Brand said in a weary voice, "He's dead."

"Yes, we supposed so. But what did Richard want with you?"

"To know if I'd killed him. I told him 'No.' I can't be sure if he believed me. It doesn't seem to matter very much. It's a fatal tendency to allow the insignificant to dwarf the significant."

Miles said, calming the atmosphere of panic that had arisen at Brand's words, "Do you mean to imply murder, Brand?"

"Richard seems to think so. A blow on the temple. It doesn't seem likely that he did it himself. Why should he? Besides, Romford thinks so too."

That silenced even Amy for the moment. Then she exclaimed; "But who—how...?"

"They found the window open."

"Then perhaps someone broke in and father interrupted him, and he killed him. And all of us in the house. How—how appalling!" The inadequacy of the expression was obvious even to her, and she sank back in her chair, her head theatrically sunk in her hands.

Brand moved away to a window, that commanded a long view over the dales. The snow had been much trampled by now, and black, unsightly patches marred its glittering whiteness. Without looking back, he called softly, "Isobel." She came, stepping nervously, and looked at him in an enquiring manner. She was so seldom addressed, except by Amy in a hectoring tone, that she seemed genuinely perplexed at his invitation.

He slipped an arm through hers. "None of us knows how this is going to end," he said. "And, whichever way it does, it means a change in our lives. It must. You can't have your background broken up and not be affected by it to any degree. I hadn't realised that till I saw Richard. Let's not anticipate the future. It'll come upon us soon enough, and what it will bring we can none of us tell. Do you remember that governess you had, who used to take all our pleasure out of snow by saying that before it was trodden it was like one's record in life, and how quickly it was ruined?"

"She wore whalebone supports to her collar, and had a huge brooch made of someone's hair at her bosom."

"And she took us to see those people who, when we asked if the church was old, because father always wanted to know, said heartily, 'Well, it's been here longer than we have, and that's over forty years.'"

"I remember. That was the day we saw a stoat cross the road like a flash."

"And Miss Gowan—that was her name—told us how stoats killed rabbits, and took all our pleasure out of stoats."

"And rabbits too, Brand. I couldn't bear to see them afterwards, thinking they were either going to be killed by stoats or slit up and hung in rows in poulterers'."

"You were always too soft-hearted. Do you remember when we found the thrush that had dashed itself against the telegraph wires, and you thought the devil must have inspired their inventor?"

"And you said it might quite as easily have dashed itself against a tree, and asked if the devil inspired that inventor, too."

"It's a question I still can't answer. What a lot of things we used to talk about."

"And what fun we had. Do you remember getting up and looking for mushrooms when the dew was so thick the grass seemed black with it?"

"And when it was so misty we couldn't see our own feet."

"And all the things we meant to do. Have you ever thought, Brand, how many things there are in life, and how terribly few we manage to keep? They go slipping past, and we're left in the midst of plenty with nothing in our hands."

"It's our own fault for not holding on to things. Or sometimes not reaching out far enough. Too risky. Too expensive. Those are the real reasons why people don't have what they want. I was to have a great body of fine work; and you were to be happy."

Isobel drew so deep a sigh it seemed to cause a shudder through her whole body. "We haven't got very far, have we? And there comes a time when it's too late. Why, Brand, do you suppose we've made such a mess of things?"

"Because we didn't care enough."

She turned startled eyes upon him. "Oh, but I did. You can't realise how much…"

"But even that wasn't enough. If it had been, you'd have held on to what you wanted."

"Nobody could hold on to Harry."

"You hold on till death to the thing you mean to have. If you let go, it's because something else has a superior claim in your heart. Besides, you're confusing Harry with happiness. You've lost happiness precisely for that reason. If you'd made up your mind to that, you'd have allowed no obstacle to deflect you. Losing Harry, you'd have found happiness elsewhere. I'm the same. I don't condemn you. Heaven knows, I'm not in a position to condemn anyone. I've always believed that work is a man's indissoluble link with life. It outlasts him; it matters more than anything he is in himself or anything he owns. If I'd really meant to be an artist I should have let nothing stop me. Not Sophy or the children or my own need or misgivings."

"But there's such a thing as right, Brand. You were right to support Sophy and your children…"

"Not by my theory. To admit that would be to admit that ethics are more important than art. We do the thing—whether we realise this or not—that we've set our hearts upon. If morality or religion or conventional considerations guide your course, that's tantamount to admitting that they're of more importance than what you've always sup-posed to be the mainspring of your life. To the man with a set purpose, laws don't exist. He makes his own; he's the only man who's strong enough to make them."

Isobel's breath came sharply; he had opened to her imagi-nation a new country, rich with promise, denied the fact of her futility, shown her a hope. She said, "Brand, why didn't we talk before? Why have I been down here so long?"

He said, "That's one of the minor tragedies of life. One drifts because it's so difficult to fight the tide, of course. There's so much darkness ahead. At this instant you're immersed in some bright dream, but reality isn't so simple. You can say, 'I won't be beaten; I'll achieve happiness,' but you don't know how to set about it. You've no compass. I doubt if you even know what happiness means to you."

She said quickly, "Ah, I do know that, Brand. Once it meant Harry. That's past a long time ago. But to be free, to live where one pleased, to have books and leisure and tran-quillity, to be able—laugh, if you like, but this occurs to me so often—to go into some restaurant and have a scratch meal, with one's book; to feel oneself in life, part of it, belonging to it, drawing vitality from it…"

Brand looked at her in amazement. "And all these years you've been storing that in your heart? And staying here!"

"It's you, I think. I haven't felt sufficient ardour even to feel so keenly until you began to speak."

Brand said soberly, "No, it's father. When you see how his life's over, and there's nothing to show for it—the waste. When I was confirmed, the angular Protestant bishop who performed the ceremony said, 'There's one unpardonable sin, and that's waste.' Life's full of it; waste of opportunity, talent, time. And generally the reason is fear."

"Perhaps you're right, and that is what I meant," she agreed.

Then Amy called authoritatively, "Isobel!" and she turned, the bright colour in her cheek, her smiling lips automatically composing themselves to meet her sister's glance. Brand, watching her walk towards the speaker, noted a new buoyancy in her step, a spring, an eagerness, a sense of advance and hope. Like finding some blossom alive under a frost, he thought.

Miles had been carefully working his way round the room. Now he paused at Brand's side, and said quietly, "As a lawyer, Brand, and speaking quite without prejudice, let me from my experience give you this bit of advice. We're all bound to be questioned pretty closely about this affair, and I don't suppose any of us will enjoy it."

"You've nothing to be afraid of," said Brand belligerently, resenting this suggestion of guidance.

"No? My position is less enviable than you seem to think. We all suspect some kind of hanky-panky about these financial affairs your father was unwise enough to confide to Eustace. I shall very probably be asked—it's not really relevant, but all manner of irrelevancies crop up in these cases—if I knew what Eustace's professional reputation was. And, knowing it, why didn't I warn my father-in-law that he was playing with fire and could count on being badly burned? The obvious implication is either that I didn't know about these companies, and am therefore a fool whom no man in his senses would ever employ again, or that I did know and kept my mouth shut for reasons of my own, connected with pickings. In which case I'm a knave. No, don't imagine you're the only person who's going to have a bad time. We're practically all of us for it."

"Do you think I did it?"

Miles said kindly, "My dear fellow, it's no use asking me questions like that. I'm a lawyer."

"Still, you're not here in that capacity. You must have some private opinion."

"Even so, I couldn't answer such a question. There are codes of behaviour in all classes and callings. Think for yourself of the psychological effect of my telling a man in a highly nervous state and a dangerous position that I consider he's a murderer. Immediately the balance would swing down, and, though you might know yourself as innocent as the archangel Gabriel, your position would be weakened. Of course, if you were proposing a confession of the crime, that would be different. But I gather you're not."

Brand agreed. "I'm not. Though not for want of encouragement. Richard did all he could to persuade me." But despite the lightness of the tone his expression was so heavy with melancholy that Miles was moved with compassion. He was aware that the family on the whole had accepted without question the theory of Brand's guilt, and the effect of so general a belief on the atmosphere in which the man moved must be to depress and to dishearten. He went on, "It isn't a desire to intrude on your affairs that makes me say this, but as a lawyer one sees so many false steps taken that a word in season would have prevented. If they can't prove that Eustace or anyone else was in the library after you admit to being there, you will, all things considered, be in a very awkward position. I don't know, of course, what took place at the interview, but my advice—and I give this to every client I have—is to stick to the bare facts. Don't, if it was a bit stormy, pretend it was plain sailing. And if you had, practically speaking, to wrench the money out of your father's hands, say so. You'll create a much better impression, and though, of course, men do have second thoughts, these don't obliterate the first ones. If they think they've caught you tripping once, they'll take everything else you say with a grain of salt."

Behind them they heard Amy say to Eustace, "I wish you would be frank with us. We have all guessed that things were not going so well as he had hoped. My father admitted as much, so I don't think there's any need for secrecy among ourselves, at all events. Perhaps he asked you to keep that final conversation private, but then he couldn't have foreseen this position. And, whatever it was, I do think you owe it to us to tell us anything that may bear on the case." She observed him with a piercing gravity, but he only said with added emphasis, "I assure you, Amy, I saw nothing of your father after he went to the library, when we had finished bridge. Certainly there were some points I was anxious to discuss with him, such as the advisability of making one or two changes in his investments, new developments that have only just occurred, but I had not intended to trouble him before to-morrow. A man, when he has his family round him, doesn't want to be plagued by business details."

Even the solemn Miles grinned at that. Brand laughed too, and Amy, who believed in describing a spade accurately, remarked in forceful tones, "It was when my father had his family round him that he was perpetually plagued by business details."

Eustace said furiously, "That may account for his persistent letters to me, asking for larger dividends, greater scope for his capital. If you suppose, my dear Amy, that acting for one's father-in-law is a joke or a sinecure, let me disabuse you. I wouldn't have stood so much interference and complaint from any other man, but one tries to make all the allowances possible, and I knew he was being pestered by his family."

Olivia burst into a flood of tears. "Oh, this is the most horrible Christmas Day I ever remember," she wailed, quite unmoved by any sense of the enveloping tragedy. So she would sob if the turkey failed to arrive or the pudding were burnt.

Eustace, torn between irritation at her collapse and relief at an opportunity for escaping his sister-in-law's grilling examination of his motives and actions, took her away.

"She was always like that," said Amy carelessly. "She cried for hours when she was a little girl, just to attract attention."

Many of Eustace's thoughts, passing and repassing in his mind, were as clear to Miles as though they were goldfish swimming in a bowl, and his suspicion coincided with Amy's. If Eustace didn't go down there last, why is he so nervy, so jerky, why afraid to enter the library? Why did he eat no breakfast, so swiftly lose control of himself? Possibly, thought the shrewder Miles, because something as bad as a murder charge awaited him. Nothing but Adrian Gray had stood between him and ruin forty-eight hours ago; now Gray had been removed, and he stared dishonour in the face. Miles, who detested rogues, felt, nevertheless, a moment of pity for this one—not for his fate, but because of his lack of courage to meet it.

There was the sound of subdued voices rising from the hall below, as a door was opened. Then feet were heard on the stairs and Richard came in, looking fine-drawn and exhausted. He glanced round the room and said instantly, "Where is Laura?" Miles said that she and Ruth were with the grandmother, who had wished to be quiet.

Amy asked, "What is happening now? Do those men want to see any of us?"—and her glance indicated Brand.

Richard replied, in preoccupied tones, "They will let us know. At present they want the room to themselves. They have examinations to make. Of course, no one will go out."

And, turning, he left them again.

Part IV

Aftermath of a Crime

1

Ross Murray, the sergeant in charge of the King's Poplars Mystery, was a man of remarkable personal history and outstanding personality. Born and brought up in circumstances of comfort and luxury, in anticipation of stepping eventually into the shoes of his father, Lord H——, he learned by chance, at the age of eighteen, that he had no right to that honourable name. H——, taxed with written proof in his wife's writing, stiffened, turned white as death, but did not attempt to deny the truth.

"You've always known, sir?"

"Before you were born."

"Yet you've treated me as your son?"

"There was no choice. In law a man's wife can only bear his children."

"Meaning you were responsible for me?"

"In law you are my son. I repeat, there was no choice. As Catholics, divorce was impossible."

"And you accepted me as your heir?"

"You are my heir."

"No, sir. Philip's your heir. And if anything happened to him, there'd be Robin."

"What are you proposing to do?"

"I must clear out, sir, and find my own niche. If there is any purpose in things at all, we must all have some particular place in the scheme of things. I thought mine was here, but it isn't. There's one thing. My father..."

Lord H——'s face was riven with a kind of anguished shame.

"I can tell you very little. He was younger than your mother, and not entirely of her class. He was, I believe, very attractive, and she assures me that they attempted to be honourable. Pure ill-fortune threw them together in compromising circumstances, and apparently it was too much for both of them. Your mother wanted a divorce—of course, I couldn't agree to that. I believe she never saw your father again."

Ross's brows drew together, but he said nothing. He thought, "What a welter of suffering. How damnably they must both have been hurt, and yet they never showed a spasm. My God, there's something to be proud of!"

H—— interrupted his meditations to ask how he proposed to avoid scandal. He could hardly abdicate in Philip's interest without causing a great deal of comment.

Ross said, "I think, sir, you had better let me go abroad. It's so much easier to die there. No official investigations, no public funeral, no awkward questions. Swamp fever—something convenient of that sort. It involves a certain amount of duplicity, I know, but at least it wouldn't mean a lifetime of it, as any other plan would."

"And Philip?"

"Oh, he and Robin would have to know the truth. It would leak out a bit, I daresay, but we can trust the discretion of our friends. Besides, there probably are people alive now who know the facts."

H—— lifted his hand and touched the young man's shoulder. "Believe me, Ross, I am more than ready to forget all this. I forgot it eighteen years ago. I've never let myself think about it. Stay here and inherit. You aren't of my blood, but I should sleep sound enough knowing the place was in your hands."

But Ross refused; he had his own philosophy of life, and he insisted that he had yet to discover his personal vocation. He carried out his suggestion simply and with despatch. As he remarked, it would cause far less comment for him to vanish now, when there was no question of a successor to the estate, than to go after H——'s death, when all manner of ugly rumours would lift their heads.

Which explained why, several years later, there came to King's Poplars Manor House, to investigate the mystery of its owner's death, a man strikingly resembling the eldest son of Lord H——, who had died in such tragic circumstances in Africa in his nineteenth year.

2

From a stile in one of the fields he traversed on his way to the Manor, a short cut normally marked by a footpath but to-day concealed by the heavy snowfall, Ross saw the house bleak against the hillside. It stood solitary, like some accursed building, halfway up the barren slope. To-day it was softened by the snow that still enveloped everything, but he could imagine that, even in the warmth of summer, it bore an aloof appearance, as if it were for ever cut off from the friendly companionship of men. It was curiously built, on two floors that contained, however, an unusual amount of space, though the general appearance of the exterior was narrow and furtive. The roof was very steep and dark; the windows were set flush with the walls, and were too close under the eaves, giving the place a sinister and somehow dishonest aspect. Ross was reminded of a peculiarly haunting aquatint he had once seen, called "The Evil House," that had stirred his imagination and chilled his blood. And to-day he experienced precisely that eerie sensation of discomfort. The Manor, he thought, looked exactly the type of house where one might expect a crime to be committed; the most bizarre story connected with it would not be incredible.

Having lived for some years in the neighbourhood of King's Poplars, and being a man of observation and discretion, Ross had a reasonably accurate notion of the relations existing between the various members of the Gray clan. He knew, moreover, that of late letters had been received from London—so much was village gossip—following whose arrival Gray would be less approachable than usual, accusing his daughter of wilful extravagance and irresponsibility. The frequent visits of Moore to the house had not gone unremarked, and there was a widely spread belief that the old man had allowed himself to come under the thumb of the foreigner, as the fellow was generally regarded. The younger son also was known to be a firebrand and something of a mendicant. Of Isobel, Ross had heard only the legendary stories of the neighbourhood, that was rich in such tales; men declared that she passed through the village without casting a shadow, that she was to be seen walking on the moors on dark nights with a lantern, and that when a mortal approached her, she disappeared, leaving the lantern hanging in mid-air. Ross could dismiss all this at its true value, but he was astute enough to guess that a situation of some gravity must have arisen during the past months, that had been difficult enough for the well-to-do, and practically ruinous for the small speculator.

The Grays, unquestionably, had come down in the world. Once they had been landed proprietors of some standing; during the past twenty or thirty years, however, their fortunes had sunk and they had parted with much of their property. At the same time, the family began to break up, various members migrating to London and other large towns, some of them even going abroad. The lands that remained were leased to farmers, the family keeping only the Manor House. The life of the village that had once centred round it now swept past its doors. No one dreamed of going there in difficulty and anxiety, for consolation, assistance, or advice. It was the old story of a new order stealing the charm from the old. But with the break-up of the county tradition had come, too, so far as an outsider could gauge, the break-up of the family itself. A steady deterioration in character was obvious in the various members; their point of view had changed. They now desired the ambitions of the common herd, that once they had despised. Place, possession, authority—these were now their gods. The generations of Grays in the churchyard would scarcely have recognised their descendants, and would certainly have been reluctant to acknowledge their kinship.

"And now the old man's dead, presumably murdered by one of his own children," Ross reflected, swinging out of the last field and approaching the house. "They'd scarcely send for the police to take his temperature. You don't call us in, especially on Christmas Day, if you can help it, not when you've gone walking through the village for years, like a cock among a lot of shabby hens that he can have for the asking, and doesn't think worth the trouble."

3

Richard met him in the hall and took him to the disordered library. The feet of so many people passing in and out, their aimless gestures and the flurry caused by the lifting of the old man, had disarranged many books and papers. Ross saw that scattered on the table and carpet were several letters and notes that had presumably been kept in place by the slab of brass that, Richard said, was believed to have been used for the murder. There was also a number of pamphlets and prospectuses lying about the room, referring for the most part to companies not very well spoken of on the London Stock Exchange—to copper and ore prospectors, to men full of wild schemes for abstracting gold and gems from remote parts of the earth, for crazy inventions, and for pioneering work that promised substantial rewards. If Gray had been induced to lodge his money in any of these concerns, he could know very little of industrial affairs.

Ross was inclined to be impressed by Richard's aloof dignity, a certain calm and reticence that were arresting. Tall, spare, grey of face, he appeared a sombre man emerging from a natural secrecy to accept the challenge of the event. Ross appreciated his attitude. The notion that anything within the family circle can empower curious strangers to come in against the owner's will and ask impertinent and intimate questions is bound to be peculiarly galling.

"There is also the rather odd matter of the open window," Richard wound up his brief explanations. "It seems unlikely that my father opened it, since he suffered habitually from the cold, and Moulton remembers closing and fastening it during the evening."

Ross made his first mental note. Richard Gray seemed anxious to show that the open window had no connection with the crime, thus disposing of the only alternative to a family murderer. Why?

Richard left him presently to his task of examining the room. Ross was aware of a curious sense of depression very foreign to him. It almost amounted to embarrassment; and it was difficult to trace it to its source. It was not as if this were the worst case in which he had as yet been involved; he had had murder cases before. Rather his dejection was due to a certain sense of inhumanity and irritation that the house seemed to exude, as though the people in it were touched, not by pity or by grief, but by anger at the manner of Gray's death and the discomfort and publicity they must themselves endure.

"Goodness knows, the dead are forgotten soon enough," he reflected, "shovelled underground and given the tribute of a flower at stated intervals, and a fee for the decent conditioning of the memorial stone. But here somehow there's a feeling that all these people care about is their own future and its prospects."

4

During the hour that followed, the family gathered in the morning-room and exchanged few words. Brand, inwardly rigid, outwardly composed, maintained his position by the window. He watched the movement of life in the quiet world outside, the changing shapes of clouds, the flight of small birds, their dun-coloured bodies flinging a dark shadow on the unbroken expanse of snow. At any moment, he felt, his crucial hour would be upon him. All that had preceded this moment was evanescent, insubstantial as a shadow, distorting, as shadows do, the reality following on its heels. It seemed to him that to fail now would be treachery, not to his relations or to his father, but to his own personality, to the spirit informing the wayward flesh. Only by a rich fulfilment of his dream could he justify the mad act of last night. A man not unaccustomed to thought and to the arguments of philosophy, he could even find a certain irrational seemliness and worth in his own deed, provided he did not permit the fruit to turn rotten. "Like trees flourishing on a stinking corpse," he thought characteristically.

Once, Olivia, who with her husband had rejoined the group, said with a sharp gasp, "We shan't be implicated, Eustace, surely?"

Eustace returned, "We are implicated. How can we help it?"

Glancing from the impassivity that he instantly resumed to Richard's remote air, that might conceal any emotion from stark fear to a blank resignation that neither hopes nor believes anything, Brand was impressed by the Power that, creating men with visible features, had made it possible for them to conceal every trace of sensibility, so that onlookers could watch them, spy on their quiet moments, but still learn nothing. Under their masks, what emotions racked them, these two men for whom so much was at stake? They must know that their individual relations with the dead man would be the subject of public discussion, and that such discussion was bound to react on their careers and ambitions. Were they afraid, even though they were aware of their own innocence? Or did they think of those revelations that were bound to be made, and that must affect their professional lives? Was there a shadow of pity in either of them for the dead man or for him who bore the weight of the knowledge of his death? For surely his was the worst position of them all. If the truth were discovered, he would, though he would suffer another kind of disaster, be relieved from the tremendous pressure he must endure now, this sense of unbearable knowledge. Last night, standing by his father's body, he had restrained a desire to summon the household with some cock-and-bull story of having heard strange sounds and come downstairs to investigate—anything, he had felt, rather than bear the burden of knowing the truth, unshared by anyone else. And to-day that weight pressed yet more heavily upon him. One part of his nature struggled to conceal every trace of evidence that could point to him as the victim of the situation; but there was another clamorous instinct that assured him that to share his knowledge would be blessed relief. It would imply the end of this inward torment, this sense of being helpless in the dark, without the slightest notion of where he was placing his feet. At any instant he might plunge to disaster; a chance word, a heedless reply, might mean self-betrayal. He saw himself as the fox torn and bloody in the jaws of the hounds; his inward being panted and exerted, as the hunted fox must do to escape pursuit, but he wondered how strong that instinct for life remained in the creature which knew that, escaping this time, it must be captured and rent to pieces at the last.

He moved uneasily, one hand holding fast to the dark window-sill. "Pull yourself together. Think of the future. This is a nightmare, but it will pass. All things pass. Only the spirit of man is indomitable." As he had waited, stupefied, beside the body some hours ago, repeating that formula, "He's dead. I've killed him. I'm a murderer. Murderers hang," so now he repeated in his heart these encouragements to preserve him from the worst of Judas-acts, the betrayal of the inner man through fear.

He received assurance from the sight of Eustace, smooth, sophisticated, uncaring, with his air of bestowing patronage on the men among whom he moved, men less worldly than himself and, therefore, less successful; only to-day he detected signs of that arrogant pose shaken, fear peering through the cracks. It strengthened his resolve to maintain the part he had created for himself, and his sense of responsibility ebbed.

Amy cried in petulant tones, "What a long time that man is in the library. What can there be for him to do? And how insufferable to have a stranger" (and such a stranger, implied her tone, a common man probably related to half the servants, who are always eager to spread gossip and make bad blood) "turning over our intimate possessions."

Richard spoke heavily. "There's a good deal for him to examine, I suppose. And I don't doubt there's plenty of local gossip that has already reached his ears. People in a small place like this have very little else to do but talk." Despite his experience, he believed, with Amy, that the working-class population, as they were termed at a time when to work openly was a subtle disgrace, were maddeningly engrossed in the affairs of their social superiors; and if anyone had attempted to disillusion him, and point out that their own lives were of infinitely greater importance to the men and women to whom he referred than the most sensational crash in—say—his own life, he would have shrugged the information aside. For Richard, the world had not marched on for nearly a generation.

Eustace put in abruptly, "I've always been against Amy's practice of engaging local servants. It's bound to make for trouble. You can trust this fellow downstairs to make the worst of a bad job."

Miles observed, "He's got his work cut out, if you stop and think for a minute. Half his case will depend on what he can compel the library to tell him. The rest he hopes to get from us."

His remark deflected the trend of Brand's thought. Instantly self-forgetful, his imagination presented him with a picture of the silent, intent man, separated from themselves only by a partition of plaster and wood, invoking the aid of inanimate objects to solve the problem that had been deliberately tangled and twisted by men, who regarded him as an interloper, an intruder on their privacies—an enemy, in short. Where would he start? On what would he base his conclusions? How differentiate between the significant and the trivial? What, for instance, would he make of the open window, of the forged document, of the ashes in the grate? Might he conceivably set them together in a pattern that was neither the truth nor the lie that Brand had offered him, but some version of the crime totally dissimilar to anything that had passed through his (the murderer's) mind? For the first time, Brand saw himself pitted against this man alone. It was to be a battle of wits between them, and if he could fabricate and distort evidence, this other also could keep his own counsel. They would presently face one another, each ignorant of the other's moves and counterplots, of the line upon which he worked, to that extent moving in the dark. The pitfalls on his own road now appeared to him with astonishing clarity, as he reflected, with some dismay, that his was not the only intelligence capable of setting snares and laying false clues.

Brooding thus, he paid no heed to his companions until Richard's voice, saying, at first with insistence and then with impatience, "Brand, the police want to see you," roused him from his thoughts.

5

As he entered the library, Brand directed a keen glance towards the man who was about to examine him. He discerned no outstanding characteristics, none of that gimlet-eyed alertness for which he had been prepared, no sign of any intention to fasten on to his lightest word and turn it to ill account. The man facing him was cool and non-committal. He asked the simple questions regarding his interview with his father that Brand had anticipated.

Brand matched his coolness with an appearance of unconcern. His answers slipped from him as easily and with as little effort as though he were conducting a normal conversation at his club (supposing him to have been a member of such an institution). Presently Ross said, "About that window,

Mr. Gray? I suppose your father didn't open it while you were in the room?"

"No," said Brand, who was prepared upon this point also. "It was shut when I left him."

"You can't think of any reason why he should have opened it?"

"None. Is there a suggestion that he did open it?"

"Who else?" asked Ross blandly.

"There seemed some feeling in my brother's mind this morning that an entry might have been forced from outside."

"When?"

"After I left the room, I suppose."

"But you met Mr. Moore coming downstairs."

"Then after he also had left the library."

Ross shook his head. "I think you can dismiss that notion from your mind. Are you aware at what hour it began to snow?"

"I don't remember." He suspected a trap here, and an admission might involve him in explanations that would begin the weaving of that mesh of suspicion, crystallising into an accusation against himself, that he must at all costs avoid.

"It happens that I do. The snow began at 11.15. If, as you say, you did not leave the library until nearly a quarter to twelve, and Mr. Moore succeeded you here, an interloper must have put in an appearance after midnight. By that time the roads were heavy with snow. I can vouch for that, because, as a Catholic, I went over to Nunhead for the Midnight Mass. It meant starting at eleven o'clock, as, of course, it was necessary to walk, and at a quarter past, quite unexpectedly, the snow began. When I came out of church at one o'clock, it was thick enough to make unpleasant walking. Anyone entering the room by the window, as you suggest—although opening a casement from the outside, without leaving marks on the frame, is a difficult thing to do—must have left marks of snow on the carpet. And, as you probably have realised, there were none. No, I doubt if the window played any considerable part in the affair. One more thing. When Mr. Gray made out his cheque on your behalf, did he take it—the book, I mean—from the safe?"

Here Brand, had he realised it, was on more dangerous ground. Behind that casual enquiry was a whole wealth of vigilance. But Brand only said, "No. I didn't even know he had a safe. At least, I did wonder sometimes, but I never located it."

"Among the books," Murray told him. "Very neatly concealed."

"That's typical of him, isn't it? Why on earth hide it? Did he think he'd have all the family at it if he let 'em know where it was?"

"He was apparently a cautious man," was Ross's equally cautious response.

Brand nodded. "Whereabouts was it?"

"Behind the *Hakluyt's Voyages*. You know where they were?"

"I'm afraid I've never taken much interest in my father's books. Where were they?"

"There were two sets; that's what attracted my attention. One in the recess near the fireplace and the other in the shelves by the door. Fake, of course, the second lot."

Brand frowned. "It seems more reasonable that the fake ones should be in the recess. Then he could indulge his secrecy to his heart's content."

"Oh, they were," agreed Ross, looking a little surprised.

"I suppose one of the family told you about them?"

"I don't know how many of them knew."

"I expect my brother would, and Mr. Moore. I don't know about the others. Mr. Amery, perhaps, but I'm not sure. I don't fancy he and my father were on the best of terms."

"No?" Ross's voice was non-committal. Brand amended himself sharply.

"I beg your pardon. I was thinking aloud. I don't mean to imply that there were any serious disagreements between them. I don't believe they often met. But I know their standards were different, and my father was displeased at what he considered Mr. Amery's lack of ambition. That was all I intended to convey when I said I doubted whether he'd be in my father's confidence."

"I see," said Murray in the same tone. "To go back to the matter of the cheque. Your father wrote it out while you were in the room?"

"Yes. He hadn't anticipated giving me one. He'd hardly have it prepared."

"Quite. He didn't say anything about a cheque for Mr. Moore?"

"No. But he did give me the impression that he would not be altogether surprised at seeing him again before morning. It was obvious to us all that there was something serious on my brother-in-law's mind."

"And you necessarily associated that with Mr. Gray?"

"The only basis on which my father and Mr. Moore ever met was a financial one. They'd nothing else in common. Besides, even I have heard how rocky some of the companies are in which my father and Mr. Moore have investments. And this wouldn't be the first time he has come down here to ask for funds."

"He said nothing of this to you—Mr. Moore, I mean?"

"Mr. Moore regards me as a congenital idiot, on whom words and ordinary common sense are wasted."

"I see. Thank you. There's one more point. This document you signed. Was that awaiting your signature or did your father draw it up in your presence?"

Here Brand paused an instant, suspecting a further trap. "He drew it up while I was in the room," he replied, after that moment of hesitation. "He didn't know he was going to give me money; he'd hardly have had the document in readiness, would he?"

"Quite. I wonder if you'd oblige me by letting me take an impression of your finger-prints."

Brand was startled; yet an instant's reflection assured him that he had nothing to fear from this procedure. He had acknowledged his presence in the room, and in the circumstances it would be reasonable to expect to find traces.

But he did ask, as he complied with the detective's request, reflecting gloomily that he would have to wash his hands before his return to the morning-room, "What's the idea? Or is it just a formality?"

"Oh, no," Ross told him, in placid tones. "There are some finger-prints on the safe that we want to identify. Of course, if you didn't know it was there, they can't be yours, but as a matter of routine I must test every member of the household."

"They may be my father's."

"Oh, very probably. But it isn't safe to act on that assumption. Thank you, Mr. Gray. I wonder if you'd let Mr. Moore know I should like to see him." Brand mounted the stairs two at a time, lithe and silent as a cat. He thought rapidly, "Must be on my guard, without appearing to notice anything unusual. I mustn't seem anxious and I mustn't go to the other extreme and look too casual. After all, I am involved, some people would say heavily involved. It may seem odd that there are none of Eustace's finger-prints in the room. A fellow like that one will be sure to comment on that. How does a man behave who knows he may be arrested for murder, that everyone believes him guilty of murder, but who is actually innocent? That's the attitude I've got to adopt."

He put his head into the morning-room and gave Moore the detective's message.

"Where are you going now, Brand?" asked Amy hungrily.

"To wash my hands. This stuff in which they take your finger-prints—oh, yes, it's all very official, like something on the pictures. Good luck, Eustace."

He lingered in the bathroom, trying to determine the best line to follow. If he appeared too greatly alarmed at the prospect he would arouse suspicion; and if he were devil-may-care and defiant he would probably confirm a suspicion, not in the minds of his relations, who did not, actually, matter, but in the mind of that silent, astute, and vigilant man who was as resolved to come to the bottom of the mystery as he, the murderer in their midst, intended to escape the consequences of his deed.

Drying his hands on the blue-and-white checked towel— "What cheap towels Sophy buys," he thought; "it's a pleasure to feel this thick, soft material under one's hands"—he went on in his mind, "How much does that fellow know? What has he discovered? He gave nothing away. Whom does he suspect? Has he examined the fireplace? Suppose that doesn't occur to him? What"—and this was the crucial question— "what does he know that I don't know he knows?" Therein lay his true danger, and once again he was impressed and appalled to think that he had stood face to face with a man, not more than two feet distant, had been free to observe his expressions, gestures, and the movements of his body, and yet had no key whatsoever as to what was passing in that calm and reasoning brain. He put the towel down untidily, and went back to the group in the morning-room. Eustace was still, presumably, undergoing examination. Perhaps he, too, was having a gruelling time.

Brand spoke suddenly. "How much authority have these police fellows got? How many questions can they ask, and is there anything sacred to them? Can you refuse to answer anything?"

"Honest people with nothing to fear don't mind answering questions," Amy ripped out viciously.

"Quite. But are any of us that?"

They turned their faces towards him. "What on earth do you mean?"

"In these circumstances, is there one of us who hasn't got something he'd like to hide? You, Amy, if you were asked what were your relations with our father, were you always on the best of terms, wouldn't you like to refuse to answer that, knowing that he is at liberty to examine the whole household staff, who may or may not corroborate your story? And Richard, do you really want to tell an outsider what happened between you and our father when you came down yesterday? I should imagine Eustace is in the same boat."

"What did he ask you?" his sister demanded.

"He might have been understudying yourself. And I gave him precisely the same replies. Oh, and I did tell him I hadn't been tampering with the safe. Unfortunately, I didn't know where it was."

Richard said apprehensively, "Who is talking about the safe?"

"Authority on the floor below. There are finger-prints on it. Very damaging, perhaps. I don't know. I've suggested they belong to the safe's owner.

"I think that sounded normal enough," he reflected, concealing an inward anxiety, that was rapidly increasing, under an aspect of derisive calm. "The type of thing they expect from me, anyway."

The door opened, but it was not Eustace but a servant who appeared. Would Mrs. Moore go down to the little room behind the library? Olivia asked quickly for her husband. The servant murmured, in discreet and formal tones, "I couldn't say, madam," and stood holding the door.

Eustace came in a moment later, pale and guarded. He answered one or two questions with brevity, and looked with malevolence at Brand, who had resumed his stance by the window. Richard said something in a low voice, and he replied, "God only knows where this will end. Gaol for half of us, probably. The fellow's a scorpion. Our distress is simply his chance of promotion."

Richard stood back, and began to talk in low tones to Amery. Eustace strategically worked his way round the room until he could speak to Brand without attracting attention. Brand, who had watched him secretly, was thinking, as he was bound to think with the return of each member of the clan from that cool but deadly examination downstairs, "What did he get out of him? How much does Eustace know? What passed between him and my father yesterday?"

He had turned his back on the rest of the room, with these thoughts in mind, and it came as a small shock when he felt a hand close on his wrist. Eustace's voice said, "What did you tell the police, Brand?"

"Just what I've told all of you. I've answered that question once at least."

"I've only this to ask you. Where's that cheque?"

"In my pocket."

"My cheque?"

"Your cheque?"

"Yes. They've examined his cheque-book, and they find that he drew a cheque for me immediately after drawing yours—a cheque for ten thousand pounds."

"And to hear him talk, you wouldn't have believed he even had so much money."

"That's not the point. I've got to have that cheque, Brand."

"Why come to me? I haven't got it. I wasn't even in the room when it was drawn. I didn't stay long after getting the money. After all, that was what I came down for."

"That cock won't fight. No one saw Gray after you did…"

"That's rather a bold accusation, isn't it? Tantamount to saying I killed him. But I suppose you think I did."

Eustace sketched an impatient gesture. "That's beside the point. The matter's out of our hands now. But I want to know about that cheque…"

"My dear fellow, be reasonable. I know less about it than you do. I know precisely what you've told me, which is merely that it exists. I haven't even any proof of that. By the way, if you haven't seen it, what proof have you?"

"The police have seen the entry on the counterfoil."

"Ah! True. I'd forgotten that piece of evidence. Well, it doesn't seem likely that my father would have made such an entry without drawing the cheque."

"The cheque itself is missing."

"What about the safe?"

"Oh, they've examined that." Eustace's voice was very bitter. "It's a combination lock, and I've never been allowed to know what the combination was. But they got it open all right. I'd not realised before what opportunities the police have."

"Did you tell them that?" Brand looked interested.

"I congratulated them. That fellow—confound his impertinence!—said coolly that if all safes were impregnable the police wouldn't have nearly so much to do."

"Well, if it wasn't in the safe, where could it be? Are there any other hiding-holes in the room?"

"None I know of."

"Then I suppose we may take it there are none. By the way, you knew about the safe?"

"Well?"

"What was my father's idea in concealing it so elaborately?"

"Your father, Brand, was a very strange man. If you think it was advantageous to work for him, and in his interest, you're greatly mistaken. If any of his shares dropped a couple of points there would be letters and telegrams and accusations, until the time came when I deliberately kept him in the dark, knowing that it was a matter of days before the shares rose again."

"Did they often fall?"

"Of course, they weren't stationary. In a situation like the present, with the whole world's standards changing from day to day, with uncertainty on every hand and the most reliable companies passing their dividends, with unemployment and idle shipyards and trouble all over the East, with no money in people's pockets, and strikes and disorders in industry, with falling Governments and all the rest of it, do you suppose his wretched little investments were going to be immune? No one but an egotist would have expected it."

Brand, smiling drily, observed, "You haven't a great admiration for my father, it seems."

"I wasn't sufficiently disaffected to murder him, all the same, though it might suit your book to say so. Just as you've made the position as awkward for me as possible with your lying story of seeing me on the stairs at midnight."

"If you're anxious to deny that, my dear fellow, I should imagine you'd have no great difficulty. Surely Olivia can vouch for you at that hour?"

"Unfortunately, that isn't the case. Had it been yourself involved, no doubt your wife could meet the situation. But Amy is kind enough to arrange for us to have a dressing-room if we require it, and on a night when I was perturbed about our affairs, as I was then, I prefer solitude."

"It only shows, doesn't it, that the slovenly makeshifts of the poor, whose dressing-rooms have to be utilised as additional bedrooms for the children, have their advantages? As you remark, Sophy would certainly have been in a position to vouch for me. But surely Olivia isn't so squeamish that she'd hesitate over a trifle like that?"

"I really can't tell you what Olivia will say. No doubt she can satisfy your curiosity on her return. Though as to that," he added, on a sudden note of rage, "I fail to see what damned business it is of yours how my wife and I spend our nights."

"Normally, I agree it would be impertinent on my part to raise the question, but in the present position, when so much depends on where the various members of the family were at stated hours, you will admit it is important, particularly as the tide of suspicion seems to be running heavily against myself."

"And you've no one but yourself to thank for that. But about that cheque. I'll swear you know more than you'll say."

"So far as I'm aware, such a cheque was never even drawn," said Brand earnestly, and, as it happened, with accuracy. "But perhaps he changed his mind and destroyed it later."

"There seems very little point in drawing it in the first place if he meant to do that. And he would certainly have cancelled the counterfoil in that case."

"You think of everything, don't you? You're right. He was a methodical man. Still, have they examined the wastepaper basket?"

"I understand that they have. The basket, I'm told, contained some torn envelopes, and your own letter demanding assistance."

"That they'll glue neatly together, no doubt. It may be useful to them. I wonder what I said."

"By this time you should be pretty familiar with your own demands."

"This was more ambitious—more outrageous, as you and Amy would say—than my previous suggestions."

But though he was inwardly cool, and even gave the appearance of enjoying this sparring-match, Brand's heart jolted uncomfortably, as he was compelled to realise more and more the immense paraphernalia of the law against which he had pitted himself. His roving glance took in the whole room, so full of enemies, eager to see him condemned and put out of the way, so that they might themselves take up their own lives and forget him as soon as might be. Only Miles Amery watched him intently, and it was impossible to gauge the quality of his thoughts. Ruth, who had also returned from the grandmother's room, stood, pale, serene, untouched, like the young Christina, against the wall. Somehow she seemed aloof from all this noisy business of scandal and greed. Probably, reflected Brand, because she had no ambitions that any of them could destroy. But Eustace, seeing the thin, keen face of the lawyer, experienced sudden, unreasoning rage, and that sense of inferiority, that he knew to be unfounded and absurd, attacked him again. This shabby fellow, whom he never met in his own more exclusive circles, never ceased to give him that impression, as though he, Eustace, were in some way insignificant, all his fine plans so much tinsel and his hopes as worthless as the paper hoop through which the clown in the circus leaps to amuse the crowd in the auditorium.

6

One by one the family was put through its paces by the thoroughgoing young man downstairs. At the end of the ordeal, a few significant facts emerged. Chief among these was Eustace's inability to deny Brand's story of seeing him on the stairs; before she realised the implications of the admission, Olivia said vaguely that her husband had left her before midnight. Later she had tried to retract that, putting the hour of his departure considerably later, but Murray would not let her off, and she left him disturbingly conscious that she had on the whole made things worse for her husband. And, being in his confidence, she realised that a very black case could be brought against him.

One question she had failed to understand until she received his explanation. Ross had said unconcernedly, "It was a great relief to you, wasn't it, when your husband could tell you that he had every hope your father would help him?"

She said blankly, "I didn't really know the position. My father had been busy all day, and I didn't know whether he actually appreciated how we all stood."

"But if your husband mentioned the cheque to you...?"

"The cheque?"

"That your father had promised him."

Olivia stared; it would have been difficult to recognise in this haggard, distraught woman the beautifully manicured, waved, and sophisticated creator of Dot and Lalage.

"I know nothing of that."

"I beg your pardon." But Ross offered no explanation. Not until she had her husband to herself could Olivia say, "But, Eustace, why didn't you tell me? How could you let me go down there unprepared?"

"Tell you what?"

"About the cheque."

"How could I? I never had the chance."

"You could have told me this morning before the police came. There were plenty of opportunities."

"I'm trying to make you understand that I'd never heard of the cheque until that fellow flung his questions at me."

"Then there was one?"

"Apparently."

"Where is it now?"

"He says they've searched the room with a microscope and there's no sign of it. But it may have been burnt, of course."

"By father? Why, if he'd just drawn it up?"

"Not by your father. By that precious hangdog brother of yours."

"But how would Brand get hold of it?"

"My idea is that in some way, probably dishonest, he persuaded his father to part with two thousand pounds. Then Gray, realising the inequality of the position, and the hopelessness of persisting in his attitude of stubborn refusal, came to the conclusion that the only thing to do was to face up to the position and pay out the money. Brand, I fancy, must have repented of signing that paper, and came back in the hopes of reclaiming it, only to find your father still in the room. I daresay they had hasty words, ending in a scene, during which Brand, whose temper is as violent as the devil when he's roused, struck your father, possibly without meaning to do any serious damage, and found he'd killed him. Then he discovered the cheque made out to me, and destroyed it."

"But didn't destroy the paper he had come to fetch?"

"That's easily explained. If you suddenly kill a man and realise you are likely to swing for it, you're likely enough to overlook something."

"On the other hand, one might think such a man would be more likely than usual to be careful, since so much depended on it."

"The history of criminal law tends to support my argument," snapped Eustace.

"Did you make that suggestion to the police?"

"I didn't say that I thought Brand was guilty. I told them I thought probably your father had drawn the cheque intending to give it me this morning."

"What did he say?"

"He asked sarcastically if I thought it was intended as a Christmas present. Of course, the fact that this is Christmas Day is pure chance. The fact is, these people have much too much licence, and are only too apt to abuse it. It's a scandal, the amount of rope given to coroners and policemen these days."

7

In the privacy of their room, Richard said uneasily to his wife, "Frobisher's coming down first thing in the morning. It's unfortunate, this affair occurring at Christmas-time. It would have been much better if we could have got him in the house to-day, before we were cross-examined by the police."

Laura looked astonished. "But you're perfectly safe, Richard. Half a dozen lawyers couldn't have altered your replies, any more than they could have altered mine."

He said testily, stripping off his collar and wrenching the links out of his shirt, "My dear Laura, you seem quite unable to differentiate between truth and discretion. Of course, one doesn't wish to conceal essential facts, but the truth remains that we are in the hands of the law, as represented by this sergeant and any assistants he may have—the coroner, for instance—men chosen quite haphazard to deal with this particular case, and quite liable to over-estimate the importance of certain admissions or to lay undue weight on what other members of the family see fit to tell them. Frobisher, with all the facts before him, might have been of considerable value to us. We have, after all, our position to consider."

"I thought we were agreed that we hadn't one any longer. I assure you, I find it a relief to feel myself a free agent."

She was, indeed, conscious of a certain sense of excitement. She had at one time employed a lady's-maid, a girl very apt with her needle, quick, tactful, and charming. At the end of a year the girl gave notice.

"But why, Lessing?" Laura wanted to know. "Aren't you comfortable here? Is it anything to do with the other servants? Have you been offered better wages or an easier situation?"

No, said Lessing, it was none of those things. It was (though she did not phrase it precisely in this fashion) a fear of developing roots, becoming so much a part of her environment that her personality became blurred, insensible to the shock of change, until at length it ceased to desire change, became afraid of it. All her interest, she explained, quickened at the thought of new contacts and new experiences. She was not alarmed by hard work, even by what her contemporaries would think derogatory work. She felt, she said, a great sense of excitement and anticipation while she waited for news of a fresh post; she enjoyed answering advertisements, picturing to herself the type of people with whom she would find her new life, the countryside, the conditions, all the novel and unknown circumstances into which life might be about to lead her. Talking that day, Laura realised for the first time the source of that peculiar charm whose radiance had touched her during the first weeks of the girl's service. It lay in the sense of surprise and of hope in the atmosphere wherein she lived. She was not, like the majority of human creatures, moulded by her circumstances. She adapted them to her own needs, grew rich, and absorbed. Nothing, thought Laura, could wholly defeat or dismay her. She remembered her to-night, as she looked into the pinched and woeful face of her husband. How quickly, she thought, he has crumbled under this blow, realising that the primary wound he endured was to his own esteem. If you peered into his mind you might find in the second chamber the body of his father, for whom he had cherished a certain affection;

but in the first room of all would be the image of a ruined man, hurriedly scanning the newspapers to see how much could be salved from the wreckage, and it was that ruined man whom she loathed.

"A free agent?" he retorted bitterly. "Sometimes, Laura, I think you're out of your mind, don't realise what you're saying. My work is my life; you may be capable of building up another out of the things that matter to you. I've never been able to discover precisely what these are, but if they are things that won't be touched by this *débâcle* I must congratulate you."

Laura, smiling in that strange, aloof fashion that had always angered him, said, "No, I don't think they'll be touched." She felt completely apart from this man with whom her life had been shared for thirteen years; endeavouring to feel sympathy for him, she could discover only distaste, and in her interior consciousness she had visions of a life in which he played no part, a life of different values that would enrich and satisfy her own hungry personality. Thus, leagues apart in their outlook on life and on this situation, they prepared themselves for sleep.

8

Frobisher arrived next morning. Ross had departed the previous day without voicing any suspicions, but everyone realised that he was waiting for the result of the finger-print experiment. Not, said Richard impatiently, that it proved much, those marks on the safe; they might have been there for days. He had asked the sergeant whether anything had been removed from it. Ross had replied blandly, "I don't know what was originally in it, Sir Richard. I was hoping you might be able to help me."

"I didn't know, either. Perhaps Mr. Moore..."

Eustace, recalled, said, "I always understood he had documents of some value in it. I've often seen papers in the safe when it was opened, though I've never actually handled any of them, any more than I have ever been allowed to open the safe."

Then he asked what had actually been found there, but Ross did not satisfy his curiosity. Eustace came upstairs and sought out Miles, in a fine rage and anxiety.

"It's infamous," he exclaimed. "How do we know how far these men are to be trusted? Oh, yes, our splendid police force, the high morale of the service and all that—I daresay in ninety per cent of their activities they're reliable enough, but they are subject to temptations like other men, and the fact remains that you do every now and again hear of policemen who have taken advantage of their circumstances, and themselves figure in the dock. We know nothing about this fellow, and we—at least, I—do know that my father-in-law had a number of valuable certificates and so forth in the safe."

His connection by marriage remarked mildly that if they were in Gray's name they wouldn't be much use to the sergeant, and anyway he didn't suppose the fellow wanted to encompass his own ruin. "Moreover," he added, "we're all in his hands now. Oh, I grant you it's illogical enough, but it's the law of life, so far as we can tell. The innocent suffering for the guilty."

Eustace cried fiercely, "We know well enough who's guilty."

Miles stopped him with a sharp, "Take care! There are such things as slander actions, and we don't want to increase the scandal. It'll be bad enough in any case."

Richard saw Frobisher alone. He was by this time trembling with anticipation, and did not make a good impression upon his man of affairs. Frobisher said, "Well, this is a mess. I suppose it'll be all over the town to-morrow."

Richard agreed bitterly that no doubt it would, and that they'd be inundated with reporters.

"Well, there's no need to see them. Give instructions that you've nothing to say and no interviews are being given. As a matter of fact, in a case of this kind it's very important that there should be no leakage. Can you trust your servants?"

Richard said weakly that he wasn't sure. He mentioned Amy.

"Is she on good terms with them? Do they like her?"

"I couldn't say."

"Then presumably they don't. Well, if you take my advice, you'll forbid them to speak to anyone. Things are going to be quite unpleasant enough without that. How do they stand at present?"

Richard began to explain, but his habit of public speaking, that was apt to be oratorical and ponderous, irritated the lawyer, who interrupted him with a testy, "Yes, yes. But have you any idea whom they suspect? Whom, for instance, do you suspect?"

"My brother seems the most likely person to have done it—temperamentally, I mean. He holds to his story of seeing Eustace Moore on the stairs as he himself left the room, but I don't know that that's been substantiated. I suppose, in the circumstances, it isn't likely that it can be."

"He admits to seeing your father, then?"

"Yes." Richard continued his explanations more briefly. "I suppose," he concluded, "there's bound to be a good deal of publicity about the case."

"I don't see how you can avoid it. Not so much on your father's account, or your own, as on Moore's. His name's going to be very much on everyone's lips in the next few days."

Richard turned white. "It's true, then? He's in for a smash?"

"A criminal smash, or I'm mightily mistaken," returned Frobisher grimly.

"Would my father have been involved?"

"I should imagine that all Moore's dupes would be. The long and the short of the matter is that he's been running a ramp and the facts have come out. If you ask me, I should say he was safe for a good five years."

"Everyone knows, then?"

"Anyone who doesn't will know very soon. And it won't be possible to keep your father's name out of that. There'll be a lot of ugly suspicions voiced. Brand won't be the only man to stand the racket, particularly in view of his story."

"I daresay his wife can vouch for Moore."

"And I daresay there'll be a good many people to whisper collusion, if she does. I don't think a wife's unsupported word will help our financier this time, particularly when it comes out that he's had every penny of your father's capital."

Richard started. "Every penny? But, Frobisher, it's only a few months since my father was discussing his position with me. He distinctly mentioned a sum of fifteen thousand pounds that he didn't propose to let Eustace get into his hands."

"Man proposes and financiers dispose," Frobisher assured him gloomily. "Moore got hold of a lot of that. In fact, the position got so bad that your father was raising mortgages, and not always paying the interest involved. I had to speak to him very gravely on the subject this summer. To my certain knowledge he's mortgaged every security he possesses. We shall be lucky if we can pull anything out of the mess for his mother. She has practically no means. And I doubt if we can satisfy all the creditors. I don't know about your financial position?"

Richard spoke hoarsely. "Is that the truth? Are things really at that pitch?"

"I don't see how they could be worse. And now that he's involved with Moore it seems to me it will be impossible to avoid a scandal. If it had been some other means, I should have been inclined to suggest suicide. But that appears to be out of the question."

"I'd never imagined anything like this," said Richard, too much appalled to be discreet. "What a scoundrel that fellow is! If they don't take him for the murder, I hope to God they get him on this count."

Frobisher regarded him piercingly. "About your own financial position..." he insinuated.

"I came down here hoping to induce my father to give me some assistance. I'm temporarily very much embarrassed." Even in moments of crisis, he could not altogether shed his rather pompous manner of speech.

"Then that looks bad. Had you asked your father, by the way?"

"For help? I'd told him my position was..." he hesitated.

"And he refused?"

"He said he understood from Moore—who categorically denies most of this conversation—that he was to all intents and purposes a ruined man. I must admit that didn't greatly impress me. I have heard my father so frequently employ similar expressions when he was up against some quite trivial temporary loss that I didn't believe this time to be any more serious than the others. I suppose it will be impossible to avoid scandal, as you say?"

"Quite, I should suppose. Not that I imagine there's any likelihood of your being involved in the murder." But at the back of his sharp, attentive mind he posed the comment as a question.

Richard looked startled. "I should suppose not. Matters are quite unpleasant enough as it is. Personally, I fancy they'll drop on Brand. It's known that he and my father were always at daggers drawn, and that he's never forgiven him for marrying that abominable wife of his."

Frobisher was thoughtful, apparently considering the wisdom of some admission to whose nature Richard had no clue. He himself, however, gave the lawyer the requisite encouragement by remarking, "Things would be even worse, of course, if my father had occupied any public position. He's not in the general eye—a retired country gentleman. That's pretty cold comfort, though."

"Colder than you suppose," agreed the lawyer unsympathetically. "In fact, about freezing-point. There's something, Richard, that it might be as well for you to hear. I don't say this will be remembered against him, but you know the condition of the Press. Some of the papers are dignified enough, but there are some scurrilous rags being issued who're simply out for garbage, and you can trust them to rake up any muck that's going."

"And is there any—muck—going where my father is concerned?"

"Yes. I wonder if it's ever occurred to you, Richard, to be surprised at your father's quite disproportionate ferocity against your brother as a young man? I'm not holding any brief for loose living, but the lad had no home ties, he was under twenty, he had practically no money, he was living in a strange country—in a word, he'd no background to his life. It's the background that counts at that stage. When that's withdrawn…"

"When you deliberately slash it to pieces," interrupted Richard coldly.

The lawyer looked impatient. "The precise phraseology doesn't matter. The point is that he did nothing that thousands of other young men don't do, but your father treated him with a quite abnormal severity. I don't know whether you know that it was a positive passion of his to discover domestic scandals in the lives of prominent men and attempt to expose them. More than once he has been in danger of libel actions, but, of course, nowadays no one pays any attention to his letters. He's a monomaniac on that one point. That mania ruined your mother's married life, and in my opinion it has helped to destroy Brand's."

"You mean he had an intense aversion from all forms of immorality?"

"Not all forms, but from immorality in the limited sense in which the word was employed by the late Victorians. It became a craze as he grew older and had no other outlet for his feelings. He was on the look-out for evil everywhere."

"But why?" asked Richard, in puzzled tones. "Yes, I know he was very bitter against Brand; he could scarcely control himself."

"Precisely. It was the only refuge he had."

"Refuge from what?"

"His contemplation of himself. You don't remember your father as a much younger man. He was tormented by what's called nowadays the sex urge, and he despised himself unutterably. He despised what he believed to be the weakness of marrying your mother, and he saw to it that she paid heavily for his wretchedness. Did it ever strike you that, with the exception of yourself, he heartily disliked all his children? He couldn't take a normal view; he saw them all as concessions—or the consequences of those concessions—to what he regarded as something revolting. He girded at your sister, Amy, because she either hadn't endured his torment, and was therefore in his estimation a finer creature than himself, or, if she had, she'd beaten that desire down. After your mother died he became worse. Of course, he ought to have married again, a sensible woman with a capacity for warm feeling, and they'd probably have got on quite well. But he didn't. Instead, he took the other way out, and spent all his time nosing into other men's lives. The war gave him a splendid chance. You remember the outcry there was in 1914 and

1915 about war babies, unmarried mothers, and so forth?
Your father, and a number of other men and women of
the same sort, got together and formed themselves into an
organisation for reporting on immorality and purifying society. They were perpetually on the watch for misconduct. It
was the mainspring of their lives. They couldn't see a young
man and a young woman together without suspicion. It's
a horrible disease, and more widespread than you'd ever
guess. Ask a neurologist; he'll tell you. They discovered all
manner of things in every kind of home; they seemed to have
spies everywhere. They found that no two people crossing a
meadow or walking by the river are moral; they learned of
second establishments maintained by well-known people,
and practically blackmailed them into obscurity. Of course,
the thing flourished with the stuff it fed on. They attacked
public schools, private houses, hotels; Society, they said,
was riddled through and through with this disease. They
even issued a magazine full of warnings and anonymous
contributions. They quoted stories they'd read and their
own experience. They got a lot of correspondence and, of
course, a pretty fair circulation among the morbid type. It
was a very good advertisement for them. As a pornographic
experiment—done in the name of the Lord, if you'll believe
me, with texts on the front cover and gleanings from the Old
Testament on the back—it was unique. There was a queer
cross of pride in it, of course. They were so bloody moral
themselves they meant everyone else to be bloody moral,
too. They weren't going to have other people taking illicit
paths to happiness. But if you'd been able to show them
that sin had been slain in the night, and we were all as pure
as daisies, they'd have been outraged. They knew, you see,
they were better than other people, and they weren't going
to share their virtue with the common herd."

"I remember now, when I was in France—that would be the beginning of 1915—my father began writing me the most extraordinary letters, all on this subject. I supposed he'd heard stories, as people at home seemed to at that time, and didn't pay much attention to him. I'd no idea anything of this kind was going on. When did it stop? I was back for good in 1917, and he was out of London then."

"Yes. It was too hot to hold him. The obvious thing happened. This work had become his life; he laboured, slept, ate, and moved in an atmosphere of unhealthy speculation, and one day the society was horrified to hear that one of their foremost directors was himself in the habit of visiting a questionable flat in the Tottenham Court Road. It was the strain, you see, coupled with his own temperament. There's no need to go into details, but they proved their case. Your father collapsed into the neurotic, sometimes scarcely sane man he's been for years. He threw up all his London activities and came down here. The basis of his rage and bitterness against society as a whole was in his knowledge of his own failure; he could forgive the world anything but that. He'd failed, been weak—was a ruin rather than a man. And, of course, the incident only increased his feeling about such behaviour in the world at large. That's why he swore he'd never forgive Brand. That's why he loathed having him down here."

"There was no open scandal?"

"The society couldn't have afforded one. There'd been trouble over the paper already, and it had had to be withdrawn, after a particularly salacious issue. It closed on a very high moral note—the wrong people were buying it, to the pure all things are pure, and so forth. I suppose eventually it died a natural death. No one cared two straws for it except the prurient-minded busybodies who composed it. But your father got worse and worse. He wrote innumerable letters—I've read some of them—to the papers on the subject. He said it was the duty of every righteous-minded citizen to disclose anything that came to his ears on this matter. He even went so far as to swear that he wouldn't spare his own son, if necessary. No man holding a position of trust should be permitted to be anything but a Galahad. And there, Richard, he spoke the truth. He'd have flung you to the lions as readily as he'd have flung any other man's son. Well, that's the story. I don't say it will come out. I hope it won't. It's quite ancient history. But I thought you ought to be warned. There are men who have every reason to have a grudge against him."

And then, disregarding Richard's look of shock and horror, he proceeded to discuss the terms of the dead man's will. He had left two-thirds of his property to his elder son, and one-third to his mother, after allowing Amy a legacy of fifty pounds a year. The rest of the family had nothing. He stated that Olivia, through her husband, had profited to the utmost in his lifetime, that Brand had had from him the last help he need ever look for, that Isobel appeared to take no interest in finance, and that he was taking Ruth at her word. This last clause referred to an incident that had taken place a year or so previously, when the Amerys were staying at King's Poplars. Gray had made one of his most disagreeable scenes, accusing all his relatives of scheming to obtain his money from him before his death. Miles had said nothing; possessing a remarkably cool head and a logical outlook on life, he seldom paid much attention to these storms, but to his surprise Ruth cried out passionately that they at all events never visited the house for what they could get, and didn't want a penny from the old man here or hereafter.

"She was quite genuine, I've no doubt," Frobisher remarked. "That couple isn't out for graft, if I'm any judge of human nature." And to himself he added, "I couldn't say as much for any of the others, except that wretched married daughter whom they all treat as half-witted."

Richard said slowly, "I wasn't aware of the terms of the will, but I suppose I am to understand from your previous disclosure that it's scarcely worth the paper it's written on."

"As I said, we shall be lucky if we can pull fifty pounds a year out of the wreck for your grandmother." He was silent a moment, tapping with an irritating movement on the table, in a way that enraged the half-frantic Richard. "A vindictive will," he continued thoughtfully. "Have you any notion what your sister will elect to do? Amy, I mean. I take it that Devereux will continue to provide for his wife."

"I've no idea at all," returned Richard shortly, not at all concerned for his sister's condition. After all, she had had the house and the control of it for a good many years, while other unmarried women had to go out and earn a living for themselves. Probably, knowing her temperament, she had a very pleasant nest-egg laid by. It was easy to read his father's mind. He'd been brow-beaten by her for so long that it gave him pleasure to think of her eventual humiliation. Of course, as a family, they were all dog eat dog.

9

He escaped presently to his own room and achieved blessed solitude. He walked up and down in a frenzy of anticipatory despair. This news that Frobisher had, with comparative light-heartedness, disclosed to him, altered the whole purview of his position. He had agreed with Laura that it was unlikely that anyone would attempt to fasten the crime to his shoulders. Where, they would ask, was an adequate motive? But this recent revelation changed the whole situation. Suppose the Greta Hazell business became public property? Suppose someone suggested, as inevitably quite a

number of people would suggest, that Gray had become possessed of the information, and had threatened his son with
public exposure? In the light of Frobisher's story, Richard had
little doubt that his father would have followed that drastic
course. And all Richard's friends were aware that his career
was the meaning of his life. His father's publication of the
Hazell episode would undoubtedly mean the break-up of his
public career. He would not be able to remain in Parliament,
and there was more than a chance—though he had never
hitherto admitted so much, even to himself—that Laura
would leap at this opportunity of obtaining her freedom.
Panic invaded his mind. Come what might, this piece of
information must be suppressed. His enemies, and he had
many, would be only too eager to seize upon this excuse for
hounding him into obscurity; it would mean the abrupt
finish to his ambitions, and his own ruin. This financial
strait that had, until this morning, seemed momentous,
faded into insignificance. Another consideration entered his
tormented mind. What if Greta should somehow learn of
his predicament? He knew her well enough now to realise
that she was incapable of compassion; she would merely see
a fresh opportunity for exacting sums he was in no position
to pay. Now indeed his peril loomed up before him, as a
wall or some great bush will loom suddenly before the eyes
of the fog-distracted traveller from the opacity of the night.
He could find no direction in which he could, with safety,
turn. Not to Laura, not to Frobisher, not to any friend or
counsellor, dared he reveal his plight. Like Brand, he felt the
burden of knowledge weigh upon him like a load intolerable to be borne; but, unlike him, he anticipated no relief
when the truth was made manifest. His normally sluggish
imagination stirred to unreasoning frenzy, he saw himself
arraigned for every kind of crime—for murder, sedition,
adultery, embezzlement, perjury—and his blood ran chill,

though he knew himself innocent of four of these charges. He turned and halted and went on again. In the scheme of his days, those busy unremitting days in which he barely allowed himself a sufficiency of leisure and sleep, he found no source of solace or of strength. An immense despair fell upon him. He thought, "If it's coming to that, let me be out of the way. I can't face it." But at the thought of a self-inflicted death his meagre spirit recoiled. No, not that. Not that. Nor arrest either. Nor, if he could help it, suspicion or exposure. Somehow there must be a way of ensuring silence. His thoughts whirled like a wheel of fire in his distorted brain: Greta—Father—Brand—Eustace—Exposure—Bankruptcy—Shame—Failure—Obscurity—Greta... and so on, round and round.

...Up and down, up and down, while, like the wheels of a railway carriage, beating out a monotonous rhythm, his thoughts took possession of him, expressing themselves harshly, unmusically. Up and down—down and out—no way out—out and down— And so on, until someone came seeking him, and he had to mask his terror and join the community once again.

Part V

The Verdict of You All

1

On the day of the inquest the ground was starry with frost.
From both the Poplars, from Munford, from Greater and
Lesser Uppington, from Rest Wythies, from Stoneford and
Bringham and Leaford, the cars came crunching the keen
surface of the roads, filled with people in fur jackets and
warm overcoats, talking, posturing, speculating, all intent on
the event, unaware of their similarity to their early Roman
prototypes who gathered with the same abominable expectancy to view some young girl racked on the Little Horse
or torn with the pincers. They said (one carload so nearly
resembled another that the conversations might be taken
as identical) that this might have been expected; that the
family was about as friendly as a host of Kilkenny cats; that
there were ugly rumours about a criminal charge on quite
a different ground; that you couldn't trust these smooth-
tongued Jews; that the younger son had come down with
unmentionable threats; that he had his father and his elder
brother in his power; that there had been ferocious debates
between Richard and Amy for ascendancy... Excited and
pleased at this new sensation, they drove up to the door of
the Assembly Rooms at King's Poplars where the inquest
was to be held, and descended with much shaking of rugs,

chatter, banter, exchange of greetings, agitated murmurs of the necessity for haste lest someone else secure a coveted seat.

Frobisher was attending the inquest on behalf of the family generally; but Eustace had sent to London for his own solicitor, knowing that against him, at the last, public opinion must inevitably turn. Hinde was a tall, thin man, with a decisive profile; he had heard Eustace's story and his face was forbidding and sceptical, though he appeared bland enough as he entered the court. He sat with folded arms, his wrists, unexpectedly bony, protruding from the flannel shirt he affected. Brand's attention was caught and held by him from the first. There was in that austere, cynical face so much strength, character, and courage that he sketched it surreptitiously, feeling that even he, on such an occasion, could scarcely defy the conventions and do his work openly.

The evidence was not sensational until the end of Ross's history of his investigations. He spoke of the handkerchief, of the burnt blotting-paper—clearly, he said, burnt to conceal the record it contained, since there was a practically empty wastepaper-basket at the dead man's elbow—other ashes that could not now be identified, Brand's document, and the finger-prints on the safe. No explanation, he said, had been offered by any member of the family concerning the missing cheque, whose counterfoil indicated that a sum of ten thousand pounds had been made over to Eustace Moore in the early hours of Christmas morning. No amount of search had revealed it, and although the counterfoil had been blotted, as was clear from the appearance of the ink, no record of this could be found on any of the blotting-paper in the library. Ross then detailed his search of the room, his discovery of the safe and of the finger-prints that, he informed the court, had been discovered to be those of Eustace Moore.

At this sensational revelation the excitement rose to fever-pitch. The evidence of other members of the family was scarcely digested; the attention of the whole court focused on the figure of Moore, who was presently called to explain the position. His explanation was strange and unsatisfying to practically everyone present.

Circumstances compelled him to admit that he had, despite his earlier denials, been in the library in the early morning of Christmas Day. He had come down to King's Poplars with the intention of explaining to his father-in-law the difficult position in which they found themselves. He had been singularly unfortunate in his explanations. Gray had not shown a trace of reason, had accused him of being a common thief and embezzler, of tricking him out of his money, and had finally declared that he would himself bring an action against his son-in-law. Moore added that he had no belief in this bombast, which was simply the old man's way of letting off steam, but he was convinced that he would obtain no financial assistance from this quarter.

In reply to questions from the coroner, he repeated in some detail the conversation that had eventuated between them. It appeared to be violent and decisive. Racked with anxiety as to the future, seeing no one else to whom he could turn for assistance, he determined to make a second appeal the following day. In the course of a chance conversation with Richard, however, he was compelled to realise that there was no possibility of Gray changing his mind. During the day—that is, on Christmas Eve—he saw both his brothers-in-law enter the library, with the intention of tackling their father for monetary help.

The coroner here interrupted to say that, so far as he could see, Mr. Moore had no definite proof as to this last statement. Eustace stared at him, incredulous that anyone should suppose either of Gray's sons to be visiting at King's Poplars for any other reason. Then he continued his story. He had heard from his sister-in-law of Brand's suggestion that Sophy and her children should make their home at the Manor for an indefinite period; he understood that that plan had been refused consideration, but that Brand was now demanding a lump sum down, to enable him to get away, preferably abroad, and shift the responsibility of his family on to other shoulders. Amy had also spoken in furious tones of the iniquity of purchasing titles and expecting other men to pay for them (Richard winced and flushed at that); and she had followed up these comments by a long and depressing harangue on the impossibility of housekeeping (with cream and Benger's for the old lady) on the meagre sum allowed her by her father, with details as to personal expenditure, her own fastidious habits, and the rising prices of butter, coal, and meat.

Eustace continued that he had despaired of making any of his relatives understand the seriousness of their father's situation. They seemed under the impression that a man could be a director of a foundering company with no more inconvenience than if his shares had depreciated slightly. He had, therefore, in desperation (and here Eustace showed traces of an overwhelming apprehension and nervousness) formulated a plan that, he admitted at once, was criminal in intent. It was obvious that he confessed to this only as the final expedient, the sole alternative that presented itself to an accusation of wilful murder.

When the household retired for the night, he had come to no decision, and for some time had discussed the problem with his wife. She had then expressed herself as exhausted, and he had left her alone in the bedroom, going to the dressing-room, where he made no attempt to go to bed, but sat brooding over the position. He denied, of course, Brand's story of seeing him on the stairs at midnight, but admitted that at about half-past two he remembered his father-in-law telling him that he had valuable documents in the safe. These documents were to be Gray's standby, and in no circumstances would he allow Eustace to handle them. He, Eustace, knew the whereabouts of the safe, and he determined to try and discover the combination and remove the documents. This, he said passionately, was a final endeavour to save an intolerable situation. He had forgotten, if he had ever known, that it was Gray's habit to lock his door when he left the library at night, and so it did not strike him as strange that it should be open when he went down. He had met no one; and the room, when he entered it, was perfectly dark. The curtain had blown across the window that was opened, and in his haste and anxiety he had not realised that it was not closed. The safe was set in a deep recess, lighted from the floor by a discreetly concealed electric bulb that flung radiance into the safe without illuminating the rest of the room. Gray, he understood, had had this fitted in, so that if he were suddenly disturbed while examining his securities, he could extinguish the light without moving, and foil the curiosity-mongers. He was always unnaturally secretive about his affairs. He, Eustace, had crossed the room in bedroom slippers, felt for and found the switch of the light, and set himself to open the safe. This, however, he was not able to do. He supposed he was in the room for the greater part of an hour. It did not occur to him that there was any way of entry except by the door. He kept a sharp look-out for the signs of a light being switched on in the hall. The recess was deep enough for a man to hide, unless anyone came directly into it. At the end of an hour he had desisted. Panic had increased in his breast, and he dared not risk being found by any member of the family. When he heard from the police that they had opened the safe and found it practically empty, he had been half distracted.

That was the substance of his story, and most people who heard it found it quite inadequate. They argued that on so cold and windy a night a man must have become aware of the open window; that it would be impossible to spend so long in a room where a man lay dead without seeing the body; that it was absurd to suppose the police could with little difficulty open a safe that had defied his efforts; that the whole explanation, in short, was lame and improbable.

The jury, and even Moore's own lawyer, took the same view. The former were away for about forty minutes, during which a number of people in the court stirred and came outside into the pale sunlight to discuss various aspects of this most exciting mystery.

2

The jury discussed the position with animation.

"We take it for granted that the doctor's right in saying the slab of brass was the implement used?"

"It seems likely, seeing it was bright and polished like nothing else was. Besides, two people—Miss Amy and a servant—remember it being on top of a pile of loose papers, and it was not on any papers at all when they found it."

There was general agreement with that. The foreman continued, "I'll tell you how I see it. I believe he did come down, as he says, and began tinkering with the safe. I daresay he didn't notice about the window. When all your mind's set on one thing you're absorbed. Heat and cold don't seem to strike you in the same way. Well, there he was, trying to help himself to Mr. Gray's papers, when through the open window comes Mr. Gray himself. There's a wide verandah outside, as happen you know, and he might have slipped out there when he heard footsteps, not wanting to be disturbed by anyone else that night. Then he watched, and found this fellow trying the safe. Mind you, I don't for a minute believe he stood there for an hour, but this chap wants to make out the best story he can. I daresay the old man watched him for some time; then he came in and took his son-in-law by surprise. Terrified and taken unawares, the fellow hit out..."

"What about the cheque?" interrupted a more far-seeing juryman. "That wasn't drawn till the morning."

"That's true. We shall have to alter that story. Look here. Suppose Mr. Moore made Mr. Gray understand how bad things were, and persuaded him to give him a cheque? Or p'raps he threatened him, standing over him while he wrote it out. And then Mr. Gray told him in that sarcastic way of his that it wasn't worth the form it was written on. He'd be glad enough to have the last laugh. And then Mr. Moore, wild at being cheated, and not seeing any hope anywhere, hit out, just to make him stop talking, perhaps, and not meaning to kill him at all. When he saw what had happened he put the cheque on the fire and wiped the paper-weight and came upstairs again. He didn't think about finger-prints on the safe. How does that fit?"

At the end of forty minutes the jury returned, with a verdict of wilful murder against Eustace Moore.

3

There was little surprise though much excitement in the court when this verdict was announced. It had been obvious from the trend of examination and argument in which direction the tide of suspicion had turned. Yet it seemed, for a moment, as though, of all present, Eustace himself had not anticipated this consummation. For a minute his control broke utterly. He glared wildly round the court, rose to speak, could not command his voice, clutched at a chair with both hands, and trembled violently from head to foot. There was something so repulsive, so divorced from normal human dignity in the spectacle of this pale, middle-aged man in impeccable morning garb, clinging to a chair-back and shivering with fear, that even his lawyer could scarcely conceal his disgust. But when he was taken away by the police a little later, his expression had changed already. Now it was that of a man who is accustomed to bathing among sharks, and, instead of expending time and energy bemoaning his present humiliation, he was even now laying new schemes for regaining his liberty. The long, sallow face, with its flat cheeks, resolute nose, and keen, prying eyes, all these were expressive of his invincible determination to extricate himself from this extremity, as he had done from others.

4

The affair involved all the family in very disagreeable publicity. The papers made a good deal of it, and shortly after Eustace's arrest a number of little paragraphs appeared, chiefly in local and evening papers, with melodramatic headlines, such as son finds father hanging; found in the river; wife's terrible discovery in barn, and so forth. Most of Eustace's victims were small men who had put their life's savings into what appeared to them a safe and remunerative market, and when these little men of Highgate and Peckham and Barnet were forced to realise that nothing would ever be recovered, numbers of insignificant anonymous tragedies were reported in little towns and suburbs and the remoter districts of London. Isobel and Laura said candidly that what Eustace was known to have done was worse than any murder, but Richard told them bitterly to stop that folly. It did no good to anyone, and it blackened the case against their brother-in-law.

Richard was paying his share of the general expense and it was proving a heavy one. The appointment for which he had run such risks and schemed so dearly went to Pollenfex after all. (In point of fact, though Richard never knew this, he would have been defeated in any case, the history of Eustace's defalcations not affecting F——'s decision. Ironically enough, it was the very expense and luxury into which he had plunged that had destroyed Richard's chances, F—— shrewdly observing that a man so reckless with his own money would be even less temperate when he had control of public funds.) Laura took the affair far more phlegmatically than he, but then she had nothing to lose—except her lover, who retired completely after the *débâcle,* leaving her to put the pieces of her life together in what proved to be a quite satisfactory pattern. Anyway, she was happier after this than she had been since her marriage. One or two people, including Miles Amery, were privileged to hear a point of view so unconventional and so much at variance with her husband's interests that the majority would have been shocked at her heartlessness and lack of co-operation with Richard's ambitions.

"All these years, Miles," she said, "I've never had any life of my own. Richard's friends have come crowding in, claiming my attention and my hospitality and my brain-force. There's never been anything left over for my own enjoyment or profit. Now all that crowd will disappear; we're pretty sure to be more or less ostracised in the fashionable and influential circles Richard loves. I doubt if he's ever able to climb back. Besides, it's been such a blow to him, I think it will be a long time before he recovers his second wind. And this is my turn. Now, at last, I shall have my house to myself, where my friends can come in, and where I can be alone." (But she didn't, of course, refer here to any house made with hands.) "It's what I've dreamed of, hoped for, prayed for, for years."

Olivia made the Manor House intolerable by her hysterics and the numberless scenes in which she insisted on implicating every member of the family. She fainted, she cried, she raved about traitors and plots and snares. She called perpetually for her sons to come to her, but they were spending their holiday in Switzerland and could not be reached at a moment's notice. When she was not fainting or screaming, she went about like a madwoman, silent for long stretches of time, and then suddenly bursting into wild and unfounded accusations against each member of the household in turn, even abusing the servants, to the effect that he or she was responsible for a diabolical trap into which her innocent and unsuspecting husband had been enticed.

Amy was too much enraged at her own position to pay much heed to anyone else. Blind with passion at the cruel trick her father had played upon her, she demanded ferociously whether she was expected to find some remunerative employment at her age, she who was trained for no particular work, and who had, naturally, expected to be left provided for.

"What am I supposed to do?" she cried in turn to each of her embarrassed relatives. "I'm a woman of forty and I haven't been taught to earn a living. It's all very well for young girls; their position's quite different. I suppose you all expect me to take a post as a working housekeeper somewhere, doing floors and emptying slops and peeling potatoes."

In due course, she addressed this rhetorical question to old Mrs. Gray, who replied in a remote and tranquil voice, "I'm sure I don't know why you should expect anything so foolish, Amy. You will live with me, of course. Mr. Frobisher says he can find just enough to pay the rent of a little flat somewhere—at the seaside. I've always hoped I should die by the sea—Felixstowe, perhaps, or Worthing, or Bournemouth, but that's rather expensive. I'm sure we shall manage quite well. We're accustomed to one another, and at my age I should have to have some kind of companion."

She actually smiled as she spoke. Amy had become something very remote in her imagination, of little more consequence, really, than the furniture among which she moved. Miles was astounded at the eagerness and warmth in the old voice. He had, like everyone else, taken it for granted that the old cease to experience desire, that their passion is spent, their feeling, even, numbed. They become, in fact, like the chairs and cupboards among which their days are passed. The old lady was the one redeeming feature in this sordid case. No one but herself genuinely grieved for the dead man. To her, he had been primarily the son she had borne nearly seventy years ago. And he remained at once the child for whom she had dreamed, and the disappointed, embittered creature he had become. She had watched him change, lose his first fine ideals, seen him gradually sink, lose hope, go down and down. And her affection for him had remained stable; it was rooted in no fineness of his, no achievement, not even in the qualities he possessed. It lay in their common blood and heritage. And now he had gone, and she preserved an attitude dignified and remote. Yet, despite her years, her sorrow, and the cumulative experience of her days, she still retained sufficient vitality to have desires and hopes, and at length to achieve them. They were little things, perhaps, but desires are comparative, after all. And it was to such things that the attention of old people instinctively turned, thought Miles, when they were at too great a remove from the fierce ambitions of their youth to be stirred by them any longer.

There was in these bleak days something beautiful about her, as she spoke, listened, and suggested in the midst of her kinspeople, herself tranquil and unattainable. Into that secret chamber where the spirit sits alone she admitted no one. But, above all, beauty remained. It was not, in essence, any beauty of feature or even of bone or expression; springing from a certain graciousness in her own nature, and the courage the old will often display, it held the attention of all the more thoughtful of the household—the Amerys, Laura, Isobel, Brand.

Isobel had reacted oddly to the position. Since her father's death she had changed, awakened, begun to glow; as a piece of silver that has not been polished for years, suddenly receiving attention, catches the light in a dozen places, reflects, burns, almost illuminates the room where it is placed, so Isobel flashed with an ardour that had been typical of her early years, but that had been quenched for so long that few recognised its return. She said to Brand, shortly before their separation, "You're right, my dear. It's a terrible warning. It would be frightful to come to death with no more to show or to carry with you than he had." She left the house before her grandmother and sister departed to the Worthing flat, and found herself work in London. Brand, hearing of it, thought, "That alone would be justification for what I did. She was a prisoner so long as he was alive. And whereas his life held neither promise nor hope, hers is chock-a-block with both."

5

Brand returned in due course to his wife in Fulham. Walking up the dreary road, carrying his shabby case, his senses exulted at the prospect of leaving this behind for ever. Since Eustace's arrest he had put the whole affair of the murder out of his mind; he no longer identified himself with the man who had cringed and scraped and quarrelled with Sophy for so many years. It was as though a new personality, purged by his ordeal and the weight of knowledge that still lay upon him, had risen in the dark library on Christmas morning, its face set towards the dawn, its being cleansed from fear.

The house presented its usual ramshackle, slovenly appearance. It was one of a long terrace, each house separated from its neighbour by a thin, dingy wall; a long flight of cracked steps led to the front door, whose dirty paint was peeling. Some of the houses had inartistic little excrescences bulging from the ground floor, square green or brown painted boxes, ludicrously christened conservatories, with panes of blue and red glass, alternating with the opaque oblongs found in bath- and waiting-rooms. The houses were Victorian, heavy and ungraceful, inconvenient and ugly, displaying none of the beauty of antiquity or the brisk cheerfulness of good housekeeping. Brand mounted the steps, noting that it was several days since they had been washed, and stood for a moment under the pretentious, hideous portico. Trails of ivy coiled over the windows, soiled yellow blinds hung awry on the further side of the glass, that was further obscured by long lace curtains. The whole aspect was one of a cheap and sordid poverty.

The door was opened by his second daughter, Eleanor, a child of nine years old. Her face was a travesty of youth, though the features were immature enough in their pinched and colourless fashion. Her fair hair hung over her eyes and was untidily cut on the nape of her neck. Neither her face nor her hands was clean, and her frock was torn. Yet she would never, in any assembly, be overlooked. It was, perhaps, the expression that held the stranger's gaze. It was arresting, fierce, and withdrawn. After seeing father and child together, there could be no doubt of their relationship. The little girl, also, had none of the candour and vitality of her years, but resembled a creature perpetually on guard, prepared for any new torment or alarm the days may hold, armed with a bitter stoicism that, in a less inattentive parent, would have touched and cut the heart.

"Where's your mother?" Brand asked.

"She's upstairs. She didn't know you were coming to-day."

"She doesn't have to make any preparations for me. Tell her I'm here."

He turned into the living-room to the left of the front door; the other side was a blank wall, separating them from the next house. He had neither offered nor expected a kiss or any sign of affection from the young creature whom he had begotten. He heard her going upstairs slowly, and the thought went through his mind, "More fuss with Sophy, I suppose. It's a wonder she hasn't killed some of the brats before now."

This was a typical sloven's room—dirty plates on the table, a torn cloth, rags of garments lying about on the chairs, and dust everywhere. But, though he had often railed at his wife for such matters, today he was scarcely aware of them. The present held him in too light a grasp; beyond lay the glittering future, and to that he looked forward, as a traveller, solacing himself with the thought of the sea round the next bend of the road, can face with courage the wind, the heat, and the grit in the air because they will so soon belong to the past.

Eleanor came back, saying her mother was just coming down.

"Wasn't she dressed?" asked Brand indifferently.

The child shook her head. "She said, 'God knows there'll be no peace when he comes back, so we'll take it while we can.'"

He looked at her for the first time with curiosity; she had spoken with a certain defiance and spirit, as though to assert herself, not to him, but to her own heart. A momentary sense of fellowship for her loneliness and determination moved him.

He said, smiling faintly, "Manners aren't your strong suit, are they? In fact, in a properly constituted household, you'd probably be beaten for that. But, of course, those tests don't apply here."

She folded her hands behind her back, and regarded him steadily. He returned her gaze, and suddenly he saw her tremble. In an instant she had recovered her self-control, but the fear remained in her mind, though her flesh denied it. Observing her more closely, and with a growing sympathy, he realised that she feared he might put that careless threat into action and was resolved to withstand his power, though she could not evade the consequences of it. Even at her age, he thought, she commanded attention, even a kind of respect. Already her personality was forming, and he reflected, "Courage; that's the answer to her attitude. It's the one thing that matters. That and knowing the only thing in your life that counts and never letting go."

Sophy came in, dragging a shapeless coat over her shoulders; her dark hair straggled from its untidy knot down her back. Her features were sharp, inquisitive, and acquisitive; she had the look of some horrible bird of prey, agape for carrion, and in the very stoop of her shoulders, the curve of her hands, the malevolent gleam of her eyes, she expressed a cruelty innate in her temperament. So shabby did she seem, so poor and ugly and unclean, that Brand was smitten with a feeling compounded of disgust, compassion, amazement, and awe.

"Can it be true that I was so low, so stripped of all decency, that I was compelled to take any pleasure I could get even from that?" he thought. "My God, I've been down. It takes a thing like this to open one's eyes. Well, this is the end."

Sophy said in a harsh voice, "What's this bastard been telling you? You know what you can expect, you ——, if you've been opening your mouth. I never knew such a bloody little liar in all my days," she added to her husband. "They fall out of her like water out of a tap."

Eleanor watched her, pale, defensive, guarded. Brand knew now why the woman had been in bed when he returned. Those prolonged drinking-bouts had been one of the horrors of his married life. Even now she was not sober, and he felt her as some loathsome disease touching and defiling his own life.

"So you've come back?" she said, slumping into a chair.

"You didn't expect to see me?"

She shrugged. "How could I tell?"

"You thought, like everyone else, that I'd done it?"

"Well, I don't suppose you're very sorry, anyway."

Brand asked, "It wouldn't trouble you, would it, if I were guilty?"

"Why the hell should it? We weren't good enough to know him. He's no loss to us." And then, leaning forward, her stupid animal face twisted into a leer of mingled greed and coaxing, "How did you get the money, Brand? Don't tell me he gave it you."

Brand replied callously, "Oh, you won't see a penny of that."

"What d'you mean?"

"I mean that cheque's not worth the paper it's written on. He's broke, like the rest of us."

"And what are you going to do about that?"

"Clear out, of course."

"You haven't the money. I know that."

Brand's laughter jarred. "Been through my pockets, have you? God, you're a decent wife for any man. Anyway, I'm going. What's it to you where I get my money from?"

"You mean that? You're going to desert us?" Her face was dreadful.

A nerve of brutality in Brand was rasped by her voice, her appearance, the recognition of the havoc she had already wrought in his life, all that she might mean, her frustration of his hopes. He exclaimed bitterly, "Yes, and thank God for the chance."

"And we're to starve, I suppose?"

They argued furiously, hurling abuse at one another. Sophy shouted that she had five children to maintain. Brand retorted that she had worked before and could work again, and had, doubtless, other money-making devices at her finger-tips.

"For instance, you might try Ferdinand's father," he suggested brutally.

Sophy became so abusive that even the child, accustomed though she was to such scenes, shivered and withdrew behind the ragged tapestry chair near the fireplace. It was a dreadful scene, not so much on account of the language in which their ugly conversation was couched as in their frank and shameless revelation of themselves one to the other, unconcealed even by the barest of draperies of decency and self-respect. Towards this woman, who invariably aroused all the most bestial passions in his nature, Brand felt himself incapable of pity. Every past occasion of infidelity or ill-usage, every head under which complaints could be lodged, every instant of mutual surrender to a base instinct that neither attempted to clothe in the garments of reticence, all these recollections, bitternesses, occasions of ugliness and cruelty, were flung like actual missiles by one of this deplorable pair at the other. For Brand, it was a lowering of the gates of self-possession that had withstood the tide of his own fears and the suspicions of other people for the past week. As for the woman, she was too far past any considerations of self-respect to be even conscious of the degradation of the scene.

Presently Brand said carelessly, "Be reasonable, my dear Sophy. Within a month you'll be as thankful for the change as myself. It'll give you more scope." And he laughed.

Sophy demanded furiously whether he proposed to abandon the children altogether.

"It won't make much difference to them," said Brand. "One man or another…"

Eleanor felt a sudden reaction from this wild interchange of insults. She, a personality distinct from either of them, with already her own dreams and visions, was being set aside like any inanimate thing that may be alternatively placed on a shelf or in a cupboard, a thing not worthy of consideration. She emerged from behind her chair; her instincts were those of any wild thing that is accustomed to thongs and pursuers.

"I suppose, mother, when father's gone, the gentleman who's been staying with us this week will be here for good, won't he? I like him. He gives me pence sometimes."

The air with which she flung up her small head, the calculated insolence of her bearing towards both parents, stung Sophy to an ungovernable half-drunken rage. She rushed at the child and boxed her ears till Eleanor was dizzy and aghast. Brand, seating himself on the edge of the table, had begun to laugh. As on that occasion on Christmas Day at the Manor, he found himself incapable of immediate control. He seemed unaware of his wife's treatment of the child, whom she now thrust from the room, crying, "Go on up and wait for me. I'll teach you to hold your tongue, you little devil, if it kills me."

With the abrupt closing of the door Brand's laughter became more temperate. He said mockingly, "My dear Sophy, I congratulate you. You don't suppose that child told me anything I didn't know already? I'm glad to hear the gentleman is likely to be faithful."

"Yes, you'd be glad to be free of having to keep me, wouldn't you? But you won't get off as easily as that. What if you have got this other fellow taken instead of you? Do you suppose I don't know you did the murder?"

Brand, still in that mocking drawl, replied, "Well, and suppose you're right? What do you expect me to do? Make a magnificent gesture? Gentlemen, you are deceived. Your prisoner is innocent of his crime. Behold the man!" He smote his breast dramatically. "But surely that wouldn't suit your book? And mightn't it scare away your devoted protector? After all, a murderer's widow…" He began to laugh.

Upstairs, standing in her dingy chemise by the partly opened window (the cords were broken and the window stuck; no one could shut it even in the most bitter weather), the child, Eleanor, caught fragments of this conversation. Her sharp animal brain pieced them together. It did not shock or frighten her that her father should even jeeringly acknowledge his guilt; whether he had killed his father or not was no concern of hers. But she realised that he was going away, and, though she had no affection for him, she regarded him in some sense as a background, and to that extent she resented his going.

The door opened and Sophy whirled in, her face dark with passion. The child stiffened at the sight of her. The foul words she used fell unheeded on ears to whom lewd language was as natural as the baby-talk of more fortunate children; but even her courage was not finally proof against the fury of her mother's blows. Bruised and stripped of that quality of self-respect that is a lonely child's armour against despair, she was helpless in that powerful grasp. It was several minutes before Brand, fallen again into a rhapsody, was aware that the shrieks assailing his mind came from his own house. Flinging himself up the stairs, he rushed into his daughter's room and dragged her from her mother's hands.

"My God, Sophy, isn't one murder in a family enough for you? Can you never let your filthy temper be?"

He thrust the stupefied child into bed, saying harshly, "Stop that noise. Why don't you keep your mouth shut, if you want any peace?"

Blind anger against these degrading circumstances, and a dreadful fear that a momentary compassion for youth assaulted would destroy his strength, drove him to a ruthless cruelty. When Sophy gibed in spiteful tones, "An affectionate father you are, aren't you?" he returned, in tones that were deliberately hard, "Oh, it's her turn now. But let her wait a few years and she'll be making hell of some man's life. It's what women are for."

He went into the room they shared and began to fling some clothes into a box. He paid no heed to Sophy's shrill disclaimers and insults; inside his head a pulse had begun to beat, warning him that not for much longer could he safely remain under the same roof as this woman to whom he was married. As he walked up from the station, he had contemplated a brief and effective scene, never this disgusting exhibition of a man's worst feelings and compulsions. It was like stepping into a shed full of dirt, and emerging stained and repulsive. He slammed down the lid of the box—it had neither locks nor straps—and carried it into the narrow hall. Sophy followed him, still shouting her accusations against him for a murderer.

"You wait till the trial begins," she jeered. "Who's going to believe your story? Adrian Gray wouldn't have given you two thousand pounds or even pretended to. Why should he? No one would believe a word you said. You couldn't frighten him. You don't count, you don't, for all your bloody fine opinion of yourself."

Escaping from the house, Brand felt all that squalor and shame fall away like the husk of a nut. Now he was, at length, free. He did not contemplate the future except as a blank canvas for the purpose of his own achievement. He did not consider the possibility of a jury releasing Eustace and putting him in the financier's place. It would be some weeks before the trial was held, and that interim space he regarded as the span of his personal life. During that period he must be uninterrupted, untouched by the wild flurry of suspicion and fear in which this trial would be engulfed. He left England that night, and was instantly swallowed up in the purlieus of the Paris he knew. Anonymous as a shadow he went in and out of the tall, narrow houses, spoke with men at corners and in cafés, drank and worked and conceived, a man so divorced from the occurrences of all previous time that he might have no connection with any other Hildebrand Gray the world had known. It was not fame and not hope that he pursued so relentlessly during that period. Having beheld the work he must do, he proceeded to achieve it; as to the consequences, he found them no concern of his. Like some tense, electric, indomitable spirit of Labour, he exhausted his actual life.

Part VI

Witness for the Defence

1

Miles Amery, travelling back to town with his wife, observed in troubled tones, "I'm not happy about this, Ruth. I'm in the position of a chap who was at Charterhouse with me. He was an R.C., destined for the priesthood. He was a nice chap, but one day (he was about eighteen) he came to me and said, 'It's no good; I can't go through with this.' I asked him what was his difficulty. I thought perhaps he was jibbing at the discipline the Catholic Church imposes on her priesthood; they have to go where they're sent, can't marry, and so forth. But he said, 'No,' it wasn't that. It was the dogmatic side of it that finished him. 'I envy your true believer and your convinced atheist,' he said. 'I'd stand thankfully in either camp. But I'm in the damnable position of knowing that the Catholic faith is true, without believing a word of it.' That's my position at the moment."

"About Eustace?"

"Yes. I know, from all the evidence, that he's guilty, but I don't believe an atom of it. To begin with, why should your father have given him that money? Secondly, do you think a man like Eustace, who's accustomed to risks and evasions, and has been all his life, is going to fling away all his hopes (and they were centred in Mr. Gray) for an infantile flash of temper? It's so much more typical of Brand than of anyone else in the house that my suspicions, in spite of the evidence, keep turning in his direction. If it had been a premeditated murder, then I'd believe readily enough that Eustace was guilty, and be prepared to swear on oath that it couldn't be Brand. Psychologically it would be as impossible for him to sustain such a mood as it would be improbable for Eustace to take up a paper-weight and hit another man over the head. You have to remember that the man's a gambler, a speculator, accustomed to risks; he must have had several narrow shaves before this, and so far he's managed to come out all right. That kind of experience breeds a caution—a reckless caution if you like, but a caution nevertheless. It puts a man perpetually on his guard, and though certain things may have the power to break through that guard, I don't believe your father was one of them. A man of Eustace's experience doesn't see red and commit murder because of a few hard words he must have anticipated. Besides, he could make things uncommonly bad for your father, if they were both alive, while, dead, Gray was no manner of use to him. This affair is the London and New York Exchange ramp over again, and I don't see how your father could have avoided implication. Even if he got off scot free, his reputation was bound to suffer. And there's something else. That cheque. If Eustace had got his hands on that cheque, no power in this world would have persuaded him to destroy it. Literally, he wouldn't dare."

Ruth said, in distress, "Oh, Miles, you aren't going to try and come into this on Eustace's side? Even if he didn't kill father, what he has done in ruining thousands of poor people who trusted him is much worse. Already there have been heaps of suicides, and what are they but deaths lying at Eustace's door?"

Miles touched her hand affectionately. "Don't forget you're talking to a lawyer," he said. "That's not evidence."

But, although he was determined to put the matter out of his mind, since it was clearly no concern of his, he discovered himself examining the evidence during every leisure hour that fell to his lot, endeavouring to trace some leakage, some false trail, some place where the police had gone astray. As always, when this mood was upon him, he lost sight of personalities. He was not *pro* Eustace or *contra* Brand. He was for the true explanation and against obscurity.

2

There is a theory that a man attracts to himself those qualities, occurrences, and fortunes with which his thoughts are most constantly engaged. Miles had never held such a belief; never, indeed, considered the subject. Yet, shortly before the trial, he was unexpectedly drawn from his comfortable insignificance, and confronted with a situation that was to tax to the uttermost his integrity and his personal feeling. He was working at his desk one morning when his clerk came in to say that a young woman wished to see him. The young woman had given no name, saying he would not recognise it.

"Tell her I must have a name, that I don't see anonymous clients," said Miles, accustomed to the army of deranged men and women with appalling imaginary grievances, who are anxious to occupy, gratuitously, so much of a lawyer's professional time.

Edwards returned to say that the young woman called herself Teresa Field, but said she did not suppose Mr. Amery would remember the name.

"Remember it?" repeated Miles thoughtfully. "No. She's quite right. It conveys nothing to me. I wonder who she is."

"I'll bring her in, sir?"

"Yes. Bring her in."

Edwards ushered in a very neatly dressed young woman of about four-and-twenty. She had the square, rosy appearance of the country girl, and was tidily dressed in black, with fabric gloves and sensible square-toed shoes, extremely well polished. Her manner was deferential without being in any way fawning or eager. Her expression was quiet, her eyes clear. She took the chair Miles offered her, sitting with the straightness of those unaccustomed to lounge in the presence of superiors. Miles decided she was a shop assistant or some kind of servant in an upper-class establishment. Her features were vaguely familiar, though he could not place them, and this vexed him, since he was apt to pride himself on his memory of the individual.

She spoke, in a soft clear voice indigenous to the county whence she was sprung.

"I'm sure I'm sorry, sir, if I've done wrong in coming to see you, but this is the kind of thing that's never happened to me before, and I didn't know what to do. No one could tell me anything for certain, and I remembered you were a legal gentleman, so perhaps you wouldn't mind telling me."

"Telling you what?"

"What I ought to do. I know you must be busy, what with this dreadful affair about Mr. Gray..."

He remembered her then as one of the servant-girls at the Manor House.

"Of course. I saw you there at Christmas, didn't I?"

"Yes, sir."

"Are you there still?"

"Well—not exactly, sir. It was about that I wanted to tell you. Now that Mrs. Gray and Miss Gray have gone, of course there isn't any need for us to be there. A new gentleman has bought the house, they say. Mr. Richard said he never wanted to live there now."

Miles, who had known that already, deflected her on to the line of her own dismay. She spoke sensibly and clearly and answered his questions without hesitation, gently smoothing a little fawn-coloured tippet over her knee as she spoke. After the break-up of the household, she said, she had applied to Mrs. Cochrane, the housekeeper, who was acting as caretaker till the new gentleman moved in, for a reference for a better-paid post in the neighbourhood. The new lady seemed quite satisfied, provided her references were good. To Field's amazement, Mrs. Cochrane refused to say a word for her. Miles remembered the woman, tall, sour-visaged, with a tight mouth.

"She told me she wasn't the fool some people took her for," Field continued, "and she hoped she was a Christian."

"That's only another way of spelling trouble," Miles assured her.

"I asked her what she had against me, seeing I'd been three years and no complaints up at the Manor," continued the girl earnestly. "At first she wouldn't speak. Then she said she knew what she knew, and she'd been against it from the beginning."

"Been against what?"

"Me coming to the Manor, sir. Everybody knew about my sister, she said, and these things run in families."

"What did she know?"

"There wasn't anything against Betty really, only she was a bit silly, through being so bright and fond of a bit of fun. But folks talk, whether there's anything to talk about or no, so she didn't stay down at Munford, but came up to London and got work as a chambermaid in a big hotel. Married now, she is, with a baby, but, of course, Mrs. Cochrane said that didn't make any difference."

Field had pressed for explanations, definitions, something concrete, and after much trouble the story had resolved itself into an accusation of misbehaviour at the gardener's cottage by the big gates on Christmas Eve. Another servant had reported to the housekeeper that a young woman from the servants' quarters had been seen creeping out of the cottage into the house at two o'clock in the morning. She, the servant in question, had had severe toothache and had been applying laudanum. From her window she had a good view of the gardener's cottage, and she had seen the young woman emerge, and steal up the drive, and in by a side door.

"She says it was me, sir," Field told Miles, in evident distress, yet displaying an admirable amount of control that compelled his immediate interest, "but that isn't true. Even if I'd take that kind of risk, which I wouldn't, I—I mean to say, that sort of thing wouldn't interest me."

Miles supposed she meant she had a regular follower, but she negatived that, saying, "No, sir, it's just that I don't care about that kind of thing. It doesn't lead anywhere."

Miles observed reasonably that it led to a home and family.

"I meant, sir, it doesn't lead anywhere that I want to go. I've got two married sisters, and I've stayed with them both. Well, it's all right for them, because they like it, but it's shown me that isn't what I want."

"Do you know what that is?"

"Oh, yes, sir. But if I don't get this situation there's nothing to show I'll get any other. It 'ud be bound to come out that I hadn't got a reference. And then I'd never get anywhere."

"What is this ideal job of yours?"

She was too ardent to feel any embarrassment at describing her vision. "To be a housekeeper myself, sir," she explained, her eyes bright, her expression warm and hopeful. "To have my own room, and a big house, with me responsible. To go through the linen cupboard of a Friday and see all the towels and the napkins and the table linen in piles, all perfect, and me responsible."

Miles was carried away by her enthusiasm. She spoke as pilgrims speak viewing the promised land, as artists have spoken all down the ages, seeing herself the servant of this beautiful and gracious house of her imagination, walking in finely appointed rooms, perpetually serving. A certain kindling vitality informed the most commonplace phrase that she employed. To her, that house of perfection was the flawless poem, the astounding canvas, the actual work of art.

Miles let her talk. She recalled to him a friend of his own, a man of delicate perception and artistry who occupied himself in designing suburban houses, in violent contra-distinction to the mass of jerry-builders who were defiling the countryside from Newcastle-on-Tyne to Cornwall. He made them beautiful, these little surburban villas, that would be regarded by their owners purely from the points of view of cheapness and convenience. There was, he saw, the same root in all these people, lowly or ambitious, a root he had long since discovered in Brand.

Field continued, "As a matter of fact, sir, I couldn't have been with the gardener, as Morton says, between twelve o'clock and two, because I was in my room, thinking about the sort of house I'd have one day, and thinking, too, about Christmas. Christmas always meant a lot to us at home, and we never had a Christmas without a tree and a party and a bran pie, and a dance at the Town Hall. And, of course, down at the Manor, you couldn't call it gay exactly. It's one of the between houses."

Miles, intrigued, asked what that meant. Field explained seriously that poor people, the sort who did not mind the Grays, for instance, describing them as common, were gay, because they saw no objection to exhibitions of animal spirits. And rich people and high-born people were gay, also

because it would not occur to them that they could be criti-
cised, or that it would be of any consequence if they were,
but that people like the Grays were solemn, because they
did not desire to identify themselves with the uncontrolled
lower orders, and were not sufficiently sure of themselves to
be immune from criticism.

Then she went on, "I didn't go to bed when I got into
my room. I had the sort of excited feeling I always do get
at Christmas. I'd had my home letters and parcels, but I
hadn't opened any of them. I thought I'd wait till it was
really Christmas Day, as we always did at home. And I liked
the idea that, though we couldn't be together, we'd all be
opening our presents just about the same time. So I waited
up till after I heard the clock strike, and then I began opening things; I had quite a lot, because we always send one
another something, if it's ever so small, and there's nine of
us. When I'd read all the letters twice over, I went on sitting
by the window and just thinking. I felt I couldn't go to bed
yet. This was going to be all my Christmas. Afterwards it
would be all hurry and bustle, getting things done in time,
with heaps of extra people in the house. Of course, at home
we all went to church of a morning, and we'd hurry out
after the service and all the Christmas hymns and holly and
cottonwool and red berries on the windows and round the
pulpit, and dish up the dinner. After I went into service, that
was what I missed most, and it didn't seem to get any easier
as time went on. It's five Christmases now since I've been
home, and each year I keep wondering whether anything'll
happen so that I can go back, though there isn't so many of
us left now, only mother and my two sisters and a married
brother and his wife, and their little girls that always go over.
And now and again one of the others can come. Well, as I
say, I sat by the window and looked out at the snow, and was
glad about it, because it made it seem more like Christmas;

and I didn't think much about the people downstairs or sleeping each side of me, till of a sudden I saw a light spring up in one of the windows to the right. You know the way the house is; kind of L-shaped; and so I knew it was one of the ladies or gentlemen of the house coming to bed, and I thought, 'They'll see I've got the light on still, and it's two o'clock nearly, and if they say anything to Miss Amy, there will be trouble.' I knew it was one of the visitors. Mrs. Gray and Miss Amy and Mrs. Devereux, they sleep further along. Then a man came across to the window and stood at his, like I was standing at mine, and he opened it at the bottom and looked out. And I saw it was Mr. Brand. I could see quite clearly, where I was, and his face looked so different from most of the people at the Manor that I stopped for a minute where I was, just to look at him. He was so—so full of life, if you know what I mean, as if he saw his housekeeper's room just ahead of him. He looked so glad I felt a sort of warm feeling, as though there was someone else in the house that knew the way I felt, though he didn't know I was feeling it. Then the clock struck two, and he turned his head and looked straight at me. I'd pushed aside the blind to look at the snow; and then I felt a bit silly, and thought he might be wondering what I was doing there. Things, you know, that seem sensible enough when you're alone seem all different when there's people watching you. So I turned out the light and undressed in the dark, and hoped he wouldn't tell on me. For, of course, if Mrs. Cochrane had known I was keeping the light up all that time, there would have been trouble."

Her face had been warm and eager during these last few minutes, but now her eyes clouded again. "I don't know whether any of that would help, though. I suppose some folk might say I wouldn't have had the light up if I hadn't had reason, and they wouldn't believe mine. But I wanted to know, sir, if there's anything I can do."

Miles asked if Brand had been fully dressed as he stood at the window, and Field said confidently, yes, in a blue suit. He had stopped there for some time; because, even after she was undressed, she had not at once been able to sleep; she had been too happy in her tranquil solitude, and it had been some time before he left the window and prepared for the night.

3

Miles left the office, his brain in a turmoil of excitement and dismay. This sudden new light cast on the proceedings disturbed him, even angered him. For he had no desire to play any prominent part in the coming trial. He walked along the river-bank towards Westminster. He had an engagement to dine with a client to-night, but he felt so much disturbed and bewildered that he paid no heed to clocks. The oily water moved sluggishly, with a slow, deliberate swell that set all the moored boats and barges rocking. A German trading-vessel, with coloured bands round her funnel, sailed by, with a squat dignity; some time later came a trail of barges, linked together by ropes, in a long straggling line. On the first sat a man, smoking idly, and staring into the early February dusk; the second flew the pennon of a line of washing, pink shirts and a blue pinafore, elongated vests, socks, and a shapeless nightgown, ballooning a little in the cool breeze; on the third, a girl in a pink flannel blouse and bare legs boiled a kettle on a small stove; in the fourth, an enormous blowsy woman was combing her hair. Miles stood still to watch them go slowly by. Other elbows beside his own rested on the worn parapet; some of their owners were watching the blazing electric signs of whiskey, flour, and cigarettes on the opposite bank. The sturdy outline of cranes and dredgers stood out smoke-grey against a pearl-coloured sky, one of those dark pearls, he thought inconsequently, that Ruth admired so much. Shy lovers stood close together, whispering and touching hands; girls carrying attaché-cases went briskly past; astounding, the nervous capacity of these trim slender bodies, that they should look so fresh at the end of a day's work in warm, noisy, ill-ventilated rooms. Young men, looking less alert, moved along the crowded pavements, talking of electricity and speed, the age's God. At the kerbstone a woman was offering jaded bouquets of chrysanthemums; further down an old man peddled studs and bootlaces. The long array of Green Line buses was rapidly filling. Miles overheard snatches of talk, fragments of indecipherable conversations, confessions, doubts. They were far too inadequate ever to present a complete situation, yet they aroused in him the instinctive curiosity that made all life a rich and brilliant pageant, and this affair of Brand, after all, only an incident in a crowded canvas.

"And if there's no room in the pit, we'll have to go to a movie. I can't run to five-and-nine to-night."

"What about the Croon at Victoria Station? I know they're not quick, but they do you a good Welsh rarebit for a shilling and it's not so noisy as most."

"What he wants is an automatic machine. Put in a shilling and you get so many letters. You can kick it, too, and it can't kick back, so you're quite safe. That's what he wants for a secretary."

"My dear, you never saw anything like it—pyjamas and a vest and the most awful toothbrush."

"Peter's offered to lend me fifteen pounds, if I can rustle the other ten. Of course, it isn't what you'd call smart, but who cares? We're not going to take a lot of girls about in it. But, I say, think of Sundays, going off when you please and where you please, no crowding for the hikers' train, or standing in a queue for a bus—and going where they damn well like to take you."

"And evenings in the summer, old man—there's a bathing-pool near Leatherhead..."

The young excited male group passed on. The air all about Miles was heavy with the fumes of petrol, of cheap cigarettes, of face powder and the scented artificial bouquets the women wore pinned into their coats; but it was vibrant, too, with life. Miles re-experienced a familiar sense of being part of some tremendous circus, full of lights, voices, adventure, risk, and enchantment. That thought brought another, inevitable, in its wake. Eustace—who, in his own calculating way, enjoyed life, though he saw little enough of its colour and shifting, elusive beauty. For the lawyer in Miles prevented his accepting Ruth's passionate, "But he's a murderer a dozen times over," or Isobel's candid, "What right has a man like that to live?" Eustace had, by the law of the land, as much right to live, provided he was not Adrian Gray's murderer, as the most ardent of his traducers.

"The point is," argued Miles restlessly, walking towards Westminster Bridge, where the laden omnibuses passed and repassed one another, and bicycles, carts, motors, lorries, and trams clattered and rang and flashed against a background of the Houses of Parliament and the darkening night sky, "the point is, am I compelled to come forward? I can prove nothing, except that Brand didn't stick entirely to the facts. I can't prove that he had anything to do with his father's death. I can't clear Eustace. I might be able to stir up a lot of mud and start a new theory. But would it lead to anything?"

He examined the problem from every aspect as he swung abstractedly into Victoria Street, making his way towards Sloane Square, where he had his engagement. The unpleasant notoriety that would attach to his name weighed lightly with him; lawyers early become hardened to obloquy.

"Of course, it is significant that Brand should falsify the hour of going to bed," he told himself, "and that he should further cover himself by saying he saw Eustace on the stairs. And it does seem rather unlikely that Eustace would deny seeing him, if he'd really been there. And he did deny it from the start. Just as Brand said he went to bed before midnight, before officially any of us knew anything about the murder. His story is precisely the kind of thing you would expect if he were guilty. Let's follow on from this new scrap of evidence. Allow that Brand was downstairs, in the library, at two o'clock. Where does that lead us? Romford said that Gray was killed in the early hours, probably between one and two, but possibly later, as the open window would induce *rigor mortis* unusually early. It's easy to assume that there was a row. But what about the cheque? Why should Brand want to quarrel with his father when he had got the one thing he came down for? And would he be likely to strike out because of some chance insult, when, for the first time for years, he had an opportunity of shaping his life according to his own desire?"

There was also, he reflected, the problem of the cheque made out to Eustace, that had been drawn on the morning of Christmas Day. If Brand had slain his father, that cheque must have been drawn before his (Brand's) arrival. Had Eustace, then, visited the library before his brother-in-law? And if so, how was it his cheque had been drawn later than Brand's?

Between this Scylla and Charybdis of evidence Miles endeavoured to guide his craft. He came back again and again to the problem of the cheque. Brand must have received his cheque on Christmas Eve; then suppose he went up to his room before midnight, while Eustace took his place downstairs. Then imagine Brand going down for the second time. Reason instantly asserted itself, demanding "Why?"

He had the cheque. So much, in the circumstances, must be allowed. He would not, Miles was convinced, even want to destroy that extraordinary document he had signed, since it strengthened his position. Without it, it might be difficult to make anyone believe that Adrian had parted voluntarily with so large a sum. Then—what excuse could he have had for his return? Moreover, there was Eustace's own story of descending to the library at three o'clock. Since Gray could clearly never have left the room, Eustace must have examined the safe after his death. Which brought Miles wearily back to his first point.

Had Eustace or Brand committed the crime?

4

His arrival at Sloane Square drove the problem for the time being from his mind. He had an entertaining and spirited evening, and returned home at midnight. He said nothing to Ruth at that stage, although the problem continued to torment himself. Two days later the second brick of the wall to be reared against Brand was slid unobtrusively into position.

Still having taken no steps to correspond with the authorities, Miles was walking down Charing Cross Road under a sunny sky. The wind, that had been piercing the previous day, had dropped, and the afternoon was pleasantly warm and cheerful. A sense of gaiety was infused by the bright air and the eager appearance of the men and women strolling up and down the road; at every second-hand book-store stood men turning over the volumes in the shelves that stood on the pavement. In the book-lined intimate interiors an occasional figure, as indefinite as a shadow, could be spied stretching an arm to abstract a book from a high shelf or stooping nearer the door or infrequent window that the light might fall on a certain page. Miles, desire stronger than any sense of duty or expediency, paused with them. He presently bought a volume of letters, edited by Mr. L——, and, seduced by haunting coloured plates in bright purples, yellows, and dark reds, a book on French painting. In the shop, waiting to have these wrapped up, he pulled out an illustrated edition of *Hans Andersen's Fairy Tales,* with entrancing coloured pictures and innumerable designs in black and white. Moira and Pat, he thought, would be crazy with delight if he took it back to them. But the price was high—half a guinea. He hesitated, turning the pages with renewed pleasure and recollection.

He was still undecided when a cheerful voice observed in his ear, "Hullo, Miles. That looks rather jolly."

Lifting an astonished head, he saw Isobel smiling at him. But an Isobel transfigured. Gone were the languor, the timidity, the apathy that had characterised her for years. In their place was an assurance, a charm, a sense of health and expectancy that warmed the air and his heart.

He said, "Hullo! Is this one of your haunts, too?" and Isobel laughed and replied, "It's one of the many new vices I'm acquiring—virtues, you'd call them, of course. I've got a job now, so I can afford to indulge them."

He asked her what it was. She told him, "Nothing terribly important. I'm cataloguing a library for a bewildered elderly spinster who's been left an enormous legacy of literature by a scholarly brother. Poor dear, she's quite terrified by the weight of learning, and she's torn between a contempt of anyone who can waste his life absorbing other people's thoughts, and a feeling that so many books, so sombre, so heavy, and so difficult to read, must be immensely valuable. So I'm cataloguing them, and when that job's done she's going to take the list to an expert and see what she'd better do about them."

"And you like it?"

"I do, Miles. I've discovered a dormant hunger for books that I believe will swell eventually to a passion. I get pleasure just from handling them. I begin to find a room empty and spiritless if books don't form part of the furnishing. I've even begun to buy books of my own. Look here!" She showed him a volume she had been carrying under her arm. It was a gift edition of *Chaucer's Tales*.

"Where did you pick this up? It's not very easy to come by this edition nowadays."

"This is my lucky day. Everything in the garden's beautiful. I was actually given some primroses by my employer this morning. She had a hamper up from the country. And now this. And meeting you. Are you buying that for the children?" She nodded towards the Hans Andersen.

"I'm striving against temptation."

"The temptation of buying it? Oh, Miles, give in at once. Nothing is so heavenly as an un-birthday present."

She was so glowing, so persuasive, so confident in her hope, that he yielded with a laugh. "And I don't mind taking that book off you at cost price," he added, laying a finger on the Chaucer.

"I couldn't, Miles. I couldn't really. When I think of the time I've spent, all this week, quieting my Nonconformist conscience, the agony of indecision in which this very afternoon I walked from Oxford Street—no, I couldn't. I've been waiting a whole week for enough money to buy it, and I was paid last night. I was terrified lest it should be snapped up."

"Why has conscience been so active in the matter? Is it against your principle to buy books?"

"It's a question of £ s. d. Conscience insisted that if I didn't spend the money on handkerchiefs, I should be reduced to the sort of painting-rags that Brand pulls out of his pocket in company. Poor Brand!" Her expression sobered. "He's had a horrible life with that woman, you know. You don't realise how she's kept his house all these years—it's filthy and full of the most contemptible rubbish, everything shoddy and broken and worthless. Those handkerchiefs were typical. Though, as a matter of fact"—she smiled again—"he'd unearthed a silk one from somewhere that last night. I teased him about it."

Miles's heart gave a sickening jolt. While they waited for the Hans Andersen to be wrapped up, he asked her casually which night, and, without arousing her suspicion, learned that she referred to Christmas Eve. It was clear that she had no notion whither his enquiries tended; she was too happy for the shadow of that tragedy to touch her to-day. Miles envied her; she spoke lightly of so many trivialities that pleased her, and caught him with a detaining hand when he would have gone away without his change.

"Day-dreaming?" she accused him, laughing.

He pulled himself together, made her some appropriate reply, and walked with her to Trafalgar Square.

"Have some tea," he offered her, with a sudden effort, realising that it was now five o'clock.

She shook her head. "I've got to get back. Any time you want your library catalogued, Miles, ring me up, and I'll give you special terms."

5

Miles walked blindly under the Admiralty Arch into St. James's Park. Destiny, it seemed, was determined that he should be heavily implicated in this affair. He wondered whether it would later occur to Isobel what she had said, what far-reaching results might spring from those lightly uttered words. For if Brand had a silk handkerchief on Christmas Eve, that, surely, must be the handkerchief found in Adrian Gray's fireplace some hours later. If it hadn't been burnt, it must have been discovered by the police among his belongings, for they had examined every pocket, drawer, and soiled-linen basket for handkerchiefs made of silk and had found none, except in Eustace's luggage.

"It must have been his," argued Miles desperately. "It's no good fighting against facts. There are too many fools doing it all the time, as it is. Brand must have killed his father. He killed him, in the heat of passion, with the paper-weight, that he afterwards rubbed clean with a handkerchief, that he later burned in the grate. Presumably there was blood on it—must have been, when you remember the state of Gray's face. And now we're back at the old question—Why?"

Round and round, like a dormouse endlessly turning its wheel, he drove his familiar arguments. Presently, like an infuriated dormouse, seeing no way out, he was striding through the London streets, repeating the same facts and phrases again and again, as though their constant repetition would give them a fresh meaning.

There is a game played in childhood, particularly among the Boy Scouts of the last generation, that consists in changing a word, a letter at a time, into a totally dissimilar one. Thus

CAT
COT
COG
DOG

though the examples are never so simple as that, and the words never of fewer than five letters. But some such game Miles was playing to himself now. He began with the position as it was known to the public, and strove to change it, a fact at a time, into a proven case against Brand.

"Of course, Eustace's cheque is the problem," he told himself. "If we could put Eustace out of the affair, things would be a lot easier. Brand gets his cheque, quarrels with his father, murders him, no doubt accidentally, and slips off to bed, presumably removing any clues there may be against himself."

But this version seemed to him woefully unsatisfactory. He was by no means intimate with Brand; nevertheless, he was convinced that, having obtained his money, nothing Adrian Gray said, no matter how bitter or insulting, would arouse in his son any appreciable feeling, certainly not to the extent of murder.

"There's something else," he decided, turning into a Tube station, and holding out his season-ticket for the benefit of the man at the barrier, "something he destroyed or something he's hidden. The point is, what? And what has it got to do with the *two* cheques?"

The following day he determined to sift the matter as far as he was able, and he went, therefore, to a newspaper office, where he read through the detailed accounts of Gray's death and the subsequent reports. He examined each detail minutely, and presently a fresh consideration occurred to him.

"Whoever burnt the handkerchief burnt the blotting-paper," he decided. "A man doesn't burn blotting-paper, when there's an empty basket at his elbow, unless he's got some specific reason. I don't suppose Gray had written any-thing he wanted destroyed. There was too little paper ash— an infinitesimal quantity, according to the police; certainly not enough to account for letters or anything damaging of that kind. Besides, if it had been incriminating letters, they wouldn't have been written and blotted in that room; they mightn't even have been in Gray's handwriting. So I should say the blotting-paper was burnt by someone else. And was that other man Brand? And if so, why? What record did that blotting-paper contain? We know the cheques were blotted, and Brand's document was blotted, but no one ever saw that sheet of blotting-paper. Now, why should it be burnt unless it contained some other record that it was dangerous for anyone else to see? It must have been something brief, too, because the paper-ash is so small."

It then occurred to him that the damaging paper might have been carried off by the murderer, although no ash had been found in any other room.

"And there's one more point, while I think of it, and that is the matches. Eustace has a patent cigarette-lighter; only Brand uses those horrible cheap splinters. The police don't seem to have made much of that."

Presently he turned from that line of enquiry to another problem that had troubled him from the first. How had Brand compelled his father to draw a cheque for that amount? The only answer that occurred to him was black-mail, but the question at once arose: what hold could Brand conceivably have over a man like Adrian Gray? No one would be likely to listen to anything he said. Moreover, Gray had no particular stake to lose, and Brand didn't know enough reputable people for his word to carry any weight. And then, look at that paper. It's ludicrous, thought Miles, sucking fiercely at a pipe. It's just the kind of fulsome, pompous affair Gray might have conceived—but who would be likely to part with two thousand pounds on so vague an assurance? Then, too, it must have been obvious to him that if Brand disappeared, as certainly with that amount of money in hand he would, he'd be morally if not legally responsible for those children, if it came to any question of State support. And since Brand had no legal claim on him at all, he wouldn't have given him money. It wasn't as if it would help his own position later. And as there were no obligations, that gift absolved him from nothing. Then what inducement had Brand offered?

Be melodramatic for a minute, and suppose Brand had been violent. It was quite probable, if the younger man saw any prospect of personal advantage that he wouldn't hesitate at any threat. But what threat could he use? Holding a pistol—literally, a pistol—to his father's head? Nonsense. Brand hadn't got a pistol, and wouldn't know how to handle one, in any case. Then had he threatened the old man with the block of brass?

"I'll smash your skull if you don't give me that money?" Was that the kind of thing that had gone on in the library on Christmas Eve? Miles shook his head again. That wasn't Brand's line. Besides, *cui bono*? Gray had only to refuse to surrender the cheque and Brand was powerless. A murder with no adequate reward was a form of activity that even men of Brand's erratic genius did not pursue. Besides, there were two arguments against this remote possibility. One was the presence, under the ledge of Gray's table, of a concealed electric bell; that would have aroused comment and enquiry, ringing at such an hour. The second was Gray's blatant betrayal of his son the next morning in the presence of the whole family, when he would unquestionably narrate the history of Brand's hold-up the previous night and recover his cheque.

"Brand had nothing important to sell him," concluded Miles, "because it would have been found among his papers. And even if he had compelled Gray to give him a cheque, and then murdered him because it was his only hope of keeping the money, still that doesn't account for Eustace's cheque. I'm damned if I see how we can work that in. Unless, of course, Eustace forged the thing himself. Yes, that's an idea. I wonder if there's any remote possibility of that being true. It's the precise sum he wanted; he was bound to be gaoled if he couldn't raise it, and I daresay he thought he might as well be hung for a sheep as a lamb. Then where does Gray come in? Of course, it's possible to sit at that table in a bad light and draw a cheque without seeing the body under the curtains—possible though not very likely. But surely he'd glance at the most recent counterfoil and then he'd see Brand's name down for two thousand pounds. But I'll swear it came as much of a shock to him as to anyone on Christmas morning, when he heard about it. He didn't know. I'm convinced of that. But, on the other hand, now I recall the scene more particularly, Brand was pretty certain Eustace hadn't got a penny. He taunted him with it. But if Eustace had got that cheque, why didn't he mention it at the time? That would be the obvious thing to do. And why didn't he mention it to the police? He must, if he wasn't completely imbecile, realise it would be impossible to conceal the existence of the cheque, and, anyway, what reason would he have for wishing to do so? And what had happened to it? If it had to be known that it had been drawn, where was the motive for destroying it?"

Try another thesis. Eustace hadn't destroyed the cheque. He hadn't destroyed it because he had never had it. It had been drawn, but had never reached him. Then who? Gray? He'd have cancelled the counterfoil. Brand? Why? And how did he know it had been drawn? He saw it, perhaps. But if Eustace had been unable to move his father-in-law and co-director, what conceivable argument could Brand have produced to account for this amazing *volte-face*? And would Gray have drawn the cheque in Brand's presence? Moreover, some time had elapsed between the drawing of the two cheques. It was far more reasonable to suppose that Gray would wait to find himself alone before drawing the cheque for Eustace. Indeed, he would probably wait until Eustace was with him. But if Eustace had drawn the cheque himself—well, he wouldn't have destroyed it. As things stood, it was simply Brand's alibi…

Brand's alibi! How damned fortunate for him. But—if he'd killed the old man, what time had Gray had to draw a second cheque at all? The answer was, of course, he hadn't had any time. Picture it. Here's Brand, with his father dead at his feet. In his hand is the cheque that proves he was the last person to see Gray alive. That's Christmas Eve. Think of the irony of the position. Probably for the first time in his life he has money on which he can draw; and through his own criminal folly it's going to be absolutely useless to him. Useless, that is, unless he can somehow escape the consequences of his crime. And the one way to divert suspicion is to show that someone was in the library with Gray later than he was. It won't be an easy thing to prove, because somehow this imaginary later visitor must be induced to leave traces of his presence in the room, something the police can get hold of, something that will nail him as the criminal. How's this going to be done? The cheque in his hand had probably given Brand the idea. Make out a second cheque—it's through a cheque that he'll be condemned, if he fails; it's through a cheque they shall take this other man. There's the answer for you. Neat, too. It had taken a long time to get to that solution. It answered all the points—the disappearance of the second cheque, and the riddle of its existence in the first place. Of course, Eustace hadn't got it. Eustace had never seen it. There'd never been a cheque for him or anyone else to see. The blank form probably accounted for the fragment of ash in the fireplace. But the illusion had been perfect.

6

After some inward debate Miles took his wife into his confidence, describing the position as he at present envisioned it. Ruth was aghast.

"Miles, you're not going to try and hunt down Brand? When he's got so many enemies as it is?"

"My dear, I can't stand by and see an innocent man convicted. It's no question of personalities. It's just a job, like any other."

"But—your job, Miles?"

"It seems so. I didn't seek it out. I didn't want it. The first hint I got, I evaded. But I can't hide my head under a furze-bush any longer. There are too many discrepancies in this case for an honest man to feel easy in his mind."

"Of course, your explanation is possible," Ruth admitted reluctantly. "I remember the fearful row there was years ago when Brand wrote a whole letter in father's writing and no one detected the forgery. We found out by pure chance. So I don't suppose a cheque—or do you think he forged both cheques?—would be very difficult."

Miles had suddenly swivelled round, and the pipe he was filling fell through his fingers.

"Two cheques," he repeated softly. "Two. You've put your finger on it, Ruth. What a dunderhead I was not to see it before. That's how Brand got hold of his money, of course. I've been puzzling and puzzling to understand how it was done; what inducements he had offered your father; above all, how he could have got that amount from a man who knew himself bankrupt. So far as I can gather, no one except his lawyer knew quite how deeply dipped he was. Even Eustace didn't know, Richard didn't know. And if he didn't mind making a fool of Brand, though even that seems to me unlikely, he wouldn't attempt to play the same trick on Eustace. Let's piece this together, shall we?"

He left his chair and, coming to the writing-table, took up a silver pencil and began to jot down notes.

"Eleven o'clock. Brand goes down to the library.

"Two o'clock. He's seen returning to his room.

"Eleven to two. Mr. Gray is murdered. According to the doctor, that couldn't have taken place this side of midnight, and was more likely between one and two. What on earth did those two do from eleven till one?"

"Quarrelled," answered Ruth unhappily.

"I'd be inclined to say Brand didn't go down till getting on for midnight. I don't know whether there's any possibility of proving that. I should say not, as no one's queried the evidence so far. They might easily argue for an hour, and they'd get pretty violent. At about one o'clock or a little later, Brand loses his head completely—it's a bad time for even the most temperate man to be arguing—and strikes your father with the paper-weight. I don't suppose at the time he realised what he was doing, but that cuts no ice with juries. All they'll look at is the fact that he actually killed the old man. Then see him with the body, realising what he's done. I daresay, at first, he doesn't even think of the consequences; the mere fact of the death is enough for him. But presently he sees the position as it is. He's killed a man, and he'll probably hang for it. I don't know what put him on to the cheque-book, unless it was his desperate need. His imagination might be fired at the thought of escaping, not only from the consequences of his crime, but also from the damnable life he was spending with Sophy and the children. And, of course, having forged one cheque, it would be simple enough to forge the next. And he must have written out the document as well. It was a bold stroke, but a clever one. It showed a strong knowledge of your father's temperament. I can just see him drawing up a ridiculous paper like that. Well, what do we do now?"

"Do you go to the police?" asked Ruth apprehensively.

Miles considered. "I don't see how we can, at the moment. We've nothing to show, nothing but theorising, and rather romantic theorising at that. We ought to get some foundation for our case. At present, it's too weak to stand much investigation."

Precisely how weak it was he forced himself to realise later, when he was alone. All it boiled down to was a maid-servant's story, with nothing to support it, and a casual remark from Isobel about a handkerchief. She, he shrewdly suspected, would deny that story if by so doing she could absolve her brother. Though they met seldom, there existed between them a curious, almost a subterranean relationship that was intimate and deep. Probably it was rooted in some early memory forgotten by both, but it involved loyalty to the individual (on Isobel's part, at least), without regard to that wider loyalty a man owes to the community as a whole, and that is the basis of civilisation. And, with Isobel's evidence dissipated, what remained? A servant's tale, a servant, moreover, anxious to prove an alibi for her own advantage. And for the rest—mere supposition, daydreaming, theorising.

"Not good enough," decided Miles. "Then what?"

Part VII

The Answer

1

It was a theory of Miles's that, when bewildered and even
dismayed by a position, it is wise to thrust the whole matter
from the mind for forty-eight hours, concentrating rigidly
on something else, so that, after the interval, the intelligence
returns to the conflict, refreshed and sharpened by the delay.
It chanced that a question regarding a disputed will came
into his office within a few hours of his conversation with
Ruth, and into this absorbing affair he threw himself heart
and soul for some days. Then he returned with a clear and
(so far as possible) unprejudiced mind to the King's Poplars
murder.

Being a man whose mind worked more eagerly in a
crowd, he went out of his office and walked down to Charing Cross, turning eventually into St. James's Park. It was
a very pleasant day early in February, with a clear blue sky
and silver-white clouds, very light and airy above the pointed
leafless trees. There were a great many blue pigeons about,
their feathers ruffled into boas round their necks because of
the wind. A number of people were walking in the Park, and
he was struck with a sense of their energy and their pleasure
in life. Some children bowled hoops and played games,
and fell over their own feet, and down by the ornamental

water were the pelicans and ducks. It was all very gay and cheerful, and the general spectre of destitution that spoils a man's pleasure so often in a London scene was absent. Some idlers there were, of course, but even the poorest had his paper and his pipe and was enjoying the mild weather. The general air of zest and well-being all about him quickened Miles's thought. He was tranquilly convinced that he would reach the solution, even before he knew where it lay. A sense of competence swept away his hesitations and doubts, as, having walked through the Park, he left it by the Buckingham Palace Gate. He went down to Victoria Station, that was a bustle of energy and excitement. A bevy of young students was setting off for the Continent, and they hummed round the bookstall, buying literature for the journey, bananas and sandwiches, and packets of raisins, settling their sensible berets more firmly on their foreheads, chattering, arguing, debating. It was intensely stimulating; Miles stood on one side watching them. Now he had a familiar sensation that his mind had actually seized on the missing clue, and it only required his concentration to identify it. He liked thinking in a crowd. Those who want their temples of quiet, he was wont to say, are welcome to them, but for himself he sympathised with the novelist who, when he wanted to write, went to an A.B.C. shop. He loved the sound of cars, lorries, buses, carts, and drays going by under his window; the noise of bells and hooters, of shouts, exclamations, warnings, the barking of dogs and neighing of horses, all the bustle and colour and excitement of daily life, delighted and cheered him. Which was why he had chosen the noisiest room in their suite for his own office, and given his children a nursery on the traffic side of the house.

At the bookstall the students bought detective novels with blood-curdling covers—skeletons, hanging bodies, creeping shadows, knives, poison-bottles, and huge impressions of mysterious feet. He wondered if any of the problems within those garish covers was as difficult of solution as his own; no doubt they were all more fantastic. A domestic murder can be made to sound very tame to those not intimately concerned.

A young woman went past in a blue beret, talking to an equally young man in a Fair Isle sweater and a black beret. Both carried cameras. The young man observed with a laugh, "God bless the chap who invented finger-prints. What would these fellows do without them?"

Miles didn't hear what the young woman replied. He had got his clue, and he walked away at once.

This, then, was his case. Brand Gray had murdered his father, forged two cheques and the amazing document, and got away with it. Eustace had been arrested, partly on account of the cheque made out to him, but chiefly because of his finger-prints on the safe. But what of the finger-prints on the document? No one, it seemed, had thought of that. It had been taken for granted that that was authentic. But if, as he now suspected, Brand was its originator, then, whose-ever finger-prints did appear upon it, Adrian Gray's certainly would not. Here, it seemed, was an obvious way of testing his theory.

2

Nevertheless, this discovery brought him no joy. Hitherto the zest of the affair itself had sustained him. But now he saw himself as Brand's chief enemy, the relentless pursuer who without motive was hounding down the man he had stayed at King's Poplars to help. It was an ironical situation, and to him a desperate one. Brand's personality, powerful and creative, appeared to him as a thing of value and even of beauty; for Eustace, he had no more compassion than he would have for the slug that destroyed his roses or the earwig that crawled on his table. And yet—

In an agony of indecision he returned home. Ruth met him in the hall.

"Monty's here," she said. "Eustace's boy."

"What does he want with me?" demanded Miles, outraged.

"I suppose he wants you to help."

"Well, I shan't do it. It's sheer nepotism. Aren't there enough men in this country eager to be paid to wash Moore's dirty linen in public, without his coming here? Hasn't the fellow any sense of decency?"

But when he saw Montague, his rage evaporated. The lad was personable enough and held himself with a certain dignity that, in the circumstances, was moving.

He said, "I hope you don't mind my coming here, Uncle Miles. I haven't come professionally or anything like that. Father's got a lawyer who's doing what he can. But I thought I'd like to see you."

Miles, puzzled but beginning to be impressed, offered him a cigarette and a chair.

"I don't know that there's anything I can do," he remarked uneasily, with a quite unexpected sense of guilt.

"I daresay you wouldn't be very much inclined to do it, if there were," was Montague's surprising retort. "It would only mean involving someone else, whom perhaps you prefer to father."

"My dear boy," expostulated Miles, professional dignity outraged by the suggestion of personal preference. And stopped. Because that, he saw, was precisely what he contemplated.

Montague went on, "Being in the house at the time, I thought you might remember if anything odd had happened. But I suppose if it had, and if you did, you'd have told the police already. No, I didn't really come to you because I thought you could do anything, only—it is pretty ghastly, you know. Mother's all to pieces, and Arnold—there isn't much I can say to him. And every post brings the most vituperative letters from people who're ruined by father's concerns. Of course, they put all the blame on him. People never blame themselves for being fools. Or else friends write saying how dreadful it is for her—mother, I mean—and they quite understand. Which is all damn rot. She's afraid to go out alone now, for fear of being insulted or pitied."

Miles thought of her, bone-selfish, terrified, incapable of any generous emotion, of any delicacy of thought, sitting trembling in her beautiful, absurd drawing-room, with its hand-painted walls and silver panels, seeing her life a ruin, and her death—at the hands of hooligans who booed and shouted and wrote her abusive letters—imminent as soon as she put her head out of doors. Yet, though he was by nature a kindly man, he could not kindle within his breast a spark of compassion for a spirit so despicable.

"Have you seen your father?" he asked Montague suddenly.

'I've just come from seeing him. That's why…" He left the sentence unfinished.

"I see," murmured Miles, and after a moment's silence forced himself to ask. "How's he taking things?"

"Pretty badly." Montague's tone was laconic, but a certain nervous clenching of the fingers he'd inherited from the Grays spoke more eloquently than words. "You know, it must be awful to be boxed in there and know that during the next two or three weeks you're going to be dragged into court and accused of something you haven't done, without an iota of proof that you didn't do it. Father knows he can't prove his innocence, and that everyone wants him to be found guilty. It's enough to drive a man mad. Just waiting—waiting—and seeing no way out."

He jumped up and began to lunge up and down the room; but even these movements were graceful. He was his father's son, thought Miles, ashamed at his own surprise in discovering in any human being affection for such a man. After all, there were at least two personalities in every individual, and the domestic one might function in a man who was a shark, a murderer, and a coward.

"If I could go ahead with something, even if it led us into a blind alley," Montague broke out. "It's worse, I think, when you know you didn't do it. You feel cheated into the bargain."

No satisfaction out of actually committing the murder, reflected Miles, instantly nauseated. You couldn't, it seemed, overcome the fellow's commercial instincts, even in a situation so grave as this one. Yes, Miles could imagine him raving because he was being called upon to settle an account for which he was not responsible. Fear there would be, too, horror, the desperate twisting of the panic-stricken beast.

He let Montague go without any sort of assurance, but when he was alone again he faced the new situation his nephew's visit had created. Hitherto, he had contemplated the position mainly from Brand's point of view, seeing that strange, savage, yet not wholly ignoble figure, living by its own fierce conventions, shaping itself in a mould unfamiliar to the rest of them, tasting at last the liberty of which it had been deprived for so long. And in his eager espousal of this brother-in-law's case he had spared little thought for Eustace's suffering. Honesty compelled him to admit that, although the creature might be contemptible, yet it had nerves and desires, and, by the bare fact of a common humanity, merited consideration. It had rights; it had a point of view; it had sensitive places like any other living organism. And it could claim justice and relief from the purely mental torture that now racked Eustace day and night.

"I shall have to go through with this," he decided abruptly. "I've no right to force this kind of hell on any man. Eustace may deserve practically everything that could happen to him, but I'm not his judge. In a sense, I'm responsible for what he's enduring now."

3

The document, signed by Brand, had been examined. It held a variety of finger-prints. Brand's, Richard's, Amy's—but not Gray's. No trace of Gray's anywhere, and his were decisive hands, with square, forceful tips—no, he hadn't touched that sheet of paper. And to Miles that spelt Brand's death-warrant.

There was not very much time. Somehow Brand must be warned; Miles couldn't stand the notion of his being taken like some beast in a trap, stepping carelessly over the scattered brush and undergrowth and stumbling suddenly into the spiked pit prepared for him. One fact above all others was clear. Brand couldn't escape the consequences of his deed. If necessary, he must be forced to exonerate Eustace. But at least give him the opportunity to take his own way out.

Tracking him down was not an easy task. Miles enquired of Isobel, of Sophy, and of Richard, but none of them knew where he was. Sophy, indeed, made it abundantly clear that she had no desire to know. His successor, though irregular, was, in her opinion, a great improvement; he was less critical, less fastidious, less caustic, made fewer demands, and satisfied her with a simple savagery that was the utmost she could appreciate. She had never understood that the root of Brand's brutality towards her lay in her own crudity, her inability to experience the finer shades of feeling, of any response, indeed, that was not instinctive or sensual. The children also preferred the newcomer; he was more generous, more friendly, did not abash them by mature comments they could not understand, and prevented Sophy from beating them. On the other hand, he gave them sweets and pence and absolved them from the tedium of homework.

As Miles was leaving the house, a pale, fierce little girl caught at his hand with sticky fingers and said in a hoarse whisper. "He did it. I heard him tell mother so. He said she wouldn't care, and she didn't. And he laughed. I heard him."

Having delivered herself breathlessly of this information, she folded her lips in a hard line and stared at her unknown uncle. Miles thought, "My God, the tragedy of it! What Brand's pitched away in that child. She's making a frantic bid for revenge, for the wrongs he's done her, for her instinctive realisation that she's been cheated, in telling me that." And his heart ached, and he felt fierce and bitter himself, as he remembered his own pretty children, in their innocence, their gaiety, and their faith.

When all his efforts at tracing his brother-in-law had ended in failure, Miles determined to employ a private detective. It was not a method he much cared about, nor was he anxious to help the other side, who must be almost as keen to find Brand as he was himself. But time pressed, and he dared not run further risks. In the present circumstances, pure chance might reveal Brand's whereabouts, and he had no reason to suppose that he would be more fortunate than the defence.

Ruth frowned when she heard of his decision. "Must you, Miles?" she asked distastefully.

"You may be sure I shouldn't, if any other alternative remained to me. It's the most expensive luxury I know. I once had a client, a lady, who had to employ an agent to track down an unfaithful husband. Her account was enormous, the gentleman being fond of foreign travel. When she saw it, she said ruefully, 'I doubt if Henry has spent as much as this on his mistress, and he's had a lot of fun for his money, and I've had none.' It's the last refuge of the desperate."

Carr, the man whom Miles eventually employed, also visited Fulham, and wrung from an unwilling Sophy the admission that Brand had gone abroad—to Paris, she said, but she didn't know his address.

So Carr went to Paris, that part of Paris where the artists forgather, where money is scarce, hopes high, and a thousand tragi-comedies are enacted in a month. He went in and out of the tall, grey houses with his persistent question, without result; he saw numberless landladies, students, and maids-of-all-work. He traversed first those streets where Brand had been known in the days before his marriage, but here all recollection of him had departed. It was so long ago, and the population of these houses changes and shifts perpetually. No man stays here long; some sink to the discomfort of the garret, with its nightly candle, its few sous' worth of vegetables, its rags and destitution; others forsake the world of art and enter business; *or* they marry and become successful husbands and fathers and only remember their past when they buy brushes and tubes of paint for their young sons and daughters; and of the various men whom Carr traced, some had no recollection at all of the one insignificant unit in that moving heterogeneous crowd; some remembered him merely as a name; and even those who had known him best had heard nothing of him for years. He had completely dropped out of the circle where he had once moved, abandoned now by them as years ago they had been (albeit reluctantly) abandoned by him.

In and out of the inscrutable houses went Carr, in and out of cafés and music-halls and studios, inventing a hundred reasons for the search, but never the true one, lest Brand hear of the pursuit and evade him. He discovered among the women of the quarter the models and cocottes who shared the artist's lives and pursued his search among them. This type of woman, he had found, frequently put a thread into a man's hand, from motives either of jealousy or curiosity, or from sheer stupidity. But neither from these could he learn anything.

Eventually he ran his quarry to earth by pure chance. He had turned into a newspaper shop to ask for an English paper. He was told that only one remained, and that was reserved for an English gentleman who came each morning. Yes, the monsieur might arrive at any moment. Even while they spoke, Brand came in. He had done nothing to alter his appearance; he looked thin and under-nourished and he had not yet shaved. The woman at the desk handed him his paper, saying that this monsieur, indicating Carr, had wanted to deprive him of it.

Brand looked up with instant suspicion. "There are other paper-sellers," he remarked offensively, and walked out.

Carr, not altogether convinced of his identity, followed at a discreet pace on the other side of the road. He saw Brand enter a café, fling himself down at the small circular table, and open the journal. He did not lift his head to give his order, but continued reading. He was, apparently, exploring the paper for some particular paragraph. His swift eye examined the columns methodically, page by page; as he turned each sheet he discarded it, allowing it to sag to the floor. Presently his attention was arrested; he let his coffee grow cold; his expression changed, becoming bold, resolute, ruthless. After a moment he flung the paper aside and walked out of the café. Carr darted up, snatched the sheet Brand had just discarded, and followed him into the road. A little later he saw him mount the steps of a house not a hundred yards from a terrace where he had pursued his patient enquiries two days earlier. Brand had gone straight in, so clearly he was at home here; Carr pressed the bell and learned from a garrulous landlady that the English gentleman for whom he asked, a M. Brett, was not lodging there; her only English gentleman was an artist, a M. Gray, who occupied a room at the top of her house; he received no letters and saw no friends. All day he painted, painted, painted. No one visited him but the model—a male model, *mon Dieu.*

She flung up her hands.

In a second café, where he ordered a bock, Carr examined the single sheet he had stuffed into his pocket. Tucked away in a corner he found a paragraph headed:

KING'S POPLARS MURDER TRIAL

The trial of Eustace Moore for the murder of his father-in-law, Mr. Adrian Gray, has been definitely fixed for March 8th (i.e. the day after to-morrow). The death of Mr. Gray in mysterious circumstances, on Christmas Day, attracted a great deal of attention. Mr. Moore is Chairman of [here followed a list of practically derelict companies].

"So that's what Gray saw, presumably what he's been looking for since he got here. Are they on his trail? Is there any suggestion of substituting another man for the one at present under arrest? Is he himself mentioned, either as witness or suspect?"

He felt a certain resentment at having, at this stage, to relinquish the case to Miles, after this intriguing search. Moreover, he was only imperfectly in his employer's confidence, and puzzled his brains to know what counter-evidence Miles could bring. Anyway—who wanted Moore to get off?

4

Miles received Carr's cable in time to catch the night boat. Ruth had learned early in her married life the inadvisability of attempting to alter her husband's plans; nevertheless, on this occasion she did her utmost to impede him.

"Do you want me to miss the boat?" he demanded, concealing pardonable exasperation under a smiling manner.

"It wouldn't be any use really, I suppose. You'd only take the next one."

"Why are you so dead set against my going?"

She faced him, white and desperate. "Don't you realise what you're doing? Brand has killed one man and you've found him out. That means he knows his life is forfeit, and do you suppose he'll let it make any difference to him whether he hangs for one murder or two? Besides, with you out of the way, who's to know the facts?"

"That, I admit, hadn't occurred to me," Miles acknowledged. "About going headlong into danger, I mean. But if you're going to base your life on security, you're not going to get far. I won't run any unnecessary risks, sweetheart, but this job's got to be put through."

Brand's studio was an enormous room at the top of the tall brownstone house. Light entered through a long casement in the north wall, that extended from floor to ceiling. In another corner an unmade bed was visible behind a soiled red curtain; water stood in a cheap white china basin; on a round table that reflected the cold northern light stood a lamp, a cup, and a plate of apples.

Miles thought, "He's not going in for still life? Not Brand?" For to his cool and inartistic nature there had always appeared something slightly emasculate about a full-blooded adult "messing about with a dead duck and a vase of cornflowers."

Brand was in the room as he softly opened the door, but he was engrossed in his canvas and heard nothing. So Miles stood where he was, tranquilly surveying his surroundings. Brand had his back to him; on the model stand was a young man also with his back to the room. He wore a blue suit and his dark head dropped towards the floor. His arms, with clenched fists, hung at his sides. The pose suggested a great energy shocked and arrested by the unforeseen event. The air of the room was tense with some inward urgency, as though some desperate race against time were in progress.

Miles, fascinated and intent, waited motionless for Brand to discover him. He might have preserved that pose indefinitely had his attention not been distracted by a sheet of paper that, catching a draught, floated silently to the floor. Instinctively, Miles stooped to retrieve it, but not until he had it under his hand did he realise that this was the coping-stone of the edifice against the artist that he had laboriously built up during the past weeks. The drawing in his hand represented a head, one of those self-portraits certain painters frequently affect. It was displayed in the framework of a mirror, of French workmanship and unusual design. Miles knew at a glance where the original of that mirror hung. At the foot of the page was Brand's elaborate monogram, and a date—December 25th…

Miles drew a deep sigh. No jury, he thought, could evade the implications of such a piece of evidence as this.

As though that sigh roused him from his mood of intentness, Brand turned abruptly. Miles thought that he saw and recognised him, though he displayed no surprise at his presence there. Probably, decided the lawyer, he was not yet sufficiently aware of his environment to experience such an emotion. The vision that had held him through the morning still enchained his imagination and his purpose. But when he spoke his voice sounded normal enough.

He spoke to the model. "You can go now. It's finished." There wasn't a quiver of feeling in his voice, but Miles felt suddenly reminded of another occasion when a similar expression had been employed. "It is finished." Something so magnificent that it transcended speech. Brand, too, seemed to have changed, to have matured and developed into the personality that had always been his but had hitherto been stunted and repressed. As the model took up a soft brown hat, and swept past the stranger without a glance, Miles got a full-face view of his brother-in-law. And he felt a new embarrassment. This was not the embarrassment he had anticipated, the shame of admitting his share in what now appeared an act of cowardly treachery, but the embarrassment a small man feels in the presence of a superior. Miles could not have explained precisely where the change lay, but he felt guilty of an impertinence in coming to warn this stranger of what lay ahead, in a sense of dictating to him a course of action that now he could scarcely contemplate.

"I wasn't expecting you," said Brand, and Miles saw that under the composure and the purpose in that unforgettable face was a new strength to accept whatever circumstance might be offering him. "Is anything wrong?"

"I've been looking for you," said Miles inanely.

"Complimentary of you. But why?" But he knew the answer to that question, and Miles knew that he knew it. He had, in the depths of his mind, realised that at any moment this shock might be sprung upon him, and these weeks that had intervened since his father's death had made him able to endure any consummation, even the one that already he saw approaching him.

"Have you forgotten that the trial starts to-morrow?"

"Does that interest me? I've nothing fresh to say."

"Are you sure, Brand?" And then, because he could not endure this indignity either for himself or for his companion, he added quickly, "Believe me, it's no good. We know too much. I could demonstrate to you exactly what you did—how you forged both cheques, the one for your own advantage and the other as a means of self-defence; how you burnt Eustace's handkerchief..."

Brand started a little. "Eustace's handkerchief?"

"Yes. Isobel remembers twitting you about it. Oh, it's true enough. I shouldn't have come over here to warn you if I hadn't been sure of my ground."

"No," agreed Brand slowly. "I don't suppose you would. And yet I thought I safeguarded myself so well."

"You did," Miles reassured him. "But chance was against you. You can't always make allowances for that."

"Chance," repeated Brand, "the one element that can't be squared. When you said you came to warn me, what did you mean?"

"That they may be on your track now, for all I know."

Brand regarded him curiously. "You're a peculiar sort of lawyer, aren't you? Frustrating the ends of justice. Doesn't this sort of thing make you an accessory after the fact?"

"Possibly it does," Miles agreed. "But, as a matter of fact, justice isn't going to suffer. The end, in effect..." But he stopped there. He could not voice the baldness of the truth.

"And you'll save the country five thousand pounds," applauded Brand characteristically. "How did you find out?"

Miles explained. "You couldn't allow for being seen by the servant or for her coming to me in quite a different connection. It's hardly reasonable to expect you to think of the finger-prints on the document. And as for this..." He held out the sheet of paper. "That must have been done in the library, after it happened, and before you left the room." He regarded Brand with an odd expression, no longer con-temptuous or horrified, but the look of a man who accepts another man's standards without subscribing to them.

"I called it 'The Murderer,'" said Brand slowly.

Miles allowed some of his suppressed feeling to escape in a sharp exclamation. "And it's betrayed you."

"Betrayed me?" He could not fathom the meaning of Brand's smile. "Betrayed me? Ah, no. That's scarcely fair. That, at least, is an office I have performed for myself." He motioned to his companion to approach the canvas.

Miles, curiosity tempered by awe, crossed the room; but when he saw what the picture represented, he was stricken dumb. Brand had instantly forgotten him again.

The canvas was a large one, and displayed a man in a blue suit, with his back to the spectator, staring at a figure lying at his feet. The face of the recumbent man was turned away, yet even that foreshortened profile was unmistakable. Miles halted, aghast, humbled, astounded. Now he could fit that vivid pencil-sketch into the whole scheme. For on the painted wall of the canvas hung the mirror, whose original Miles had seen in Adrian Gray's library a few weeks ago. And in the painted mirror was reflected the young man's face, a face so striking, so distinguished, so fired with some quality of nobility that he could not diagnose, that it shook the lawyer's heart. Here at last was the true man none of them had hitherto been permitted to see. So keen was the face, so eager and so proud, so marked the sense of domination, that it compelled attention from the most lukewarm observer. It belonged to a man whom it would be impossible to ignore. The force of that ardent personality filled the room.

Miles turned to speak to Brand, but paused, silenced by the flesh-and-blood reality. Brand was looking at his own picture, absorbing it, exhausted by it. All his vitality had gone to its making, and he seemed drained of desire, as of fear. Miles was reminded of a very powerful study he had once seen of an early Latin saint; he had been struck by the fanatical abandonment of self that that drawing had displayed. And here, for the second time in his life, he encountered a similar absorption in an object, greater than the individual who planned it, yet a concrete expression of his personality. Brand to-day was unaware of his danger as he was unaware of himself. And, thought Miles, watching him sensitively, if all his peril could be expressed in tangible symptoms, laid out before him on a table, he would have been oblivious to their intent. He was possessed and devoured by this indescribable force. And Miles turned back, his words frozen on his lips.

He was not, perhaps, a great judge of pictures, but this overwhelmed him, not merely by its power but by its technical excellence. In the drab futility of the dead man, in the energy of purpose of the murderer, Brand had achieved a masterpiece. Every detail—the light thrown back from the polished table, the edge of the brass weight, the sheen of the blue leather cushion in the winged arm-chair, the dead ash of the fire, the dull surface of a terra-cotta curtain drooping near the dead man's head—in all these he detected perfection. The effect of the whole, even on one to whom it had no peculiar significance, must be terrific. The white heat at which the crime had been committed was here surpassed by the white heat inspiring the painting.

"Well?" said Brand softly, emerging at last from his long reverie.

Miles said in an abrupt voice, "You do realise what you've done? What other people would say? That it's the act of a madman. What on earth possessed you to do anything so crazy?"

Repeating the interview later to his wife, Miles said, "He seemed in those last few minutes to have undergone some startling change. I couldn't get near him. No words can express the sheer magnificence of the man."

This transfigured Brand, leaning forward from the edge of the table, where he had seated himself, replied, "I wish I knew the answer to that last remark of yours. The act of a madman, you said? But how can you say such a thing? How much do you or anyone else actually know? And what's normality for that matter? Is it, in any event, worth the tremendous price—the sacrifice of originality, idealism, ambition—that we're asked to pay for it? I suppose no one could supply a satisfactory answer. Perhaps it doesn't even matter very much. When I was painting that, it occurred to me it might be its own explanation, but now it's finished I feel less assured. Probably we can't get any nearer than to say that we're bound—morally bound—to accomplish the work that is ours to do, without questioning or refusing. If it comes to that"—he smiled, sweetly, gravely, with a tender understanding of a situation that Miles was finding intolerable—"I daresay you wouldn't have chosen to hound me down. But some things are inevitable. In a sense, they don't even involve free will. I could no more not have painted that canvas than you could have kept quiet and stayed in St. John's Wood, and let Eustace hang. There comes a stage when consequences simply don't count. A picture may lead one man to the Academy and another, it seems, to the gallows. That isn't significant, though, not if you've got your values right. I think all artists feel the same. I suppose to the author the important thing is writing his book, quite apart from publication. Publication, after all, is only a sop to his vanity—except where it's his living; and most of us don't make enough for it to be that. What matters actually to him, if he's worth anything, is the quality of his work. When that's done, his essential job is over. That's the only answer I've been able to puzzle out for myself during these weeks. All our experience is fused to one point—that we may adequately produce our own harvest. And I suppose," he added reflectively, "if we were satisfied with anything less, it wouldn't be worth going on at all."

5

Evening had stolen down the street, that was now folded in shadow. The pinpoints of light glimmering through number-less curtains only served to intensify the gloom beyond their tiny radiance. Miles, standing by the cold north window while Brand wrote out his methodical confession, page after page, in the room behind him, shivered with a nausea he could not repress. The crossing had been a bad one, and the vessel had tossed about for some hours outside the harbour before she could attain port; then he had caught a slow and very bad train to Paris. It was enough, he told himself grimly, to sicken the most robust. Yet he knew that this discomfort, this sense of loss and despair, had no physical root. He thought of many things and people while he stood there, smoking steadily, cigarette after cigarette, in an effort to dull the brain. He remembered all the traitors of history, from false Sextus to Judas Iscariot, and from Iscariot to men whom he had known as spies in the last war. And he felt that their mantle lay upon his shoulders, the strain of their disease had infected him for ever. Never again, he knew, would he hear a criminal sentenced to the supreme penalty without recalling this dreadful hour in a top room in a narrow Paris house, without re-experiencing these emotions of horror and misery that possessed him to-day.

Brand spoke at last. "You'd better see what I've written. Make certain it's all ship-shape. And do I need a witness?" Disregarding Miles's shaken head, he continued, "I'd like you to see how it all happened." He passed the sheaf of thin pages to his companion. "Have I made it clear?" he questioned.

He had made it so clear that Miles, reading that long, detailed document, looked up in bewilderment, missing the heavy furniture, the books, the hangings and carpets that he anticipated finding all around him; missing, too, the figure of a young man moving swiftly round the room, distorting evidence and standing before that mirror to sign his own death-warrant.

"It's clear enough," he said heavily. Brand nodded. Untroubled of hope, he was now making his final preparations. Now it was time for Miles to go. If possible, he was not to be involved in the final act of the drama. When the newspapers announced:

ECHO OF KING'S POPLAR TRAGEDY
MYSTERIOUS DEATH OF ENGLISH ARTIST

he was to be sitting placidly with his wife in St. John's Wood, and was to exhibit as much surprise and consternation as any other man interested in the affair.

"That's all, I think," said Brand's voice. "No. I mustn't make my final bow without signing my—confession."

Miles looked confused. "You did—surely..." He thrust a finger under the envelope he held in his hand. Then he hesitated. They were at cross-purposes to the end. For Brand, without heeding him, had taken up his brush and was signing, with that elaborate monogram, his amazing achievement.

6

Miles came out blindly, the letter in his hand. He could not, all that night, blot out from his mind the thought that, by his deed, a man now vigorous and alert would in a few hours be thrust out of a scheme of life in which he gloried and that he might enrich and explain. Walking through the dim streets, he was visited by a powerful temptation to destroy the envelope and its contents, and let that grey-faced, shuddering creature in a Grebeshire gaol take his chance. It wasn't as if his life was of any value. But common sense, rescuing him from sentiment and personal desire, advised him that it was too late for heroics of this nature. In life it is never possible to go backwards, and, whatever the future held, he must advance to meet and conquer it. And so, with a sense of finality, he posted the confession in one of the grey-blue boxes, nailed to the wall, that he saw as he passed, and walked—and walked—with no sense of direction, till the day was bright all about him.

And with the coming of light, the dawn of a new era, as each day was to the individual, came reflections to soothe and console him. He remembered the opening words of a novel he had once read, and that had impressed him strongly at the time: "It is a pity that we cannot die when our lives are finished." A pity! When one remembered the army of artists and writers and poets who laboured in the pathetic self-delusion that industry can replace genius, who insisted on bombarding the public with work after work long after inspiration was dead, desperately clinging to their ancient reputation (and their royalties), what better could one hope for any of their number than that he might pass in the zenith of his powers and at the height of his achievement? Brand would never surpass that picture. In it he had given expression to all the force and vitality and power that he possessed; it was the high-water mark of his maturity, the only kind of immortality he would have valued.

And, comforted thus, Miles retraced his steps and went down to the station, where his train waited to take him back to Calais and thence to England, back to the sensations of the trial, the subsequent re-arrest of Eustace Moore, and his final sentence of seven years for fraud.

Epilogue

The critic in the —— *TIMES* of the 27th October, 1932, wrote:

> ...But the *pièce de résistance* of the Exhibition is undoubtedly the canvas entitled 'The Murderer,' by the late Mr. Hildebrand Gray, by whose tragic death in the spring of this year Art lost one of her most valuable disciples. This magnificent picture, both in courage of conception and vigour of execution, displays a nobility and promise that fall little short of actual genius. It is impossible to predict what Mr. Gray might not have achieved but for his untimely death.

Brand himself might have observed with his ready cynicism, "Since it's impossible, why talk of it? And as for what a man might have done, why talk of that either? It's what he does that matters. This," he might have said, "is what I do. And as for the meaning of it—who knows?"

To see more Poisoned Pen Press titles:

Visit our website: poisonedpenpress.com/
Request a digital catalog: info@poisonedpenpress.com